#

Jonathan Ross

New York
Harvard Square Editions (HSE), Ltd.
www.HarvardSquareEditions.org
2011

Published in the United States by
Harvard Square Editions (HSE), Ltd.

ISBN: 978-0-983-32160-6

Harvard Square Editions web address:
www.harvardsquareeditions.org

Printed in the United States of America

Acclaim for *A Weapon to End War* by Jonathan Ross

"Ross is a powerful new voice on the thriller scene. He takes the best of Le Carre, Clancy and Ludlum and winds it up with a timely, riveting commentary on the socio-political threats that lie beneath the surface of the nightly news. You won't be able to put this book down."

—RIP GERBER, author of the best-selling thrillers *Pharma* and *Killer Virus*

"Just as William Gibson introduced the world to the Cyberspace in his classic novel *Neuromancer* in 1984, Jonathan Ross introduces us to the brave new world of Nanotechnology and Microrobotics in his brilliant debut novel, *A Weapon to End War*. This is truly an intelligent thriller and a page turner. Ross displays not only cutting edge insights into the technological revolution soon to transform our world, but also a deep understanding of the unchanging nature of the human soul."

—RICHARD DUNCAN, author of the best-selling book *The Dollar Crisis*

To Mom and Dad,

V,

Julian, Sienna, Anabella,

and Blaze

"O men! Here is a parable set forth! Listen to it! Those on whom, besides Allah, you call, can never create even a fly, if they all met together for the purpose! And if the fly should snatch away anything from them, they would have no power to retrieve from the fly what it had taken. Feeble are those who petition and those whom they petition!"

—*Koran, Surah 22:73*

The technologies mentioned in this work exist today.

PROLOGUE

Even after the passage of decades, her last words to him still rang uncomfortably in his ears. *"You're insane. A weapon that can stop War?"*

It was going to be a busy night, and there was still a lot left for Carpenter to prepare before the guests arrived. But after tidying up the living room, placing coasters here and snack bowls there, he allowed himself a stop in front of the mirror for a final check of his appearance. He stood on his tiptoes to better see himself in the mirror, arranged the few remaining strands of hair on his bald pate, and adjusted the robin's egg blue bow-tie he'd chosen to match the color of his eyes. Satisfied he'd done his best to look presentable, he paused in front of the mantelpiece to take in the painting of Alice.

We'll see soon enough who's sane, Alice.

Though it was almost forty years ago, he recalled with extreme clarity the night he met Alice, *Über Alice*. It was sometime just after the dawning of the Age of Aquarius. An outdoor party on a warm, late spring night in Harvard's Radcliffe Quadrangle, where the two were undergraduates. Torch lights were flickering, and the nighttime sky was filled with stars.

* * *

He asked one of his friends who the tall blonde was, standing next to one of the torches. "She has an almost ethereal beauty . . . and a dimple to boot."

"Where you been, man? This the first time you hung your eyes on Alice Van Houten?"

Carpenter wasted no time cornering her in the drinks line and, as was his custom when quarrying a woman of interest, he spoke boldly and to the point. He knew he was not attractive in the conventional sense, but when making his approach he took assurance in his intellectual superiority, relying on a natural self-confidence that often led him to the boundaries of arrogance and recklessness. He moved close to Alice, paused for a second to watch the torchlight flicker in her eyes, and then whispered softly to her:

> "O, she doth teach the torches to burn bright
> It seems she hangs upon the cheek of night
> Like a rich jewel in an Ethiope's ear.
> Beauty too rich for use, for Earth too dear . . . "

Next came the part he liked best, the repartee to his outrageous come-ons. Sometimes even a slap. Occasionally the girl became so flustered she just left blushing, speechless. But experience proved that one in ten was seduced by his boldness and his brilliance. *One in ten is good enough odds for me,* he thought, as he took note of all the shy and awkward boys huddled in groups, standing around the periphery of the party. *Better odds than they have,* he comforted himself.

"Hmmm . . . *'Beauty too rich for use, for Earth too dear,'*" she repeated, trying to place the line. "Normally, I'd think you were a creep and tell you to go screw yourself," she said without missing a beat, "but you're lucky because I just happen to have a soft spot for Shakespeare, especially *Romeo and Juliet,* even if it is sentimental, sexist and bourgeois to its core. So instead of telling you to *f— off,* I'll be nice and just ask you to get lost."

After she had turned and left, leaving him momentarily dumbstruck, he felt a flutter in his heart.

Two days later while reading the *Harvard Crimson,* he saw an advertisement for the American Repertory Theater and couldn't believe his luck. *Romeo and Juliet!* He checked the campus directory to see where she lived. That evening, he waited outside her dormitory for her to return from classes.

"Remember me from that party last Saturday in the Quad? You said I was lucky you didn't tell me to . . . I believe 'screw myself' was the term you used . . . because you liked Shakespeare, especially *Romeo and Juliet*? So you just told me to get lost?"

She nodded cautiously, unsure what to make of his effrontery.

"Well now it looks as though you're the one that's lucky, because *Romeo and Juliet* starts tomorrow night at the ART, and guess who has two tickets?"

* * *

Carpenter looked again at the picture of Alice. *What would you think of me now? Would you be proud of me, finally embracing your Moral Absolute? No longer "Maury, the Ideological Jello," as you once labeled my political convictions? Or would you think I've now gone completely off the deep end?*

He recalled longingly his final conversation with her. It was by then seven years after he painted the picture of her hanging over his mantelpiece, and the two were living together in New York. He was completing a joint M.D. and Ph.D. degree in biochemistry at Columbia. Their relationship, always tenuous, had begun to deteriorate in earnest. While he was engrossed in his Ph.D. thesis and completely drained by the load of his studies, Alice was supporting them both by working as a research assistant to a sociology professor at NYU.

Eager to bed her, the professor had not only introduced her to various powerful mind-altering substances; he was also fueling her with notions of accompanying him on an upcoming research trip to Namibia. Never having left the U.S., she found the thought of traveling to Africa had kindled a powerful wanderlust in her. She had begun to talk of going to South Africa to fight apartheid. Her plans for the future vague and unsettled, she'd waved off Carpenter's hopes for marriage and a family with the admonition to forgo "such petty bourgeois notions."

* * *

Alice was furious. "What the hell is this?"

She shoved a set of papers in his face. The offending documents were his employment application to the Brookhaven National Laboratory. His ideological equivocation and political ambivalence had always been a sore spot with her. *But now this . . . this betrayal was too much.*

"An employment application, Alice. Please recall I'm about to graduate at long last, and presumably I need to find work, don't I?" He could see the anger rising in her face.

"In a National Laboratory? Those places were created to develop *nuclear weapons*. You want to work as a *war pig*, in an arsenal of fascist military oppression?"

"Don't be so simpleminded. They're pushing the envelope at Brookhaven — the technology has many peaceful applications. Oppenheimer, Alice, think Oppenheimer."

"Think 'Oppenheimer' what?"

When faced with Alice's fury, logic and eloquence would often abandon him. "Oppenheimer was a committed humanitarian. Nuclear weapons are terrible, but who knows how many lives were saved as a result of his invention? Millions — Americans and Japanese — might have died if the U.S. had been forced to invade the Japanese home islands." He sensed his argument was unlikely to convince her, and regretted the words as soon as they'd escaped his mouth.

"You want to go off and design *nuclear weapons?*"

"No Alice. Not nuclear weapons. MEMS. I want to work on *MEMS*. Brookhaven is light years ahead of everyone else, and the funding is almost unlimited. I'm convinced that MEMS will revolutionize our world."

"'MEMS will revolutionize our world?'" she asked incredulously. "What in God's name is '*MEMS?*'" Her face was turning red. "Whatever happened to, say . . . working in academia? What about our discussions on the importance of spreading truth and beauty through teaching? If you want to 'revolutionize our world,' then how about starting with a revolution to liberate the oppressed?"

Her eyes were now ablaze with rage. Clearly he'd failed again to live up to her standards of moral courage. With her it was all or nothing. He knew she'd never truly accept him if she felt he weren't fully committed to their mutual cause.

* * *

Why didn't I just shut up then and there? Why couldn't I have just taken her advice . . . gone into academia? He again castigated himself just as he often had over the past thirty-odd years.

He recalled wanting to share details about the direction of his intended research at Brookhaven, but remembered checking himself. His supreme idea — the idea he'd been secretly nurturing for so long — was too important and too powerful to share with anyone.

The idea had come to him early one morning in a *Eureka!* moment as he was eating cornflakes in his cramped graduate student apartment. He had been absentmindedly watching a fly crawl up the wall, and when it unexpectedly disappeared into a small crack where the wall met the ceiling, *The Idea* had burst into his brain like an electric shock. From that instant on, *The Idea* had maintained a constant, physical presence in his innermost thoughts.

Further steeling his resolve to remain silent, Alice's new crowd was heavily involved with drugs, and she was known to be indiscreet when she was high. It had come back to him that on one 'trip' she had been unflatteringly descriptive to her friends about private parts of his anatomy. So he had never shared *The Idea* with her, and wasn't about to. *Besides, she would just laugh at me.*

"Alice, I've thought a lot about this," he had offered. "I don't want to spend the rest of my life writing papers on *Clinical Manifestations of Gonadal Dysgenesis*. I need to create things. Some of the projects going on at Brookhaven could have applications in prosthetics, in medicine, or in the environment. If I'm going to work in research, I've got to work in the best facility available, and quite simply, I'm convinced that MEMS — Micro Electro-Mechanical Systems — is where I need to focus."

The reference to the technology went by her unremarked.

"You need to create things? Don't bullshit me, Maury. Everyone knows the place is a laboratory for mass murder."

He remembered trying a different tack in a bid to win her over. "Alice, I'm going to subvert the System from within. I'm going to use the System's weapons against itself."

"Not the whole 'reform from within' crap again! How many times have we been over this? You know the only way to change the System is through confrontation. You have to destroy it and build a better System on the rubble of the old. Because you know that the System is too powerful. It will co-opt you if you try to work from within it. You think you're going to subvert it, but it will end up subverting *you*. The next thing you know you'll be in the rat race, living in a little house in the suburbs with a white picket fence and mortgage payments, and you'll have become *enslaved*." She gave him a cold stare which told him that the conversation wouldn't end well.

"Listen. If I'd spent less time confronting or going to protests with you, and more time thinking, inventing, and discovering, who knows? Maybe I could have invented something useful . . . a weapon . . . a weapon that could actually stop the war, end all wars . . . a weapon for *peace*. An invention that could have saved Jimmy," he pleaded.

"I'm onto something beautiful, Alice. So beautiful . . . Trust me, please. Just trust me on this."

Carpenter would never forget that next moment.

"So you're onto something *beautiful*, are you? Well, if it's beauty you're after, then by all means don't let me get in your way," she said, her voice dripping with sarcasm. Then she added: "But just you be damned sure you don't end up with *beauty* that's '*too rich for use, for Earth too dear!*'"

A cold silence fell between them, as if both knew an unspoken line had been crossed. After a brief lull, the conversation resumed its inevitable, destructive path. He particularly recalled the look of disgust in Alice's eyes as she uttered her parting words.

"You're insane. A *weapon* that can stop war?" she said, shaking her head. "And you're tripping bad," she added, "if you think I'm going to spend the rest of my life with a fascist war pig."

CHAPTER 1

The doorbell rang at eight-thirty p.m. with three short rings that shook him out of his reverie. Seated in his leather easy chair in the living room, Dr. J. Maurice Carpenter, or "the Doc" as his colleagues referred to him, placed his wire-frame glasses over the bridge of his small, hooked nose and retrieved the remote control from the side table next to his chair. He turned down the stereo, which was playing Elgar's *Enigma Variations*, and rose slowly from the chair. Dressed in his customary mauve herringbone tweed jacket, tan oxford shirt, and khaki pants, he adjusted his bow-tie one last time, plastered a smile on his face and approached the front door. *This has to be good*, he thought with a gulp.

"Zach, come in!" Carpenter said, looking up at Zach as he opened the door. At just five-foot-eight inches tall, with a round belly, ruddy cheeks, and lively gray-blue eyes, Carpenter generally found himself looking up to greet his visitors. *Not too effusive. Just act natural. Don't make anyone suspicious,* he reminded himself.

Zach was his assistant at the laboratory. Twenty-eight years old, with deep blue eyes and curly blond hair. Master's Degree in Mechanical Engineering from Virginia Tech. Only eighteen months in the lab. *Capable enough. Worships me,* Carpenter thought with a tinge of satisfaction. *Well, I'm not going to hurt*

1

him, right? In the end, it's for his own good. For everyone's good. Can't make an omelet without breaking some eggs.

Zach stepped out of the unseasonably chilly nighttime drizzle into the warmth of Carpenter's living room. Carpenter had been careful to set the temperature just right.

"Quick, come in and have one of these," Carpenter said, offering a cup of mulled cider. He avoided looking Zach in the eye. "Make yourself at home."

Carpenter's house was a modest suburban craftsman home. Surrounded with knee-high white picket fencing and wrapped in white clapboards with dark green trim on wooden shutters, the exterior couldn't have been more plain. The interior, however, was anything but ordinary. The walls in the modest-sized living room were ablaze floor to ceiling with paintings and other artwork.

Moving into the living room, Zach stopped short as he caught sight of the paintings that decorated the walls.

"Wow!" he blurted in awe, "I didn't know you collected art."

Zach's gaze settled on a mid-sized piece hung prominently over the mantlepiece. It was the nude of Alice, and depicted a beautiful woman inclined languidly on a rich tableau of multicolored sheets, blankets, and throw pillows. The painting swirled with vivid hues of green, blue, purple and red.

"That one's amazing," Zach said, almost transfixed by the beauty of the subject. "Haunting," he added, as an afterthought.

Carpenter was pleased and mildly amused to gain Zach's approbation of his own favorite painting. An electrical engineer, Zach didn't strike Carpenter as one given to flights of romantic fancy or to aesthetic appreciation.

"I'm glad you like it," Carpenter said. "It's an original *Carpenter*. I painted that over forty years ago. I must have been younger than you are when I painted it." He thought wistfully of the subject.

"Did you paint it from a model?" Zach asked, pointing at the girl in the painting, then swatting after a fly crawling on the dimple that adorned her right cheek.

Carpenter nodded. Pointing to the fly, he gently admonished his protégé. Chastened, Zach withdrew his hand and left the fly alone.

"Was she that beautiful in real life?" he asked, refocusing on the painting.

"Well, Zach . . . " Carpenter replied pensively, weighing whether he should offer a glimpse of his private life to his assistant. After a moment's reflection he spoke.

"She was my first and only true love," he finally offered. "Beautiful beyond words. Had the heart of an angel, but a temperament to match the Devil himself."

As Carpenter checked himself and betrayed a hint of impatience, Zach refrained from further inquiry. Carpenter stole a glance at the painting, and then at the fly still stationary on the frame. *If you only knew what I'm about to do, Alice . . . If you only knew.*

After Carpenter excused himself to go into the kitchen to check on the evening's meal, Zach returned his attention to the collection of artwork. Not long after the scientist had left the room, Zach felt a slight twitch in the left nostril, as if a small insect had flown in. He tried to blow his nose to remove the foreign object, but couldn't be sure if he had successfully dislodged it. After a moment the sensation in his nose was gone, but a short time later he felt a blinding headache that lasted no more than an instant. The flash of pain elicited from him a startled gasp, and caused him a momentary unsteadiness on his feet.

"Everything OK?" Carpenter called out, peeking out from the kitchen in time to note his assistant regaining his composure, though still mildly dazed.

Zach nodded. "Headache or something, but it's gone now." Though clearly he was shaken, at least the pain and discomfort had vanished as quickly as they had come.

"Need an aspirin?" Carpenter asked helpfully. Zach shook his head to decline. After overcoming the feeling of disorientation, he resumed his perusal of the artwork.

Carpenter explained that the artwork was arranged as a *triptych*, as he called it, or three walls each with a distinct style of art. On the wall opposite the entrance, the wall where Zach had fixed his attention on the piece over the fireplace, were what Carpenter referred to as his romantic pieces. These were realistic pictures of nudes, almost all female, lovingly rendered in deep, glowing colors and bold brushstrokes.

On the far wall were works in the psychedelic and phantasmagoric genre, evoking artists such as Wes Wilson, Mati Klarwein and Friedensreich Hundertwasser. These were brightly colored, disorienting, highly symbolic day-glo jumbles of shapes, patterns and fanciful subjects. Stylized renderings of human brains, skulls, flowers, clocks, peace symbols, scales of justice and an occasional Egyptian *ankh* were the most frequently used motifs.

The third wall to the left of the entry was covered with well-framed black-and-white period photographs. Zach recognized that all were of important events that had defined the American social and political landscape in the nineteen-sixties and early nineteen-seventies. Neil Armstrong landing on the moon. The Civil Rights marches at Selma. Dr. Martin Luther King Jr. at the reflecting pond in Washington. Robert Kennedy speaking at the Ambassador Hotel in Los Angeles on June 5, 1968, moments before he was gunned down. Mary Ann Vecchio kneeling and screaming over the body of Jeffrey Miller, shot dead by Ohio National Guard troops at Kent State on May 4, 1970. Naked children fleeing a napalm attack at Trang Bang on June 8, 1972 during the Vietnam War.

"Quite the collection, Doc," Zach called out, clearly impressed even as his senses were overwhelmed by the panoply of color and shape and movement arrayed on all sides around him.

"The term 'collection' implies a body of works collected," Carpenter said matter-of-factly as he emerged from the kitchen.

He noted a look of puzzlement on Zach's face.

"I painted all of them," Carpenter explained, motioning around the room, and allowing a hint of pride into his voice. "The photographs I bought, of course, but the paintings are all mine. All original *Carpenters.*"

Zach found himself speechless for a moment.

"Well Doc, I'm no art connoisseur, but I'd say if you ever retired from the lab, you could have a pretty successful career as an artist. I'd buy your stuff."

Carpenter smiled coolly and gave a small awkward bob of his head, which passed for modesty on those occasions when he wished to convey a measure of humility.

Zach pointed to the psychedelic wall. "But tell me Doc, what's all that about?" he asked, gesturing towards some of the more disturbing images before him. Skulls, skeletons, bomb blasts. "What does that all mean?"

Carpenter hesitated before answering. "I'm not sure, Zach, that I can distill it all into just a few sentences." He wondered if he sounded patronizing, and instantly regretted his tone. He was genuinely fond of his assistant.

5

"It would take hours, days, or longer to explain properly. But let's just say that everything you see here on the walls is in some way a representation of the three most important precepts around which I have built my life: *beauty, truth,* and *justice. The Holy Trinity.* Those are the only precepts upon which anything of value can ever be built."

Zach nodded his head, mulling Carpenter's puzzling response. "Wow, Doc. That's deep," was the best he could muster.

In preparation for the other guests who would soon be arriving, Carpenter went to the kitchen and returned with a tray loaded with reinforcements of apple cider. Zach was still scanning the artwork. Carpenter put down the tray, and then turned to look once more at the painting of Alice.

He had finished the nude of Alice in his sophomore year at Harvard where he had gone on to graduate *summa cum laude* in mathematics. The *communards* in Winthrop House had named her *Über Alice,* in reference to the fact that she was very blonde, very blue-eyed, and very well endowed. It was during a period in his life when he was called — not altogether fondly — *Pro-Patria Maury. Dolce et decorum est pro patria mori,* Carpenter recalled wistfully, expelling a sigh that echoed four decades down in the pit of his stomach. *How sweet and fitting that I die for my country.*

Über Alice. Pro-Patria Maury. He felt the appellations a bit unfair, especially to Alice, who was as *Left* as they came and bore the nickname simply because of her association with him, and because of her teutonic features and proportions. In Carpenter's case, he was hardly the chest-thumping super-patriot the nickname conveyed. A liberal of changeable commitment, he earned his moniker simply by failing to be as radical as most of his fellow students. He shared great sympathy with the progressive causes of the day — civil rights, women's rights, the environment — but oblivious to fashion, he refused to wear his hair long, dress in jeans, embrace Maoism, and take drugs ("Mathematics is challenging enough without the added burden of cognitive impairment"). Most damningly of all, he was lukewarm in his opposition to the Vietnam War. It wasn't just that he had flat feet and therefore didn't fear the draft. Hating totalitarianism, he was genuinely ambivalent about the war. That ambivalence later turned to grief and guilt when his older brother James was killed in a friendly fire incident near Da Nang in nineteen seventy.

Zach cleared his throat. "Hedlinger and McIntyre coming too?" he asked, pulling Carpenter out from his thoughts. Hedlinger and McIntyre were the MEMS team experts on semiconductor fabrication.

"Everyone will be here tonight," Carpenter replied, emerging quickly back into the moment. "All thirteen of us," he added.

"They say around the lab you're an accomplished violinist too," Zach said, pointing to a photograph on the mantelpiece of Carpenter playing in a string quartet.

"Viola, actually," Carpenter said curtly, beginning to tire of the small talk. He had more pressing things on his mind. "Lucky for you, I'm also a pretty good cook, which hopefully you'll find out in a few minutes, assuming I haven't ruined tonight's meal."

The doorbell rang. Raj Agarwal, the electrical engineer, and Dong-Su Kang, the materials scientist, arrived. "Raj, D.S., come on in," Carpenter shouted, putting down a serving tray before giving each a hearty slap on the back. "Glad you could make it."

A few moments later, Arkady Lubchenko, thermodynamics, and Rob Pittman, optics, were there. The computer programmers arrived after a few more minutes. Handshakes and hugs all around. There was a sense of celebration in the air, and curiosity. It was the first time Carpenter had had any of them to his house. Carpenter excused himself to go into the kitchen while the guests milled in the living room, many of them examining and puzzling over Carpenter's artwork.

After all the guests had arrived, Carpenter and Zach emerged from the kitchen with rack of lamb, done medium rare, steaming from the oven and dimpled with red pools of blood. Then came the wild rice, French beans, and a vinaigrette salad with toasted walnuts, brie cheese, green apple, and raisins. Carpenter laid out the food on a sideboard beside a basket of bread before uncorking bottles of Willamette Valley Oregon *pinot noir* and Mendocino *sauvignon blanc*. He then invited the guests to help themselves and watched with satisfaction as they made themselves comfortable at the dining table, on the sofa, and on the settees in the living room. Carpenter officially began the meal by passing the bread to Zach.

The guests spent the dinner focused mainly on the food, with idle chatter interspersed here and there amidst an atmosphere of congeniality and customary levity. As the guests were finishing the peach cobbler pie *à la mode*, McIntyre pointed to his dessert and proposed a toast to Carpenter. "Leave it to the Doc to deliver *peach in our time*," he said to a chorus of groans all around, mixed together with exclamations of "Hear, hear!" and "To the Doc!"

At last Carpenter rose slowly, acknowledging the banter with a smile and characteristic bob of the head. He then struck his wine glass three times with a fork. Never one for speeches, he wasn't fully comfortable upon the altar, but he felt reassured as he looked across the pews at the trusting faces of his yet unknowing disciples.

"Gentlemen," he said, as he held up his glass.. He was pleased to see that the conversation died down quickly after he raised his glass. As head of the laboratory, he was their undisputed leader, their high priest, and in the disciplines of mathematics, machine vision, artificial intelligence, and other facets of their common endeavor, he was their *Word become Flesh*. All eyes were on him now.

"You all leave me *peachless*," he began. The groans resumed.

"To a project well done!" he said, beaming with genuine pride. "I raise my glass to all of you." There was a chorus of cheers all around and a clinking of glasses.

"Now," he continued, "the reason I saved the speech for after dinner is that I have a small demonstration to make, and I didn't want to ruin everyone's appetite by holding the demonstration *before* dinner . . . "

The guests exchanged glances. *What's he up to?* Carpenter could practically hear his guests wondering what would happen next.

"So, if you'll just excuse me for one moment," he said, returning to the living room a moment later with a caged rat.

"This rat is an *ex*-rat," he began with a smile and a twinkle of the eye. There was an uneasy rustle around the room, a shifting of seats. While several present chuckled, having understood the veiled reference to an infamous *Monty Python* skit favored among the scientists, the atmosphere had already shifted. The levity that had filled the room just moments before had quickly begun to evaporate. Seasoned weapons designers all, each had witnessed the demise of countless rats. Still, it was considered politically incorrect to make light of killing a living creature. To *off* a rat cavalierly somehow violated an unspoken code among the fraternity — and everyone knew Carpenter of all people upheld the code as fastidiously as anyone. After all, weapons designers were supposed to create weapons in order to *save lives* by defending the *peace*.

Everyone there knew Carpenter enjoyed playing the iconoclast on occasion, and knew also that he reveled in overstepping boundaries. But just how far over all boundaries Carpenter would step tonight, none had any idea.

He removed from his jacket pocket a dark gray device similar to a remote-control.

"Gentlemen. May I draw your attention to the rodent," he said with a subtle hint of merriment, and pointed to the cage. He jauntily punched a few keys on the remote control, and suddenly something — which appeared to the guests as a fly or gnat, but smaller — flew at blinding speed into the cage. It landed on the rat's nose and quickly burrowed into its right nostril, to the furious distress of the rat. With repeated violent strokes of its paw, the creature attempted urgently to dislodge the insect.

Theatrically, Carpenter raised his right hand, as if he were a concert pianist preparing to unleash a dramatic *arpeggio,* and then he punched another key on the remote control device. The rat immediately went into a moment of violent spasm and exhibited death tremors. A few breaths later, with claws bent and teeth bared, it abruptly flipped prostrate, evacuated its bladder, and finally lay still.

Silence took hold. Collective breaths held. Zach looked ashen. He had just begun to draw the connection with the twitching he felt in his nostril earlier in the evening, and the accompanying headache. Carpenter returned Zach's glance with an icy stare and a finger over the lips, indicating silence. To convey his seriousness to Zach, he also made a menacing gesture with the remote control, as if to say *don't try anything stupid.*

A flurry of glances around the room reflected the shared hope that the rat was perhaps only paralyzed, but eventually gave way to the discomforting truth that the rat was indeed dead. The crowd of scientists surveyed each others' faces. Up to now, in the laboratory, Carpenter had been careful to make sure each had worked on his own small piece of the puzzle. None but he ever glimpsed the project in its entirety. Finally confronted with the full and direct implications of their two-decade-long scientific collaboration with Carpenter, the scientists now felt their glints of discomfort give way to a subtle undercurrent of terror that flitted across the room. Then Lubachenko, with his thick eastern European accent, spoke in a theatrically hushed and deep voice.

"I am become Death, Destroyer of Worlds," he said, echoing Oppenheimer after *Trinity*. The assembled crowd exchanged a collective nervous giggle. But farsighted as he was, not even Lubachenko had any idea about the plans Carpenter was secretly harboring for his new weapon.

"Now, now," Carpenter said, cutting in. "Let's not get overly dramatic. No one here has anything to fear. We're not here to destroy the world. We're here to *rebuild* it."

As the other guests were leaving, ten minutes later, Carpenter entreated Zach to stay on. A gesture to the remote device he was holding in his right hand made it clear to Zach that there was to be no consideration of refusal.

CHAPTER 2

Boxed in on all sides, Bill "Mad Dog" Maddox changed lanes and punched the accelerator on his Audi TT, only to come within inches of the rear bumper of an SUV blocking his way. The daily commute from his Victorian craftsman home in the historic Adams district of Los Angeles to the FBI field office on Wilshire Boulevard in Westwood was beginning to grate seriously on his nerves. The traffic was only one of many things weighing on him. Long-time difficulties with his wife, the recent unsuccessful conclusion of a high-profile narcotics case, *barely even a conviction,* and a profound sense of personal and professional disillusionment had reduced him to something near clinical depression of late. He checked himself in the rear-view mirror, and though still pleased with the ruggedly handsome face that peered back at him, he noticed a few more wrinkles surrounding his hazel-green eyes, a few more gray hairs mixing into his curled red-brown sideburns, and an extra heaviness weighing on his thick, clay-colored eyebrows.

He looked out the window and felt lost, a stranger in his own city. He found it disorienting to drive for miles down Olympic Boulevard and not come across one sign in English, not even in the Roman alphabet. From Beverly down to Pico, Vermont to Fairfax, the signage was all in Korean. In fact, the only English he saw was the occasional graffiti from some of the black gangs that used to rule the area. Those gangs were now in retreat in the face of Korean expansion. *At least the graffiti here is still in English*, he thought to himself wryly. Closer to his office, the signs along posh Westwood Boulevard were now mostly in Farsi. *What happened to the city I grew up in?*

A native of Torrance, California and graduate of California State University at Fullerton, Maddox had been with the FBI for twenty-two years. He started there not long after he left the Marines after stints in Central America, and before that in Lebanon. It was in Beirut in nineteen eighty-three that two hundred and forty-one of his comrades were killed in a suicide truck bomb attack. He couldn't pinpoint the moment when the enthusiasm he'd felt throughout most of his career in the FBI had started to wane, but he was sure it took a steep descent right after Nine-Eleven. The event laid bare what he could only conclude was colossal incompetence at the Bureau. He was at a loss to explain how the FBI itself could have failed to put computers on the desks of a large number of agents, or how it could have run four separate Information Technology platforms in parallel, none of which was capable of interfacing with the others. While the Bureau had made great strides in the intervening years, Maddox had still been unable to recover his earlier enthusiasm.

Adding to his malaise, an unfortunate incident in an important case in Colombia had further stunted his once-promising career. There was nothing overt in the postmortem report, just an observation that " . . . *also contributing to the mission's failure was the fact that Maddox took more risks with his agents than would otherwise have been warranted under the circumstances.*" Now, between the occasional suggestion that he might wish to mull the attractiveness of some "very generous" early retirement programs on offer to longstanding personnel, and more recent talk that he would probably soon be relegated to Vice, Maddox had started to count his days. While he realized his options at the Bureau were dwindling fast, the thought of life beyond the Bureau seemed to him a bleaker prospect still. *What will I become? Security consultant? How easy are those jobs to land? Small arms peddler? Night guard at Seven Eleven?* For now, then, he considered himself fortunate just to be punching the clock.

Maddox passed through the metal detector in the office lobby, then went to the FBI offices on the seventeenth floor. He managed a few perfunctory smiles as he made his way to his cubicle.

He passed the office of his boss, James Martin. A devout Mormon, Martin was as straight-laced, by-the-book, no-nonsense, and hard working as any FBI agent Maddox had ever seen. Fastidious in his dress, he always kept his graying dark brown hair perfectly combed with hardly a single strand out of place.

How does he always get such a razor-sharp part in his hair?

As he came to his own cubicle, he passed Janice, the secretary he shared with three other agents on the narcotics team. For Janice he was able to produce a sincere smile, even if short-lived. *Janice has my back*, he reminded himself. He wasn't surprised that having grown up in a broken family in a gang-ridden area of Compton she could be a bit rough around the edges at times, but he was grateful for her enduring loyalty, and also for the sympathy in her eyes as she returned his smile. Her cheerfulness was one of the few things to which he looked forward as he came to work each day. But when he saw the workload on his desk, his spirits sank anew.

Colombia didn't seem like so long ago. *Bianca, where are you now?*

Everything had been going so well. He, Maddox, had actually managed to turn the kingpin's moll. Or so he thought at the time.

Bianca had stunned him with her deep brown eyes, wavy, long, dark brown hair, and ample bust. They had met at a party in Bogotá, in Chapinero to be exact, with a sweeping view of the Cordillera Oriental right out the front window. They'd been seeing each other for almost a month after the party, when he pressed her to go back to the cartel leader just one last time. For just one more piece of intel. And so she did, but she never came back.

So, boom! Just when we thought we had the case nailed, the trap was reversed. The ambushers became the ambushed. Donohue, poor Donohue.

Did she play me all along, or did they find out about her and turn her? Force it out of her?

* * *

Maddox's phone rang. It was Martin calling him to his office.

In Martin's sparsely decorated office Maddox was joined by two other colleagues from the narcotics team, McDonough and Weintraub.

"We've got pressure from the top," Martin was explaining, "to produce some very high-profile arrests over the next few days." Having read the papers the previous day, Maddox wasn't surprised. Eighty-two corpses had been discovered in a mass grave outside of Ciudad Juárez, each shot execution-style in the back of the head, and the Mayor of Ciudad Juárez had received by mail a care package containing his daughter's severed head. As a result, the Mexican government was pressing hard for

15

dramatically increased U.S. cooperation in the drug war, hinting even at the possibility of withholding a key vote in the UN Security Council should the U.S. not comply.

Maddox understood what "pressure from the top to make some very high-profile arrests over the next few days" would mean in practice. He would have to lean hard on Omar Rodriguez, one of his few remaining informants in the Mexican Mafia.

Based in El Monte, California, *The End of the Santa Fe Trail*, Rodriguez was Maddox's eyes and ears into the Mexican Mafia. A senior lieutenant in *La Eme*, as the notorious criminal organization was known in the *barrio*, Rodriguez was looking to go straight, and Maddox was his only hope for doing so. Maddox had already helped Rodriguez's daughter get out of jail, away from the *homeys*, and into a good-paying job as a medical receptionist. He'd also helped Rodriguez's son win dramatically reduced charges in a homicide case, and after the son's release saw to it that he finished his high school diploma. And if it weren't for Maddox's intervention on more than one occasion, Rodriguez knew he himself would have been dead or locked away in state prison by now. Rodriguez owed everything he had to Maddox. Through years of collaboration, Rodriguez had become more than just Maddox's best informant. If such a thing were possible, he was even on some level a friend.

And so now, even though Rodriguez — having seen too many of his friends and associates end up dead or in jail — had been begging Maddox to get him out of the game completely, Maddox would have to lean on him one more time. Both knew that the Mafia was growing in sophistication and employing ever more advanced surveillance techniques, including the use of electronic eavesdropping. Any contact between Rodriguez and Maddox would risk putting Rodriguez in even more jeopardy. Both also knew about the Mexican Mafia blood oath, which stipulated that the only way out of the organization was to be killed.

"A few high-profile arrests?" Martin's words echoed in his ears. *Instead of trying, mostly in vain, to roll back the distribution networks, why don't we try to do just a little more in terms of curtailing demand for the product?* Maddox wondered. He wanted to ask Martin why, the next time the socialite celebrity London Conrad was busted on felony cocaine possession while driving in Beverly Hills in her Rolls Royce, instead of releasing her with a slap on the wrist, couldn't they send her down to Ciudad Juárez for just six months of community service? She could work with the widows, orphans and other innocent victims of the drug trade. Or why not imprison her among the general prison population until she gives up the names of everyone she's ever seen snorting or selling "blow?" But Maddox knew better than to open his mouth, so he remained quiet as Martin finished the briefing.

Once back at his cubicle, Maddox sat still in his chair wondering where he should begin his day. As often of late, his thoughts flew back to Colombia. *Donohue paid the price, and I guess I should consider myself lucky to get off with just a reprimand . . . "Maddox took more risks with his agents than would otherwise have been warranted."*

What made the postmortem report so damning, and potentially terminal to his career, was the fact that it put Maddox in an untenable quandary. If he continued to take risks on the mission, he might perpetuate the idea that somehow he was too dangerous, too trigger-happy to be relied upon. On the other hand, if he avoided risk they might say he had become too gun-shy, had become washed up. *Amazing how clear everything looks with the benefit of hindsight.*

Staring out the window absentmindedly, surveying the endless rows of crosses in the veterans' cemetery across Wilshire Boulevard, he rearranged the casework on his desk. He flipped through his folders idly. *So many cases, so little time . . . And then you do all the work, really give it your all, try to make sure you dot every "i" and cross every "t," and the bastards still walk free . . .*

CHAPTER 3

Carpenter put down his calculator one last time and nodded his head with satisfaction. *It will work.* He was in his book-lined home office, seated at his mahogany desk, pouring over an exhaustive set of plans and making a few last minute changes to his preparations. Aside from the excruciating detail demanded by the next steps in his audacious scheme, though he wouldn't have allowed himself to admit it, he also found involvement in the minutiae a good way to silence the few remaining troubling voices that struggled to be heard from deep within his conscience.

Demanding all the more acquiescence from his conscience was the knowledge that he could, in fact, still turn back if he wanted. Yes, he had infected Zach with the *microbot* a week ago at the party. And yes, three days after the party at a specially arranged "family night" open house at the laboratory, over the course of the evening he had surreptitiously infected the rest of the laboratory team along with their wives and children. But if he wished, he still could command the *bots,* as they were called, to expel themselves from their hosts and thus buy silence through his magnanimity, or leave those he infected with merely a dormant *bot* as *quid pro quo* in exchange for a promise of silence. Either way, the affair needn't go any further than his small circle of cohorts and their immediate families.

Although it had been quite a struggle, in the end he had managed to wrestle his conscience into submission, even to the point where he had obtained its reluctant support to proceed with his plans. He also reminded himself not to be naive. Having already deployed the *bots*, he had already released the genie from the bottle. There could be no turning back.

He glanced at his pills on the end table, pills his cardiologist had prescribed two months earlier. He didn't need to remind himself of the doctor's prognosis. The periodic chest pains gave him all the more impetus to seize the moment. *Who knows how much time I have left?* In fact, his growing sense of mortality had hastened his preparations to a degree with which he wasn't fully comfortable, moving forward the entire plan by six months. *If I had the luxury of time, it would have been better to wait a few more months until after the elections.*

* * *

Zach was in Carpenter's cramped den watching television. *Nothing but bad news.* The economy was going from bad to worse. President Drake's approval rating had hit an all-time low, even in his home state of Virginia. A big trial involving a large Colombian drug cartel had ended in a hung jury and, according to an interview with Los Angeles-based FBI narcotics agent, Bill Maddox, the outcome was sure to deal a huge blow to the government's efforts to stem the flow of illegal narcotics into the country.

"Zach, please be ready to leave in five minutes," Carpenter called out from upstairs.

Sequestered incommunicado in the Doc's house for an entire week since the fateful party, Zach had only television for release. With Carpenter's cable offerings being quite sparse, he was forced to watch re-runs of the news. Such was his boredom that even though he had no idea where Carpenter was about to take him, he was glad at least to be finally leaving the house.

Five minutes later, he heard Carpenter's footsteps on the stairs. Zach emerged from the den to see Carpenter struggling with his suitcase. He helped his mentor down the last few steps, his habit of respect and deference undiminished by his week-long captivity. Zach's suitcase was already standing by the door, and he placed the senior scientist's suitcase next to his. He watched the older man in silhouette for a moment.

Passing through the living room, Carpenter paused in front of the mantelpiece to stare at the picture of Alice one last time. He slowly reached out a hand towards her image. *What have I started, Alice? Please tell me I'm doing the right thing.*

As if sensing Carpenter's hesitation, Zach said, "It's still not too late to turn back."

Carpenter shook his head slowly. "Time to cross the Rubicon, my boy," he said with finality. "I'm afraid the die has already been cast, and there's no turning back now."

CHAPTER 4

D r. Heather Anderson gently shook her long mane of silky, chestnut hair, and then turned to look out pensively on the fading pastel light of day. Outside the window, a flight of geese drifted silently against the coral sky, and specks of orange light scattered languorously over the gray, undulating surface of Lake Minnetonka. The sun's last rays burnished her skin and set an ethereal glow to her blue eyes. She briefly watched her reflection in the window, and made a pout which accentuated her dimple.

She produced the pout as her moment of silent contemplation was interrupted by an annoying sound. *Boom, boom, boom* . . . the thumping sound came from the study. At first, the sound didn't register with her, subtle as it was. It merely troubled her on an unconscious level. After a few moments, though, at last it broke through the walls of her conscious mind and she recognized it for an instant for what is was — the sound of doom. *Another doomed relationship?* she wondered, before pushing the thought aside. She was not prepared at this time to allow herself to face the reality squarely.

"Honey," she said from instinct, shouting over the thumping bass as she turned towards the study, "would you please turn that down?"

No response.

She continued setting the table, laying a fork carefully here, a knife there.

"Stan, love," she repeated, this time louder, "I said please turn the music lower!"

Still no response.

The plate rattled loudly on the small oak veneer table as she put it down abruptly. She turned her gracefully upturned nose towards the source of the noise, marched to the study, knocked, and then opened the door without waiting for a response. Standing in the threshold, she mouthed "*turn . . . it . . . down!*"

Her boyfriend, Stan Garrett, made a tired show, heaved his large frame up reluctantly and turned down the music. Both exchanged glares.

"I can't concentrate, you know," she said.

He shrugged.

"I come home from a hard day at work in the clinic, and I need to decompress a little," she explained, a soft plea for sympathy entering into her voice. She disliked confrontation.

"You know," she continued, "you should put yourself in my place some time. Try spending just *one* week in the Neurology clinic dealing with terminally sick kids all day long. Anyway, I don't know why you listen to that rap garbage. Especially since you know I can't stand it."

"Sorry, gorgeous. I put it on before you got home, and I didn't know you were back yet," he retorted in the tone she always found patronizing. The tone where he slows down and puts a lilt on the word in the sentence he wants to emphasize. The tone that seemed to her to leave an unspoken '*duh*' dangling at the end.

"Cut me a little slack, will ya, babe? And by the way, it's not garbage. It's art, original *Art*, or the closest we'll get to Art in our time."

"Weren't you just going on the other day about how Art is dead?" she asked, bored.

"It is," he retorted. "That's why I say it's the *closest thing* to Art. Because the real thing is most definitely dead. Painting, theater, music, literature, poetry, cinema. All dead. Stone dead."

"Don't they say that every generation? Isn't that what they said just before Beethoven came along? Picasso?"

"Yeah, but this time it's finally true. In times past, one generation would say 'Art is dead' and then in the next generation someone, an original genius, would come along to prove the doubters wrong. More recently a Dylan Thomas or a Ginsberg. A Beckett or Stoppard. A Bergman."

"And . . . ?"

"So when's the last time a decent classical composer came along? Someone whom anyone outside of a few ancient turtlenecked musicologists buried in some underfunded university basement can stand listening to?"

She shrugged indifferently, not wanting to be drawn into the discussion, but drawn in nonetheless.

"Stravinsky, maybe?" he posited.

She shrugged.

"Kurt Weill?" he offered.

Another shrug.

"Surely not Bartók, Schoenberg," he continued, "or Alban Berg, or any other composer that followed those atonal symphonic sadists," he posited. "I mean the test of great music, great art is that it has to *last,* right? It has to stand the *test of time.*

"Can you really see anyone coming home now, or in fifty, a hundred, two hundred years from now, and pouring themselves a scotch, putting on a soft pair of slippers, and kicking back in the easy chair to listen to a Bartók string quartet? Or, improbable as it might be, actually hearing a Bartók string quartet on the radio or at the mall and then saying to themselves cheerfully, 'Oh lovely, that's Bartók's Fifth String Quartet!'"

She shrugged again.

"Here," he continued, relishing the polemic quality of the discussion, his voice taking on an ever more patronizing tone, "would you like to hear some Bartók?"

She shook her head, but he ignored her.

"Here, listen," he said, queuing up Bartók's Fifth String Quartet on the iTunes in his computer. The music issued forth with uneven rhythms and, to Heather's ear, unpleasant, screeching tones.

"Okay, enough," she said after a moment, not wanting to continue listening after the first few seconds had passed. "I'll take the *rap*. Anything but Bartók."

He ignored her, and continued to play the Bartók, though he turned it down slightly so that she could hear him continue in his argument.

"And when did Bartók stop composing?" he pursued, a bullying quality entering into his voice. She had no idea, and thus didn't answer.

"In nineteen forty-five," he informed her with an air of superiority. "That's well over *sixty years ago*! It's been almost three generations now. So much for the next generation proving the prior generation wrong," he concluded triumphantly.

"OK, smarty-pants. What about Barber?" she interjected finally. "Or Copeland?" she asked, pressing the point home. "They wrote some fairly decent stuff, didn't they? Not too hard on the ear."

"OK, fine," Garrett admitted reluctantly. "Maybe I'll allow you Barber and Copeland. But they were still, what, fifty, sixty years ago, so they prove nothing. The argument still holds: classical music has been totally dead for a long, long time."

She dipped her head slightly in assent.

"And you want to tell me music is not dead?" he asked rhetorically, shaking his head. "And what about painting? When's the last time an original painter came along? Pollock? Johns? Warhol?"

She remained impassive.

"Those guys were forty-five or fifty years ago," he said, issuing a haughty laugh. "Everything that can be done on canvas has already been done. The arts have gone silent: Art is dead." He paused for effect. "Don't you see?"

She waited silently.

"And of course you know what this all means, right?" he went on.

She regarded him skeptically.

"This can only mean we're living at the end of History. At the *End of Days*. Look here in the Bible. I was just reading this the other day."

"Since when did you suddenly get religion?" she challenged.

"Even the Devil can quote scripture," he replied with a wink.

"See here, in *Revelations*," he pointed to a passage in the Bible he was holding, "'And when he had opened the seventh seal, there was silence in the heavens for half an hour . . . '" he quoted.

He held her gaze and paused before continuing.

"Heather, I'm telling you. That silence written of in the Bible, in *Revelations*, is the silence we are now experiencing in the Arts. That "half an hour" is our Time, our Generation. And what does it mean? It means the end of the world is upon us, now, sweetheart."

With that final conclusion, he shut off the Bartók and resumed playing his rap music.

Too tired to argue, she glared at him.

"You know, arguing with you makes me feel the way I did when I used to argue with my mother," she said at last.

"Really? I wasn't aware your mother was capable of intelligent discourse," he said smugly.

"Firstly, don't flatter yourself, you inconsiderate abomination of a medical intern. Secondly, I was referring to my real mother, not my stepmom."

"Based on that one time I met your mother a few years back, the night she basically threw me out of her house, I would have thought her even less cogent than your stepmom."

"The mere fact she was sensible enough to throw you out is ample testimony to her intellect," Heather said with finality, shutting the door behind her as she left the room. As she left, she thought to herself how much she really needed a new boyfriend, maybe even a real husband.

In truth, she had entered into the relationship with some doubts: she had to admit to herself that she first saw him as a kind of fix-me-up project. Both medical students, and both attractive — on the surface their union seemed logical enough. She was also drawn to his intellect, despite its abrasive qualities. With an almost genetic propensity to believe she could change her partners for the better, to mold them to her liking, she was not initially daunted by his brash and often argumentative nature. Over time, however, she had come to realize that the project of changing Stan was becoming a lost cause.

I'd be willing to trade five points of intellect for just two points of emotional maturity.

CHAPTER 5

No wonder his approval rating is so low, thought Carpenter. Carpenter glanced up to the podium where the most powerful man on earth was speaking. Standing on the dais behind President Daniel Uziah Drake were the Governor of Virginia, the First Lady, the President's two teenage children, and the Virginia party chairman. Behind the podium was a large campaign banner that read: "Re-elect Drake," and arrayed across the back of the stage were alternating signs reading: "Vote Drake, For Goodness' Sake!" and "Re-elect Drake."

"And so, we will continue to press forward on a broad range of policy initiatives to promote fair trade, strengthen the family, create jobs, lower taxes and enhance our military capabilities . . . " the President droned on, and Carpenter rolled his eyes. *The banality . . .*

And here I am, just forty feet away. Well within range. Carpenter let show a bittersweet smile . . . *One hundred and forty thousand dollars later . . . One fifth of my entire life's saving, the fruits of all my life's labor . . . A Summa Cum Laude from Harvard . . . An M.S. from Caltech, an M.D./Ph.D. from Columbia, more than thirty years of hard work at Brookhaven . . . And one-fifth of the sum-total of all that effort buys me a seat forty feet away from the President, only to hear him mouthing twenty minutes of platitudes to the party faithful . . .*

But what matters above all is that he's finally within range. *He's now within my grasp, and the moment of truth is finally here . . .*

Two years of tantalizing the Virginia State Economic Development board and an equal amount of time courting the state party apparatus was all it took for Carpenter to make a few very well-placed friends in the President's home state. He had even incorporated a company in Virginia, and on the strength of his impressive resumé had made known his plans to set up a large nanotechnology plant in Blacksburg, near Virginia Tech. The plant, he impressed upon local officials, would eventually spawn a high-tech cluster. "What the IC chip did for Silicon Valley, nanotechnology will do for Virginia," he told the spellbound state investment officials, who lapped up his vision by the bowlful. Several strategically placed political donations, a handsome retainer to a leading Richmond law firm, and Carpenter soon found doors open wide along the corridors of power in Richmond.

And the culmination of all that preparatory work was to secure the seat he was currently occupying in the grand ballroom of the Jefferson Hotel in Richmond Virginia. He was at the second most important table at the re-election campaign function, just around forty feet away from the President, or thirteen point sixty-eight meters to be exact, according to the readout in Zach's specially designed "camera." Carpenter surveyed the security surrounding the President, buzzcuts in suits with earpieces running down the back of their necks. *Straight from central casting.* He smiled. *Little do they know just what a sitting duck the President is.*

It's now or never, thought Carpenter, and he took a deep breath. He nodded at Zach, giving the signal to begin the well-rehearsed sequence. They had practiced the sequence countless times the prior week at Carpenter's house, where Zach had sullenly served his time as both a soldier and prisoner in Carpenter's cause.

Zach shifted his digital single-lens reflex camera, adjusting its small tripod and placing it on the dining table. "My wife wanted me to get some pictures of the President," Zach offered apologetically to the other diners at the thousand-dollar-per-plate dinner. "She couldn't be here, but she adores the man." He positioned the camera squarely on the table, squinted through the specially designed lens, and trained the camera directly at the President's left nostril.

Carpenter withdrew a large metal fountain pen from his pocket and jotted down some notes. Holding the pen under the table, he removed the cap and a small mechanical fly sped out. Using precisely arranged triangulation provided by low power radio transmitters he and Zach were carrying in their cell-phones, the *bot* maneuvered through the air currents towards the President. For the last few yards of flight, the *bot* trained on the infrared laser signal emitting from Zach's camera. For the last few centimeters, it was programmed to seek out the darkness of the target's nostril. It reached the target just as the President was completing his speech.

"With your help, we will build a better, stronger Virginia and a better, stronger America . . . Thank you, Richmond." The teleprompter switched off. Just then, the President felt a twitch in his nostril, but knowing that he was on television, he fought the urge to swat his nose. By the time he'd removed his hand-kerchief and attempted to dislodge the foreign object by sneez-ing, it was too late. The *fly* was already fastened to the inside of his nasal cavity, and shortly thereafter the anesthetic coating on the outside surface of the fly had desensitized the lining of his nasal passageway to such an extent that the unpleasantness no longer bothered him. The President stepped back from the podium to absorb a few moments of scripted applause from the party faithful, and then, with a sniffle and snort, descended from the podium.

He's mine now! Carpenter took in a breath of deep satisfaction. *Everything precisely according to plan.*

After dinner, Zach quietly collected and pocketed one of the campaign donation envelopes that had been arranged around the table at each place setting. With a worried look on his face, he excused himself from the table to go to the men's room. "I'm not sure if my stomach is so good right now, Doc," he said, feigning strong and immediate gastric discomfort.

Carpenter paused for a moment to consider. "Don't be long, Zach," he said, giving Zach a steely stare. "I'll be waiting here for you." Then, thinking it over and not wanting to let him out of his sight for even an instant, Carpenter hustled after him a few moments later, pushing his way through the throng to follow him to the men's room.

With at least a five second head start on Carpenter, Zach raced to the bathroom, increasing his pace as he moved forward through the crowd. He pushed open the door forcefully and, once inside, accosted an older, distinguished-looking man finishing up at the washbasin.

"Please, Sir, I need to borrow your pen," he said, his voice and eyes betraying an extreme anxiety that was all too real. The man reached slowly for his pen, unsure how to respond, and Zach snatched the writing instrument out of the man's hand.

"Now into the stall over there. Please hurry! This is a matter of life or death!" Zach barked, finding an inner strength in his voice that he hadn't realized he had. He guided the man gently but urgently into the stall. Though confused, the man complied, and then Zach rushed into the neighboring stall.

"Now please be absolutely quiet and don't say a word," Zach whispered urgently, "I'm going to give you an envelope in a second. Please mail it for me right away. Many innocent lives depend on this."

Zach took a deep breath. This was his one chance. Carpenter had not let Zach out of sight once since infecting him with the *microbot* a week earlier. The only member of the laboratory team with no immediate family threatened by Carpenter's *microbots*, Zach had spent the entire week at Carpenter's house under his mentor's twenty-four-hour watchful eye. Despite his captivity, his previous admiration for the Doc had somehow remained intact, and he couldn't bring himself to hate the man. But he had no intention of standing by and doing nothing as Carpenter carried out his plan.

He knew with extreme clarity that his life was in danger. One wrong move and Carpenter could end his life with a single punch of a button. After causing a fatal cerebral hemorrhage, the *microbot* would exit his body without a trace, leaving only a dead body behind — *mine!*

Just as Zach finished locking the door to his stall, the door to the bathroom swung open and Carpenter's voice called out: "Zach, are you in here? Everything OK?"

"Yes, fine, Doc," Zach responded with a grunt from within his stall. "Just a bit of the runs. Give me a minute, OK?"

"Gotcha. I'll be waiting for you right here."

As quickly and quietly as possible, Zach then scribbled a note onto a few sections of toilet paper he tore from the dispenser in his stall. He found it challenging to write while not tearing the paper. The difficulty was compounded by his racing heart and shaking hands. When he was done with the note, he placed it carefully into the donation envelope he had procured from the dinner table. He then scribbled an address on the front of the envelope. The address simply had the name of the only FBI agent he knew of, a Bill Maddox, whom he had briefly seen interviewed earlier that day on WNN News in connection with a highly publicized narcotics trial.

CHAPTER 6

Maddox set to work opening the morning mail. Targeted junk mail pedaling magazines, body armor, firearms, law enforcement events and conventions; a letter from the Director explaining recent organizational changes at the Bureau. He was ready to crunch the whole pile into a ball and toss it into the trash bin when a solitary envelope caught his eye. It was a personal letter, and there was no return address. Moreover, there was barely even an address. The hastily scribbled envelope was simply addressed: "URGENT and CONFIDENTIAL for Agent Bill Maddox ONLY, Fed. Bureau of Investigation, Los Angeles."

Maddox worked open the envelope carefully and pulled out the contents. His training had taught him to treat the letter gingerly, as evidence. He noted the postmark, stamped "Richmond." He was puzzled to find that the "letter" was actually written on toilet paper. *What kind of joke is this?* Struggling to decipher the erratic scribblings, he began to read, and a few moments later when he put it down, he was in a state of raw shock. He re-read the letter again to be sure he fully understood.

PRES DRAKE IN DANGER. MICROBOTIC PLAGUE. DR.
J. MAURICE CARPENTER, BROOKHAVEN NANOSCALE
WEAPONS LAB. CONTACT DR. BERNARD LEWIS, L.

LIVERMORE ASAP. MUST PROTECT LEWIS FM CARP! STAY AWAY FROM B'HAVEN: ALL THER COMPRMISED.

KEEP TOTAL SECRET. CANNOT TELL ANYONE OR MULTITUDES WILL DIE, INCLUDING PRES. DESTROY AFTER READING THIS.

Maddox put down the letter, and his mind began to race. He got up and paced the floor, then read the letter a third time. *What do I do with this? How to proceed? I should notify Secret Service about this at once. They're responsible for protecting the President. I'm in Narcotics — I'm supposed to go after drug traffickers, so why me?*

Normally, his caseload was provided to him by the office director. He was briefed, placed into a team, the plans were agreed, and then the case unfolded. *Simple.*

Never in his career had he come across anything like this letter, which demanded total silence and total suspension of disbelief. The questions tore through his head. *How can I verify that this is not some crazy hoax? If it's not, how can I possibly proceed with an investigation without telling anyone, not even the office director, about the letter?*

One thing was clear to him: if he were to find any answers they would have to come from Dr. Lewis at Lawrence Livermore Laboratories.

CHAPTER 7

The President held the envelope in his hand and weighed it. He tried to comfort himself with the knowledge that it had been screened for anthrax and contact poisons. Still, he hesitated before opening it. He read the outside of the letter again. "Extremely Confidential, for the President's Eyes Only." If it had been a normal letter, his aides would have opened it first, but in this case, given that the envelope was official stationery from the Brookhaven National Laboratory director's office, the "Eyes Only" security level was respected. The President's aide, Mandy Garcia, was standing behind him, watching to see what he would do.

He motioned for her to sit on the couch, and then he reached for his Selangor pewter letter opener and began to work the letter open. Mandy stared at the lines of his face as he read the letter, but he was impassive as he read.

Dear Mr. President,

At precisely six p.m. tomorrow evening, you will feel a splitting headache that will last exactly ten seconds. Do not be alarmed. You have nothing to worry about.

I would like to explain your symptoms to you personally.

As a matter of life or death you must not share the contents of this letter with anyone — not your physician, not the First Lady, not your staff.

Please arrange for me and my assistant Mr. Zach Eskar to visit you at the White House on Tuesday at six p.m. for a private meeting.

Sincerely,
J. Maurice Carpenter. M.D., Ph.D.
Director, Nanoscale Weapons Project
Brookhaven National Laboratory

The President's face was emotionless as he looked up from the letter. Mandy waited anxiously to see what the President would say. He folded the letter, put it away in his jacket pocket, and said nothing.

The following evening, the President looked at his Rolex watch. *Five fifty-eight p.m.* A gloomy, gray dusk had settled around the White House. He had his doubts, but still he excused himself from a campaign strategy briefing in the Oval Office to go to the bathroom, then sat on the toilet and waited. At six p.m. exactly, just as the letter had warned, a blinding jolt of pain tore through his cerebrum. The pain was so great it caused his legs to tremble violently. Though only lasting for ten seconds, the searing pain seemed to him to last several minutes. It produced a torrent of sweat and a racing heartbeat, but when it was finally gone, it disappeared without a trace. He felt perfectly normal except for the sweat on his brow and under his armpits. He cleared his thoughts, refocused his vision, and looked at his watch to note the time. Only seconds had passed.

"Mandy, please clear my schedule for Tuesday at six p.m. I'll be expecting two guests: Dr. J. Maurice Carpenter of Brookhaven National Laboratory and his assistant Zach Eskar. And please run a quick background check on the two."

* * *

Two days later, Carpenter and Zach arrived unceremoniously in a Yellow Cab taxi and reached the front gates of the White House at five fifty p.m. Carpenter noted an impressive array of guards. *Centurions,* he thought, and for a moment his knees went weak at the sight, but he soon regained his composure. *What on Earth have I started?*

At the gate, a guard with a menacing expression squinted at the driver and carefully observed the occupants of the taxi. He asked for identification and the two obliged. He then asked the two passengers to exit the taxi, and upon exiting they were frisked carefully head to foot. Carpenter was asked to open his briefcase, which was X-rayed and inspected carefully. *A fat lot of good that will do,* Carpenter thought with satisfaction as he recalled the virtual undetectability of the new breed of weapons he had created. *Not even any biological or chemical agents to set off alarms.*

With a Secret Service escort, the two walked up the long drive to the East Wing door of the White House. Another agent gave them a cautious, icy perusal before escorting them into the foyer, down several corridors, past several sets of armed guards, up a flight of stairs and into a small spare office. The President was absent. The agent motioned for Carpenter and Zach to be seated, then went to the door, spoke a few words into his hidden mic, and stood at attention.

The President was watching on the closed circuit monitor as the two made their way to the door of the White House. He put away the security briefing on his two guests. The background check had come back perfectly clean. No criminal records. Perfect credit reports.

Dr. J. Maurice Carpenter, born January seventh, nineteen fifty, Bethlehem, PA. Education: M.D., Ph.D. in Biochemistry from Columbia University, M.S. in Electrical Engineering from the California Institute of Technology, undergraduate Harvard, Mathematics, *summa cum laude*. Marshall Scholar, nineteen seventy-seven. Shaw Prize in Mathematics, nineteen eighty-two. Currently director of the Nanoscale Weapons Project at the Brookhaven National Laboratory. Parents, Josef and Maria Carpenter, both clean. Maternal Grandfather Nathan Karpinsky, born Poland, nineteen hundred and one, naturalized in nineteen twenty-seven, name changed to Carpenter in nineteen forty-seven. Karpinsky's records include small FBI file nineteen fifty-seven to nineteen fifty-nine: participated in protests against House Un-American Activities Committee.

Zachary Eskar born May twenty-sixth, nineteen eighty-two in Morgantown, W.Va., to David and Jessica Eskar. Master's in Electrical Engineering, Virginia Tech, undergraduate in Mechanical Engineering, Georgia Tech. Laboratory assistant, Nanoscale Weapons Project, Brookhaven National Laboratory. Parents clean. Grandparents as well.

A moment later, the President came into the room and Carpenter and Zach stood up. The President measured out a lukewarm smile and extended his hand. Carpenter shook it first, and then Zach.

"You asked for a private meeting," the President said, businesslike, "and you got one." He motioned around the room to the table of empty seats.

Carpenter motioned at the close-shaven, well-built secret service agent at the door sporting a flattop haircut. He was holding a briefcase. *Presumably the briefcase with the emergency nuclear launch controls,* Carpenter thought wryly, as he recalled that the controls were always kept in close proximity to the President. *Nuclear weapons are so 'yesterday,'* he thought to himself smugly as he fingered the remote control device in his pocket.

"Normal security detail, but I can ask him to leave if you like."

Carpenter nodded, and the President asked the agent to leave the room. Only Carpenter, Zach and the President remained.

Carpenter regarded the President for a moment, then withdrew a sheaf of papers.

"Before we get started, I'd like you to look through some literature that might be of interest to you. It explains the situation in a bit more detail," Carpenter said.

The President looked down at the sheet of paper his guest had placed before him. On the sheet of paper were instructions to request a stroll in the Rose Garden. The President weighed his options for a minute before pressing a buzzer. The agent with the flattop entered the room.

"We're going for a private stroll in the rose garden, Otto. You can tag along, but give us plenty of privacy please."

"Yessir, Mr. President," Otto replied.

The President's face looked wan and tired in the fading light of the day. He read from the sheaf of papers Carpenter had handed him.

Mr. President — I've written down this information because I can't take a chance your security detail might be using directional microphones to record our conversation. Do not speak a word until I indicate, and return these papers to me when you're through reading.

As you know by now, my name is J. Maurice Carpenter. I am the director of the Nanoscale Weapons Project at the Brookhaven National Laboratory. Please call me "Maury." You didn't know me then, but we were actually at Harvard together, class of seventy-one.

I have good news and bad news for you.

Starting with the bad news: I have implanted you, the First Lady and your two children with devices that are capable of causing blinding pain or DEATH in a matter of seconds. This device was the cause of your headache at six p.m. two days ago.

Because you're meeting me now, and have received the refresh code, you're safe until your next refresh. However, your wife and children must be brought to within a range of one hundred meters from me within the next forty-eight hours to receive their first refresh code. Any of your family, including yourself, who don't receive the refresh code within the next forty-eight hours will die immediately.

From now on, through the rest of my life or until I choose to release you, you and your family must always remain within one hundred meters of me, or return to such a location at regular forty-eight hour periods, to receive the required radio transmissions from me. If you or they travel more than one hundred meters away from me at any time without a proper refresh (based on an unbreakable code algorithm), then you or they will first feel blinding pain, and then you or they will die immediately thereafter. You and your family are now permanently *tethered* to me.

In addition, as an added precaution, upon my own death my personal transmitter will TRIGGER THE IMMEDIATE DEATH OF YOU AND YOUR FAMILY. Since the fate of you and your family is now irrevocably intertwined with my own, you therefore MUST ASSURE above all else that NO HARM COMES TO ME at any time.

When you have reached this point in the letter, smile, motion to the rose bushes, and say, "Quite interesting. By the way, aren't these American Beauty roses lovely? They were originally planted by Jackie O when she was First Lady." This will indicate to me that you have read and understood what I have written here thus far.

The President looked up ruefully at Carpenter and Zach, and paused for a moment. His mind was racing. *One press of the secret alarm button in my breast pocket and a team of secret service agents will eliminate these two madmen with a few well-placed shots.* But the warning that the fate of his family was now intertwined with Carpenter's unto the point of death gave him pause. He slowly motioned to the rose bushes and mouthed his lines. It was then that his eyes began to water over with shock, anger, hate and helplessness. *Could this really be happening?*

Carpenter motioned back to the documents in the President's hand and said, "Lovely specimens indeed, Mr. President.

But there's more. Do continue reading." President read on in increasing disbelief.

> Now for the good news:
>
> I mean you, your family, and the world at large no harm. You have nothing to fear, and as long as you do nothing in opposition to my wishes, no one will be hurt. On the contrary, I am very confident that only good will come of what I have undertaken.
>
> When you have reached this point in the letter, motion to the trees and say, "Such lovely elms. I hope the Japanese beetle infestation doesn't harm them. That would be a great pity."

The President performed his lines, and continued to read at Carpenter's behest.

> The following are the rules of the game.
>
> 1. You must see at all times that no harm comes to me.
> 2. You must always do exactly as I indicate.
> 3. Tonight, you will explain to your wife and children that they have been infected with a dangerous biological agent, and that from now on they must always come back into your presence at least once every forty-eight hours to receive radio treatment. To ease their concerns, you can tell them that an antidote is being developed, and within months or just a few years, the threat will have passed and they will be completely free again with no harm to their health.

4. You must never tell ANYONE else or hint to ANYONE anything about the present matters, not even your physician, your priest, your psychiatrist (if you have one), your staff, nor any other government or law enforcement officials.

When you have reached this point in the letter, nod your head thoughtfully, and say, "Taking this stroll makes me think perhaps I ought to have done more in my presidency to protect the environment." Carpenter smiled at the letter's reference to "biological agent," a detail designed to throw the President and any possible interlopers off the scent. *There's nothing "biological" about the bots.*

Unsure how to respond, the President hesitated again for several moments and stared down at Carpenter with deep loathing. Not intimidated, Carpenter reached down for his transmitter in the guise of the cellphone, made a threatening gesture, then spoke.

"I applaud your awareness of these important environmental issues, but I don't need to remind you, Mr. President, that these are quite serious matters we're dealing with here. The health of our planet depends on your actions." Carpenter's comments were as much directed at the President as they were at any Secret Service microphones which might be recording the encounter.

Carpenter lifted his index finger, indicating that he was ready to press the button. *The button of pain? The button of death?* the President wondered, and again thought better of any attempt at immediate rescue as he mouthed his lines once more. The decision to resist was too weighty. *There will be time later to stop these lunatics.*

Carpenter motioned for the President to continue reading the final portion of his instructions, and the President obliged. The remaining directions in the letter called for the President two days hence to conduct a Rose Garden awards ceremony with a number of high-ranking officials in attendance. He was also to reserve time after the ceremony for a further briefing, and finally to reflect deeply on the critical importance of maintaining absolute secrecy.

As the last directive in Carpenter's letter described: "Consider the chaos that could ensue if word leaks that the President, the top law enforcement officials in the land, and their families have essentially become walking zombies under the control of a deranged scientist. The result could be revolution, a *coup d' état*, or anarchy. Therefore no one must have any idea about our mutual predicament: no one must know what is currently transpiring at the White House (not that anyone ever had any idea to begin with, present company included, but we'll address that issue at our next meeting on Monday)."

As the President finished reading, he asked Carpenter what he should tell his staff if asked about this stroll through the Rose Garden. "Please recall, Mr. President, that I'm an old friend from your Harvard days, and at your request I'm discussing with you some novel scientific breakthroughs related to some of the very pressing environmental issues of our time."

* * *

"Just tell me one last thing," the President whispered quietly to Carpenter as they were finishing their stroll. "What do you want? What are your demands?"

Not wishing to be drawn in, Carpenter said loudly, "And so, Mr. President, now you see why I had to maintain such secrecy surrounding this meeting. Please remember, these issues we're facing are deadly serious and very unpredictable."

At that, Carpenter extended his hand to the President and said, "I look forward to seeing you Thursday." The President reluctantly took Carpenter's hand and gave it a feeble shake. As he withdrew his hand, he looked down and noticed what he thought could only be a large round scar in the middle of the scientist's palm, the type of scar, the President thought, that could only have resulted from a puncture wound.

CHAPTER 8

It was a long, six-hour drive from Los Angeles to the East Bay, so named owing to its location along the eastern edge of the San Francisco Bay. To make the fastest journey, Maddox took the flat and drab Highway 5. Though his heart was racing with impatience, he knew he couldn't gun the Audi, but rather had to stay within the seventy mile-per-hour speed limit. He couldn't afford to get pulled over, because absolutely no one must know where he was going.

He made sure to pay all his gasoline and meal charges along the way in cash. If anyone asked, he was at home, nursing a cold. He had also been careful to leave his light timer on at home, and a trickle of water running in the bathtub to run up his water meter. A neighbor agreed to feed and walk the dog. He switched onto the 580 to Pleasanton, near Livermore.

So as not to raise any alarm bells and to make sure that Dr. Lewis was in town, Maddox had called Lewis' secretary to make an appointment for four thirty p.m. To be doubly sure Lewis did not have any travel plans, he had also checked his availability for the following morning. Maddox used a cover, having said that he was with DARPA on a routine audit of the lab. DARPA was the Defense Advance Research Project Agency, the organization that funds basic research into technologies that have applications in national defense and security. Knowing that his cover wouldn't get him through security at Livermore, Maddox then used the FBI computer system to locate Dr. Lewis' home address and car make, which turned out to be a blue Buick Park Avenue. Lewis lived in a single family dwelling on a quiet, shady suburban street, and Maddox waited anxiously for the Doctor to come home from the lab. *I hope he's not one of those types that works until three in the morning . . .*

At six forty-nine p.m., Maddox saw Lewis' Buick come down the street. He checked the plates and when they matched, he got out of his car and watched the scientist pull into the driveway of his house. When Maddox saw the garage door open, he ran over to the driveway to wave Lewis down before he pulled into the garage.

Lewis stopped the car and cautiously opened his window a crack. Maddox flashed his FBI badge quickly. Lewis appeared just as in the files Maddox had reviewed beforehand: a head of thinning gray hair, a wispy gray goatee, and a narrow face framed in black, horn-rimmed glasses.

"Doctor Lewis?"

Lewis nodded tentatively, regarding Maddox with understandable suspicion.

"Doctor Lewis, my name's Maddox. I'm with the FBI. I'm working on a case and I need your expertise, badly."

"I thought you guys have your own team of experts. Forensics? Ballistics?"

"It's well beyond that. Otherwise I wouldn't be bothering you. Believe me. Do you mind if we speak in private?"

Lewis paused for a moment. "Sure, I suppose we can talk."

"Good. There's a park a few blocks away. Maybe it would be better to speak on a bench there. I can drive you if you'd like, or if you'd feel more comfortable, I can meet you at the park.

I'll explain everything when we get there. Please. This is very important. A matter of life or death."

Dr. Lewis paused for a moment to consider, his face shadowed with concern. "OK, then, I'll meet you there."

"Then you lead the way, please," Maddox said, just to make sure he didn't lose Lewis along the way.

* * *

The two sat themselves on a bench at the park, underneath a canopy of eucalyptus trees. Children were at play on a seesaw, jumping and balancing in the fading light of the day.

"Doctor," Maddox began, "I don't even know where to start, so let me just ask you a few questions. Do you know a Doctor J. Maurice Carpenter?"

"Do I know Maury?" Lewis laughed subtly. "Sure I know him. Everyone in our field does. We go way back."

"What's he like?"

"Is he in some sort of trouble? Is he OK?" Lewis asked with concern.

"Forgive me, Doctor, but it would be better if you just answered my questions directly."

"Can you first just tell me what this is all about? You said you're with the FBI?"

"Yes, I'm FBI. I already showed you my badge. We just need to know a little bit more about Dr. Carpenter and his work."

"As with my own, Dr. Carpenter's work is highly classified. Even if I knew, I'm not sure how much I could tell you."

"Well, putting the work aside, what can you tell me about him? What kind of person is he?"

"Dr. Carpenter is probably the most brilliant mind in our field, the area of micro-robotics. He's a bit eccentric, has an unusual sense of humor. Used to be quite combative and egocentric, but he seems to have mellowed a lot with age."

"Would you say he's dangerous in any way?"

"Dangerous?" Lewis pondered. "He's a bit iconoclastic, but strange as it may sound for a weapons designer, he's very much known in the community as a pacifist, a humanitarian."

"Any grudges of which you're aware?"

"None that I know of."

"How would you characterize his lifestyle, if I may ask?"

"Lifestyle?"

"Our checks show he's never been married. Any close companions?"

"None now, that I'm aware. I believe he's very much absorbed in his work of late. Used to have a reputation as a bit of a ladies' man, believe it or not, but my impression is that those days are long past."

"No women he's close to now?"

"None that I know of."

"Men?"

"You don't mean . . . ?" Lewis paused to consider. "I wouldn't know for sure, but I don't think so. I would be completely surprised."

"On a scale of frugality to extravagance, how would you characterize his financial proclivities?"

"Based on my acquaintance with him and by reputation, he's quite modest in his means."

"No fancy cars, yachts? No nights on the town?"

"Not that I've ever heard."

"Politically, how would you characterize his views?"

"Whoa, whoa, wait a minute, Agent Maddox. I'm old enough to remember someone named Joe McCarthy. If you want to go any further, you're going to have to tell me what this is all about. Why all the questions, and the interest in Maury's political views?"

Maddox looked Lewis carefully in the eyes.

"OK, Dr. Lewis. You've been very helpful thus far, and I appreciate all your help. I'll get right to the point. It may be nothing at all, or it may be quite serious. I'm not sure yet. But I have reason to think there may be something very, very strange going on at Dr. Carpenter's Nanoscale Weapons Lab at the Brookhaven National Laboratory."

"Strange? Such as?" A wave of concern crept over Lewis' face.

Maddox paused before continuing. The mysterious letter specifically said not to share its contents with anyone, but Maddox saw no other way forward.

"Read this, but of course, you have to promise me, *swear* to me, that you'll keep the contents an absolute secret. I'm taking a huge risk by showing this to you, but as you'll see in a moment, I very much need your help."

Maddox handed Lewis a transcription of the letter from Richmond, Virginia. Lewis took the letter and read in rapt attention. When he had finished reading, he lay the letter down carefully, stunned.

Lewis said nothing, remaining silent in lugubrious thought.

"So, Doctor, here I am," Maddox said, "and I'll lay out all my cards for you: I have none, except that letter you just read. You're the first person I have approached since I received the letter two days ago. As far as I know, no one else within the FBI is aware of the letter's existence, nor, I believe, is anyone aware of any of the issues related to the letter. No one within the FBI even knows I'm here talking to you."

Lewis nodded thoughtfully.

"So you see," Maddox continued, "we're at the top of the first inning now. I don't know if the letter is a hoax or if it's at all credible. I don't know if I was a complete imbecile to give up my weekend to drive all the way up here from L.A. on my own expense account to see you. And if the letter is credible, I have no idea how to proceed. So my first question to you is: do you think the letter is credible?"

Lewis paused for a moment, then spoke. "You know, you're putting me in a very difficult situation, because as I said earlier, most of the work I do is highly, *highly* classified. So I apologize if I can't answer that question directly, or give you the level of detail that you might want."

"I'll take that as a yes."

Lewis remained impassive, and Maddox continued.

"I appreciate your situation and your concerns, Doctor, but let's put aside all of our preconceptions here. I'm here in an unauthorized capacity, possibly risking my career and even my life just to speak with you. If the letter is to be believed, then both of us are way beyond the bounds of any legal restraints or responsibilities to which we previously may have been subject."

Maddox continued. "You know now why I didn't destroy the letter as its author asked. If push comes to shove, if presented with this letter, what jury in its right mind could fault us for acting as we are? As we must?"

Lewis was unmoved.

"Assuming the danger outlined in the letter is real, which by your hesitation I'm beginning to believe is the case, then you have to see doubly why I can't possibly destroy it." Maddox paused to let his words sink in. "It's the only thing that can possibly justify the unimaginable course on which you and I are now forced to embark."

Maddox paused for effect, then continued.

"So let me put this as starkly as possible. If the letter is credible — and only you can tell me if it is — then it's absolutely no stretch to say that the President's life is at stake, your life is at stake, the fate of the nation is at stake, that indeed the future of the entire world could be at stake. So you see, you *have* to see, we have no choice. No choice at all. You have to help me."

"Perhaps what you say is true, Mr. Maddox, but I'm sorry. It's just that this is all so sudden. So *unbelievable*. I need some time to digest this. How do I know you're not a spy, for instance? I can't just go revealing national secrets to the first guy who flashes a badge and an unsigned letter in my face. There are channels. Procedures to follow. We should be handing this over to the FBI, Secret Service, I don't know."

"I am the FBI! Don't you see? None of the 'channels' to which you refer can be presumed safe anymore. Let's be realistic: your life is at stake here, Doctor."

Lewis paused again to absorb the gravity of the situation, and after several moments let out a deep sigh.

"So what do you propose we do?" he said at last, surrendering.

"All I need to know is whether the letter is credible or not."

Lewis looked at the orange glow behind the distant hills, and took a deep breath. At last he spoke.

"Alright. It looks as though I'm just going to have to trust you. But I first want to make two copies of the transcript, and I want you to sign, fingerprint and lick both copies. That will be my insurance in case this turns out to be a ruse. The saliva will provide a DNA sample."

Maddox briefly considered Lewis' proposal, and then said "It's a deal."

* * *

The two drove in Lewis' car to a nearby strip mall and found a Kinko's Copies. After the scientist had secured both signed, fingerprinted and spittle-tinged copies, the two went back to the park.

After seating themselves in the deepening dusk, Lewis paused for a moment, fixed his gaze on a lamppost starting to swarm with gnats, and then began slowly. "You asked if the letter is plausible, and I'm afraid, Mr. Maddox, that your instinct is right. As I think about it, it's possible the letter may indicate a genuine threat, unfortunately. Let me give you a little bit of background.

"I work in a laboratory dedicated to the creation of micro-robots. Some crawl, some swim, some fly. Some do all three. Our laboratory focuses on the application of these *microbots*, as we call them, to the field of electronic warfare. The idea is to unleash on the enemy a swarm of *microbots* that can jam enemy radar, cripple the enemy communications infrastructure, detect enemy troop movements, and even operate on a very personal level to eavesdrop on enemy communications. It's actually possible for one *microbot* to surreptitiously record a single conversation between two individuals."

Lewis paused to make sure that Maddox was following.

"Dr Carpenter works in the same area and we collaborate often, but to my knowledge, he focuses only on flying *microbots*. These are also known as *micro air vehicles*, or *MAVs* for short. *MAVs* are typically either fixed-wing devices, like miniature airplanes; rotary wing devices, similar to tiny helicopters; or flapping- or vibrating-wing devices that fly like birds or insects, so-called *ornithopters*.

"Now, his work also differs in some other material respects from my own. It adds a slight twist." Lewis hesitated. Maddox could just make out the scientist's eyes on him in the growing darkness.

"You see, Dr. Carpenter's work is a bit more . . . more aggressive." Lewis paused again to allow Maddox time to absorb what he was saying.

"What I mean is that his *microbots* are designed to *attack* the enemy. To inflict casualties. Think of a swarm of hornets or killer bees administering a chemical or biological sting. Almost impossible to defend against. And much more capable than a missile of distinguishing between friend and foe, or soldier and civilian. Better still, the *microbots* don't destroy buildings, and can even penetrate indoors or underground through cracks, fissures, or by burrowing."

Maddox's eyes remained fixed on Lewis.

"And wait, there's more," Lewis continued. "The casualties don't even have to be fatal. The dosages administered by the *microbots* can merely incapacitate, without necessarily killing the target. Operating on a large enough scale, it's the holy grail of weapons-making. You can overwhelm the enemy silently, undetectably, and without firing a shot. The enemy doesn't even have his boots on, has no idea what hit him. And you can potentially do all this without a single person getting killed. No buildings destroyed. Who knows . . . these types of devices could someday even end warfare.

"Now from what you're telling me, someone, whoever sent you this letter," Lewis explained, "is claiming that Maury — Dr. Carpenter — has developed a *microbot* that is designed to penetrate and possibly lay dormant in the human body. I'm just guessing, but it sounds to me like the original idea behind this probably was to say to the enemy: 'Attention! Attention! You've just been implanted with a *microbot* that will kill you within ten seconds unless you surrender immediately and come out with your hands up.'

"Again, it's bloodless warfare. Or not just warfare . . . Think of the ability to end hostage situations, or to track the movements of persons of interest unawares, or to gather intelligence."

Maddox cut in. "Or to create an army of slaves completely dependent on a single master. But is the technology *here already*? Is this a real and present threat? Does the technology exist *now*?"

"Oh, I assure you Mr. Maddox, the basic technology is very much here with us now. Or at least ninety-eight percent of it. MEMS-based MAVs on the scale of a few centimeters have been demonstrated, as have MEMS-based micro-robotic medical probes that can swim in the human bloodstream, or administer precise doses of medicine to the patient."

"MEMS?"

"That stands for Micro Electro-Mechanical Systems. Basically, we create the very tiniest *microbots* using the same photo-lithographic processes that are used to create integrated circuits. In this way, we can even combine the electronics and the mechanical systems into one unit. We can create gears that are a tiny fraction of the width of a human hair. To understand what I'm getting at, imagine a robot the size of a dragonfly. It uses wings or propellers or legs for locomotion, and possibly delivers to the target multiple smaller *microbots* or *nanobots* the size of ear mites, or even down to the scale of bacteria, complete with mechanical flagellates to control movement.

"Now I'm not saying this is all easy, mind you," Lewis continued, "especially down at the microscopic scale. It's fairly easy to create gears, but putting the mechanical systems together requires a lot of skill. The power system to drive the devices is another challenge. And then the motion-control systems to control movement and provide navigation capabilities are a completely separate can of worms. I would have thought that the technology for an entire field-operational package was perhaps five to ten years away. But what Maury — Dr. Carpenter — is doing is highly classified, and naturally we don't share everything.

"Who knows? Perhaps he has had some breakthroughs of which I, or his superiors and the world at large are unaware? Maybe he's five years ahead of the game. If what the letter says is true, then he definitely will have had *some* breakthroughs. But we're not talking about Nobel Prize-level advances in basic science. We're just talking about a number of incremental steps forward in a few key aspects of systems design, power and control."

"So. just to sum up everything you've told me," Maddox interjected, "based on your professional judgment, there's a good chance the letter is not some crazy hoax?"

Lewis paused for a moment to consider.

"Yes, unfortunately I'd have to say it is probably reliable. It definitely cannot be dismissed out of hand, and in my judgment, I'd say the likelihood is high that Maury has a leg up on everyone here."

"And he could have developed and given himself access to such a system without others knowing? Without his superiors knowing or controlling his work?" Maddox asked.

"Just look at the *Chen Wen-lai* scandal. I don't need to remind you that oversight in our national laboratories is pitiful. And since Maury's field of research and the devices he creates range from the very small down to the nano or atomic scale, it's probably very easy for him to conceal the fruits of his labor and the progress he's making. It's not as though he's constructing a rocket ship in a big space hangar, sitting in plain sight for everyone to see. It wouldn't be too much of a leap to assume that Maury could have run parallel development programs, one for his bosses' consumption, and one for his own. Especially as a great deal of the technology needed to make his ideas come to fruition actually lies in the area of software control systems. Pattern recognition, machine vision, motion control, navigation. Those are some of the more crucial technologies and they all lie in the realm of software, the development of which is very easy to conceal, duplicate and modify.

"In terms of power systems, the other main barrier to Dr. Carpenter's work in my opinion, there have been whispers, so far unconfirmed, that Maury was working on a battery that can generate power by digesting organic material. It would be able to re-charge itself *in situ*, i.e. in the host. Literally a self-sustaining mechanical bacterium that can reside within a living organism for long intervals. Such 'bio batteries,' as they are called, have already been developed and proven in laboratory conditions. I would have thought that a robust version of such a battery, one that could work in real-life conditions, would have been a few years off, but it is possible that Maury has figured it out. Again, such a battery would not require any breakthroughs in basic science, just a lot of hard work and trial-and-error. I liken this effort to Edison inventing the electric light bulb, rather than to Einstein formulating the Relativity Theory.

"So again, to get back to your question, Mr. Maddox, in my professional judgment, unless proven otherwise, we probably *do* have to assume your letter points to a direct and concrete threat."

Maddox blew out a big breath of air. *I was afraid you'd say that.* He paused for several moments, and could hear his heartbeat pulsating maddeningly in his ears.

CHAPTER 9

The ceremony at the Rose Garden was brief. The President thanked the FBI Director for his service to the country and presented him with an engraved plaque, hastily arranged and inscribed with the words "'Protector of the Nation' — from a grateful people." There was cordial applause all around.

The Director looked pleased, but puzzled, as he accepted the plaque, having only been informed of the award's existence a mere forty-eight hours prior. After thanking the FBI Director, the President lavished praise on the Secretary of Homeland Security, calling him "our nation's best answer to the ancient Roman proverb *quis custodiet ipsos custodes?* which for those who don't understand Latin — present company included — apparently means: 'Who will watch the watchers themselves?'"

Carpenter looked on, especially pleased as the President uttered those words. It was he who had written the speech, including the self-deprecatory remarks added to make the speech sound more in character.

And Lionel Gottlieb, White House correspondent for WNN News, crowding in the press gallery, furled his brows. Something wasn't adding up. *This award didn't exist forty-eight hours ago. Nothing about the award was on anyone's schedule until two days ago, and now presumably on a whim the most scripted, best-planned political office in the entire world suddenly decides to insert into the President's schedule a Rose Garden ceremony for a "Protector of the Nation" award? And what's with the Latin? The President can barely speak English, for chrissakes. Is this all part of some kind of political makeover? And if it is a makeover, what's the point? It all seems pretty pitiful, ill-conceived, and ill-executed, just like everything else out of this presidency of late.*

But as for Carpenter, he just looked on at the proceedings and smiled. With Zach's help, he'd just bagged the Director of the FBI, the Vice President, the Chief of Staff, the Secretary of Homeland Security and all of their family members. Unbelievably, everything was going according to plan. *Very much* according to plan. *And now the fun really begins.*

"Time to baptize them," Carpenter whispered to Zach on the way back into the White House.

* * *

Following the Rose Garden ceremony, the President's staffers escorted the ranking officials and their families back into the Oval Office. On Carpenter's instructions, the President was careful to make sure all of the listening devices were off in the room. After each guest was further individually swept for listening devices, and the venue deemed secure, the President asked his aides to leave the room. Last to enter were Carpenter and Zach, who assumed seats to the President's right and left respectively.

"Ladies and gentlemen," the President began, "sweetheart," he added, turning to his wife and clearing his throat, "I would like to introduce to you Dr. J. Maurice Carpenter. He will be saying a few important words to you here. It is absolutely critical you give him your undivided attention, and of course you'll see in a minute that everything that transpires in this meeting needs to remain absolutely and completely confidential."

Carpenter stood up, and moved to the head of the room.

"Thank you, Mr. President. Hello, everyone. As the President said, I'm Dr. J. Maurice Carpenter. Please call me 'Maury.' I am the Director of the Nanoscale Weapons Project at the Brookhaven National Laboratory. This is my assistant Zach." Zach smiled weakly, and there were puzzled faces all around the room.

"Zach, please say 'hi' to everyone."

Carpenter carried on in as nonchalant a voice as he could muster, studiously sounding as banal as possible. "Anyway, I need to tell you that I have secretly implanted in each of you a micro-robotic device under my radio control."

After demonstrating through the headache mechanism the potent capability of his *bots*, he noted the shock, exasperation and anger that shone on the faces of the guests. *Is this a sick joke?* He could practically hear their mental shouts.

He waited for the guests to recover equilibrium a few moments later, then asked, "Everyone OK?"

There were concerned, bewildered nods all around, interspersed with angry glares. It was now beginning to dawn upon many that the award ceremony was just a ruse to bring them all together, and several eyed the President with contempt. Drake looked down in shame.

Once the gravity of the situation had sunk in fully, a few of the mothers hugged their children and some of the men gave Carpenter hard, hateful stares, but none could bring themselves to act.

"From here, I'd like to do the following," Carpenter instructed. "First, I need to swear everyone here to absolute secrecy — *on pain of death.*" After he had obtained everyone's assent one-by-one, he asked the President, the Vice President, the Chief of Staff, the Secretary of Defense, the Director of the FBI, and the Director of the Secret Service to remain.

"Ladies and Gentlemen," he said, addressing his now smaller audience, "I have good news for you. By working together, we're going to turn this presidency and this nation around. To that end, we're going to take three steps here today.

"The first is that with immediate effect the Director of the Secret Service is going to appoint me and Zach here to the Secret Service, White House detail. There are concrete signs of a possible biological weapons plot against the White House," Carpenter said, winking theatrically to assure the guests that the biological weapons plot was just a ruse. The story would provide him cover for joining the Secret Service, and thereby gaining access to the White House. "I have with me here a sample of anthrax taken from the Oval Office," he said, waving a vial of talcum powder.

"And in this ever more dangerous era of global bio-terrorism," he continued, "it is necessary to have a specialist team of bio-weapon experts on standby with the President to guard him at all times against biological attacks," he said with a flourish. The appointment to the White House Secret Service detail would ensure that Carpenter and the President could remain constantly in proximity, as necessitated by the distance limitations in the current version of the *microbot* control system, limitations that Carpenter planned to fix soon.

"Secondly," he continued, winking again to let his listeners know he was developing the ruse further, "I have run tests and have determined that the source of the anthrax plot in the White House is the Nanoscale Electronic Warfare Laboratory, in the Lawrence Livermore National Laboratory in Livermore, California. The director of the laboratory is named Bernard

Lewis. I would like the FBI to arrest Dr. Lewis secretly under the Patriot Act, and any other anti-terrorism legislation if necessary, and have him brought to me at once as a material witness in a terrorism investigation. Do not use force to detain him. He must remain unharmed. His arrest must be kept totally secret, and his family and colleagues must be led to believe he is on a pressing business trip. If he is not brought to me within days, you're all going to be coming down with some really bad headaches. Am I clear?"

Slow nods all around.

"Finally, tomorrow, Mr. President, you will meet with your advisors and cabinet officials. You will tell them that your presidency has lost momentum and you want to start brainstorming with them to develop a new direction for the country. Tell them the slate is clean, and in each of their respective areas of responsibility they have four weeks to come up with a plan of action as to how to move your presidency and the nation forward again." This four week 'brainstorming session' was to be the means to sequester all the nation's top officials together under Carpenter's control.

"Tomorrow, after the morning cabinet meeting, you will hold a press conference to announce publicly that you've reflected deeply on your presidency, and you feel that a new direction for the Administration and for the country is needed urgently. You will cancel all your remaining campaign engagements and travel plans for the next four weeks, and will announce to the public that instead you will remain huddled with your advisers to map out a new plan for America."

* * *

"So what, exactly, do you want me to do?" the President asked once his guests had left and he was alone with Carpenter.

"Honestly, I don't really care what you do, as long as you come up with something, *anything*, that requires just about all our nation's senior government officials to meet together with you at Camp David for around four weeks or so."

"Huh?"

"And their families."

The President appeared dubious.

"Look," Carpenter explained, "I need you, your key staff, and your collective families all together, where I can watch you and administer you your periodic refreshes. I'm working on a technology that will allow me to give you your refreshes remotely, in automated fashion, so you won't all have to be together with me all the time. But the technology isn't quite ready yet. Until it's ready, you, the FBI director, the Secretary of Defense, the Secretary of State, the Vice President, the Chief of Staff, Congressional leaders — basically everybody who's anybody — together with all your families, need to be within arm's reach of me. And I need some plausible cover for that. Got it?"

"Hmmmm," the President retorted with visible discomfort. "I think I see what you're getting at. But you must know that's highly irregular. Highly unlikely. It will never work."

"I know it's irregular and unlikely, but you need to put your thinking cap on and come up with something — *anything* — we can feed the press that will justify a month-long gathering of all the important officials in the U.S. government and their families at Camp David. I don't care what it is, as long as it flies."

"So, something like a terrorist threat?"

"I thought of that. But if we go public with that, won't that raise just too many alarm bells? Won't it have the press doing backflips in search of evidence, trying to figure out what's going on?"

"So what else then? Any brilliant suggestions?"

"I think the only way we're going to pull this off is to have a big huddle for a major, *major*, new policy initiative. This will have another benefit too."

The President screwed up his brows, accentuating the quizzical expression on his face.

"Look, I'll be blunt with you, Mr. President," Carpenter continued. "Aside from having all our senior officials together in one place, there's another angle to this huddle," he explained. "To be honest, I didn't vote for you. You're not really my cup of tea, politically. But I *absolutely* need you to get re-elected. Because if you're not re-elected, then I have to start over again zapping a whole new cast of characters, and God only knows what I'll do with you and your crew once you're no longer of any use to me.

"To get straight to the point, I need you somehow to do something, anything that will suddenly make you and this administration wildly popular. After all, the re-election is less than three months away, and you're so far down in the polls now you don't stand a chance unless you pull off a significant change in course.

"Don't just sit there," Carpenter urged. "Knock yourself out and figure out what you can do to boost your approval ratings *massively.*"

"Obviously, if I knew the answer to that, I would have done it already. Don't you think?" the President retorted.

"No wonder your approval ratings are so low! May I suggest that perhaps you employ a small amount of creativity? Possibly you may for once wish to consider thinking *outside* the box a little. What do the American people really want? What do they want from their government?"

The President paused to consider, momentarily dumbfounded. Carpenter continued.

"Look, Mr. President, I don't have the answers. I'm not a politician. In fact I'm a mathematician by training," Carpenter said, fidgeting with a strip of paper on the desk. His voice trailed off and he sank into a momentary reverie.

"Which gives me an idea," he said a few seconds later, his face lighting up as he emerged from deep thought.

The President focused his attention on the paper that Carpenter had been playing with.

"Do you know what a Möbius strip is?" Carpenter asked.

"A *what*?" the President replied.

"A Möbius strip," Carpenter said matter-of-factly. He took the strip of paper in his hands, gave a half-twist to the ends, and then joined the ends to form a twisted oval-shaped loop. "It's this shape here in my hand," he explained. "It looks kind of like a three-dimensional symbol for infinity, with a little twist in the middle."

The President looked on intently.

"Do you know what the beautiful thing about a Möbius strip is?"

The President shook his head.

"It has a very interesting mathematical property: it's made from a two-dimensional, two-sided object — the paper — but in fact it only has one side."

"Huh?" the President responded. "How can that be?"

"Just like I said, it looks like it has two sides," Carpenter continued, "but it really only has *one side*."

"No idea what you're talking about. Show me, please," Drake requested.

"See here," Carpenter said, taking out a pencil. "Let's start here," he said, pointing to a spot on the strip of paper. "Now let's trace this all the way around. You'll notice that at no point will I lift the pencil off the paper."

The President watched intently while Carpenter traced a line on the paper, never lifting the pencil. He traced the length of the entire object and stopped when he reached the initial starting point.

"Do you notice anything interesting about the line I've traced?" Carpenter asked.

The President examined the paper for a moment. "You've traced both sides of the paper without lifting the pencil," he finally said.

"That's right! Very perceptive, Mr. President. As I said, it looks like it has two sides, but it really only has one side."

"In other words you want me to unite the country?" the President asked, after pondering the analogy. "Not red here, and blue there. Just red, white and blue everywhere?"

"Very good, Mr. President," Carpenter said, genuinely pleased. "Should give you a pretty strong boost in the polls if you can pull it off, right?"

"But how?"

"How do you think?"

"Well, lowering taxes is always a popular thing. But I tried that, and Congress blocked it."

"Well, then maybe Congress is part of the problem?"

"What? You can't be suggesting that I abolish the Congress!"

"Look. As I said before, I'm no politician. Politics is supposed to be your department. All I know is that the American people just want a government that works for them. That's responsive to their needs. That gives them value for their money. I'm giving you a once-in-a-lifetime chance to start with a completely blank slate, to re-invent the wheel if necessary, and come up with a system that actually works, unlike the broken, dysfunctional, partisan, pork-riddled mess we now have in Washington. And come to think of it, abolishing Congress may not be such a bad idea.

"Anyway, it's your call. I for one would not shy away from considering deep structural reforms. But something tells me, given how low you are in the polls and the generally sorry state of our country at present, that along with structural reforms we probably need to go even further. I think we also need to consider some form of spiritual reform as well."

"Spiritual reform?" the President asked skeptically, his voice betraying impatience at the direction the conversation was now headed.

"Yes, Mr. President, hence the Möbius strip," Carpenter responded. "My gut tells me that if you want to turn around your own fortunes, and turn around this country while you're at it, you're going to need to do something to heal the spiritual divide in our country: you need to come up with the political equivalent of a Möbius strip. Anyway, as I said, I'm not a politician. You just come up with a solution that works."

The President paused to consider the task before him. Before long, he began rattling off ideas for uniting the country. Carpenter rolled his eyes subtly, but smiled in encouragement as he sat and listened patiently to the President.

CHAPTER 10

If Gottlieb's suspicions were piqued at the Rose Garden, they were set afire the next day. The President had called the White House press corps and held a brief, two-minute press conference to announce that he would be huddling with his advisors at Camp David over the coming four weeks to "map out a new Blueprint for America." *Now he's really shot himself in the foot. He's got expectations running way too high,* Gottlieb thought.

Gottlieb called Phil Constantine, his editor. "Phil. Did you hear the press conference? Man, the entire White House press corps is onto the scent of blood. I've never seen anything like this. The President finishes his two-minute spiel . . . and never have so many arms shot up in unison since the Nuremberg rallies! I mean, you would have thought the press were on pogo sticks they were jumping up and down so much. And what does the President do? He declines to answer any questions and just walks off the podium. *Just walks off.* Just like that. Leaves everyone looking at each other like: 'Did you just hear what I heard?' 'Is this guy still in his right mind?' Blah, blah, blah.

"Next thing you know, he's on the White House lawn waving goodbye and taking the chopper to Camp David." Gottlieb paused to catch his breath, then continued. "And now everybody's on hold for four weeks? The speculation alone will burn out the airwaves. This is Washington for godsakes."

If he doesn't seriously blow people away when he announces his "New Direction," they'll be carrying him off the political stage on a stretcher.

"I can just see it now, yet another disappointment in a long line of political miscues from the current administration. Sorry, you're cutting out. What's that you say? The latest snap polls show his popularity trending down still further? Go figure! Man, it has never been so much fun covering the White House. I'll have the stuff for you in a few hours, Phil."

CHAPTER 11

Maddox awoke with a very stiff neck. He had parted from Lewis the previous day with an agreement to meet again twelve hours later on the same park bench. Lewis had spent the night working on a plan to combat Carpenter and his *microbotic* plague. To avoid leaving any trace that he had left Los Angeles, Maddox had slept the night in his car rather than check into a hotel. After waking, he drove over to a McDonald's, got an Egg McMuffin combo and a newspaper, then sat down to read the news. The front page headline that screamed "President to Chart New Direction" set off alarm bells. *Hard to imagine that's just a coincidence, but what's the angle?*

Maddox scanned the rest of the papers for clues as to what might be unfolding in the White House. Nothing else too unusual in the paper, but a small story about the FBI Director receiving a "Protector of the Nation" award caught his notice. *"Protector of the President's Posterior" would be more apt*, thought Maddox, recalling a terrorism case that had been squelched prematurely on orders from the top. And then his mind went over to darker concerns. *If there's any chance that the Director is already compromised, I'm already well on my way to getting myself into a whole world of trouble.*

At eight o'clock in the morning, he drove over to the park and found the park bench. Lewis was already there waiting for him.

"Sleep well?" Lewis asked, taking in Maddox's unshaven appearance and bloodshot eyes.

"Couldn't take any chances, so I slept the night in my car. Did you have time to come up with a plan?"

"Well, I've given the entire matter a great deal of consideration, and of course, I guess it doesn't help any to say it will be incredibly difficult. To make matters worse, I can't think of a more challenging opponent than Maury. He and I used to play chess often, and I never beat him once. Never even came close. And most would consider me a very strong chess player."

"I'm under no illusions regarding the odds against us here, Doctor Lewis. Please tell me you have even just a little bit of good news for me."

"Well, I think it's the Koran that says something to the effect: 'God does not send down any disease without also sending down the cure,' so you'll be happy to hear I did indeed manage to come up with something. Let's hope it works," Lewis offered.

"While I'm no ace spy," Lewis continued, "I do happen to work in communications and signal intelligence. I know broadly that there are two ways of collecting intelligence, one way though *elint*, or electronic intelligence, the other through *humint*, or human intelligence. I think the best course of action will be for me to focus on the *elint*, and you on the *humint*."

Maddox nodded. Lewis was speaking language he could understand.

"Regarding the *elint*, I think the best way to proceed will be for me to develop two specific devices that we can use to try to defeat Maury's *bots*." He went on to describe one device to be used to monitor the signal communications between the remote control and Carpenter's attacking *microbot*. By using this device to monitor the communications governing the *bot*, Lewis would hopefully learn how to disrupt or override Carpenter's control system.

"If I had to guess," Lewis continued, "I'd venture that initial guidance is through laser tagging, telemetry or GPS, with the final means of vectoring the device via machine vision. We have to assume that the *microbot* uses a MEMS gyroscope for positioning, and that it is equipped with CCD or CMOS sensors for pattern recognition."

"I'm not going to ask you to repeat any of that," Maddox said.

"The second device I'll develop will be a simple defensive *microbot*," Lewis continued without a pause. "This will be a device that can at the earliest stage block entry of the attacking *microbot* into the host, thereby rendering Maury's *bot* ineffective."

Lewis went on to explain that there would likely be three practical means of penetration into the target. Through the mouth, through the ears, and through the nose. Each presented its own problems. Through the mouth, the target's mouth would need to be open, which was not a given. Also, it would be easy for the target to spit out any foreign object perceived to have entered the oral cavity. Finally, entry through the mouth would present the danger that the *microbot* would get crushed by teeth, or possibly even end up in the target's breathing passage. "Too dangerous," Lewis surmised.

"Forget the ears. The ears would be too painful and obvious. The subject would hear a loud noise and experience significant discomfort upon penetration," he continued. "There would also be the risk of damage to the vestibulocochlear nerve."

"The nose, therefore, seems the most logical choice," he concluded. "It's always open. It offers the shortest passage to the relative safety of the nasal cavity. It's the least risky in terms of potential damage to the host. Most importantly, it is very easy to penetrate to the brain from the nasal cavity. In fact, in the past, I believe the *needle lobotomy* was a standard technique for performing the frontal lobotomy procedure."

"Needle lobotomy?" Maddox interjected.

"Yes," Lewis responded, "the doctor simply inserted a needle through the patient's nose into the frontal lobe, and by swishing the needle around, effectively severed the patient's frontal lobe. *Voilà!* Instant lobotomy.

"Now, mind you, there is always the risk that the subject has nasal congestion, but I would think that the *microbot* could be easily designed to penetrate through mucus and other nasal discharges if necessary."

"OK, so Carpenter's *microbot* enters through the nose. Now what?" Maddox asked.

"In that case," Lewis explained, "to capture one of Carpenter's *bots* and figure out how to defeat it, we simply need a counteragent concealed in the target's nasal cavity, or even in the nostrils. Upon attack by an external *microbot*, the defending *microbot* springs into action and neutralizes the intruder before the intruder can penetrate further into the target's body. These defending *bots* may be as simple as an active mesh structure that blocks and latches onto the intruding *bot*, rendering it immobile. Nothing too sophisticated at all," Lewis explained, to Maddox's relief.

"My plan is as follows," Lewis concluded, "I'm going to develop the listening device and the defending *bots*. Meanwhile, you're going to have to come up with a way to try to uncover the source of the warning letter and see if you can enlist that person's further cooperation. If that doesn't work, you have to find someone else who can get close to Carpenter, because we will need as much first-hand information and assistance as we can gather."

Maddox nodded his assent.

"A couple more things," Lewis said.

"Yes?"

"A lot of the work needed to develop the two devices I just discussed has already been done. I estimate I can complete design of initial prototypes in software in around two weeks. But to tape-out the devices and test the micro-circuitry will probably take six to eight weeks, even on a very accelerated schedule. Of course, there are risks as well. I think all of the people in my lab are reliable, but one never knows — there's always a chance that word of our intentions could leak back to Maury. But I don't see that we have any other choice, so I think this is a risk we have to take."

"There's also another issue," Lewis added, a hint of hesitation in his voice.

"What's that?" Maddox asked.

"One obvious facet of my plan is that we need someone, actually two separate people, to deliver my devices to Maury. Firstly, someone needs to place the eavesdropping device in close proximity to Maury's *bots* in order to latch onto Maury's signals," Lewis explained, "and then after we analyze the data from the eavesdropping device, we will need to deliberately send to Maury someone outfitted with the defending *bot* in hopes Maury will infect them." Lewis watched Maddox grimly.

"In other words, what you're saying is that we need two guinea pigs?" Maddox asked.

Lewis nodded, and Maddox swallowed hard.

* * *

After further discussion, the two agreed that Maddox would work on a plan to identify and recruit the guinea pigs — "refine the *humint* part of the operation," as Maddox put it.

"Just a few items on protocol as we proceed," he told Lewis, as he began to conclude the discussion. "I've got to go to work Monday in Los Angeles as if nothing has happened. The demands of my job could also take me anywhere in the country or in the world at just a moment's notice. So listen carefully to what I'm about to tell you.

"You need to get your team started right away on the devices you described to me, and then you need to be prepared to clear out of here fast. Be ready to disappear for a week or longer if needed. If the threat from Carpenter is real, if you really are Carpenter's only threat, and if he's got the President by the balls, then you have to expect he will come after you right away. We have to operate under the assumption that you'll find yourself with an FBI *APB* on you any minute now."

Lewis gulped.

"Under this assumption, you need to lay very low," Maddox continued. "Once the first of your devices is ready, we're going to need to meet up anyway to coordinate the next steps. So as not to be a stationary target, I suggest you come down to L.A. to find me, at the latest when the device is ready, or even earlier if I give you a coded message letting you know that Carpenter or the FBI is coming after you."

Tension building in his gut, Lewis let out a breath of air.

"I'll need your cellphone number," Maddox continued. "You also need to keep your cellphone charged, on and with you at all times, and you also need to check your e-mail inbox every fifteen minutes or so.

"Most importantly, when the time comes for you to skip down to L.A., you'll need an alibi."

"An alibi?" Lewis asked, concerned.

"That's right. If you disappear for a while, we need to be prepared for a time when you'll need to explain your absence."

Lewis paused to consider Maddox's suggestion.

"Typically, this type of absence would easily be explained by a woman," Maddox offered helpfully.

"A woman?" Lewis shot back. "But that's preposterous!"

"Well, if you have a better reason to disappear off the planet for a few days, please let me know. I'm all ears."

"But I've always been faithful to my wife."

"Carpenter doesn't know that. Not even your wife knows that for sure. In fact, assuming it's true, you're the only person on the planet who knows with certainty whether that's true or not."

Lewis pursed his lips, accepting the logic of Maddox's argument.

"So, excuse me for prying," Maddox prodded, "but are there any plausible candidates you can offer up?"

"Quite frankly, no," Lewis retorted. "My secretary is the only other woman with whom I have regular contact. If you saw her, you'd realize that wonderful though she is, she is not a likely candidate for my romantic affections. Not to mention, we can't make her disappear with me too, so she won't fit in the alibi."

"Any women ever work in your lab in the past? Do you ever give any lectures at a university? Berkeley? Stanford?"

Lewis paused to reflect.

"Now that you mention it, we had a fairly attractive graduate student interning in our lab a few years ago. I'm trying to remember her name."

"A name would be a good start," Maddox offered smugly.

"I can barely remember. I think she was Serbian from the Croatian part of Slovenia. Or Slovenian from the Serbian part of Croatia. Something like that. I can't remember."

"Well you're going to have to become intimately acquainted with her, very quickly. Starting with her name, please."

"It was Vera. Vera . . . Vera Draganovich. Yes, that's it. Vera Draganovich."

"Where is she now?"

"No idea."

"OK, don't worry, I'll take it from here. I'll track her down, then send you further instructions.

"But the main thing to remember is, if you receive a phone call from Vera Draganovich, or an e-mail or any other communication from her, or from anyone possibly sounding like her and purporting to be her, that means you just drop everything and take Highway 5 South straight to Los Angeles. You follow?" Maddox's eyes were set in dead earnest, and Lewis nodded his assent with an additional gulp.

"You need to have all your bags packed in advance, preferably loaded into a car at the ready. You need to brief your number two at the lab, so he can carry on your work when you're away. Make sure you have a good road map in your vehicle, along with a canteen of water and some snacks. Don't use GPS. The system might record your route, and we don't want anyone to know where you've been.

"Minutes can make a difference. We don't want you stopping for gas or food unnecessarily if we can avoid it. Have with you at all times lots of cash. Don't use credit cards. If you can do so, borrow someone else's car, someone on your team, that's even better.

"Primary communication with me should be through the following untraceable e-mail account." Maddox jotted down an e-mail address and phone number and handed the paper to Lewis. "If you need to reach me urgently, then have your wife or secretary call the following number: it's the number of a bar a few blocks down from where I live. Leave a message for Sunee. Say it's Josh calling. Clear?" Maddox said, handing the slip of paper to Lewis.

Lewis looked at the paper, then looked at Maddox with concern. "The name of the bar you want me to call is *Thais that Bind?*" he asked incredulously.

"That is in fact the name, and no, I don't frequent the establishment," Maddox responded with some impatience. "The owner is one of my better informants and it's a very secure location. Trust me, no one would ever think to look for either of us in an S&M joint," Maddox concluded with emphasis. "When finally it comes time for you to hightail yourself down to L.A., you go straight to *Thais that Bind*. Sunee will contact me from there."

Lewis nodded, vaguely stunned.

"Now, keep this card somewhere safe, and keep a lighter with you at all times," Maddox concluded. "If you think at any point that you're going to be arrested, burn the card."

CHAPTER 12

The Presidential chopper cleared the high perimeter fence and touched down at Naval Support Facility Thurmont, more commonly known as Camp David. President Drake emerged from the helicopter with a salute to his Marine guards. He moved onto the tarmac closely trailed by Carpenter, Zach, and three of his aides. Carpenter kept his hand firmly on the *microbot* remote control as he passed an honor guard of twelve Marines.

The small party made its way down the one main road that bisects the camp, military facilities on one side, and the Presidential guest cabins on the other. Vapor issuing from his moderately labored breath, Carpenter rushed to keep up with the President, who was striding forward at full pace. The group passed the camp commander's quarters, then detoured along a short mulch path through the woods, and arrived finally at the spacious Aspen Lodge. Sizing up the imposing structure of wood and stone, Carpenter instantly pronounced it his command center. "Upon this rock I build my church," he said softly, as he rapped three times on a granite cornerstone.

* * *

A few hours later in the fading twilight, after Carpenter, the President and their entourage had settled into their quarters, a motorcade pushed through the media throng at the front gate and entered the camp. In the motorcade were all of the important Administration officials and their families, who on arrival were quickly shown to their quarters. Just after sundown, a convoy of large trucks and buses snaked through the last few winding roads of the Catoctin Mountains and arrived at Camp David. A contingent of Navy Seabees and Marines was on hand to unload crates of laboratory equipment, just as all the members of the Brookhaven Nanoscale Weapons Laboratory, along with their families, descended from the tour buses. That evening, the laboratory equipment was quickly and efficiently installed into various facilities around the camp.

* * *

At dinner in the stately wood-beamed and wood-paneled main dining hall of the Aspen Lodge, Carpenter spoke to the gathering of nearly one hundred people, government officials and their families to his left and laboratory scientists and their families to his right. Each side regarded the other with a good measure of suspicion.

"Mr. President," he began with a nod to Drake. "Honored guests. A warm welcome to everyone," he offered, his voice resonating through the room with a force that surprised even him. "This will be our home for around four weeks. Of course, I don't need to repeat the rules. Just do exactly as I say, and don't do anything stupid. You'll be watched at all times by our security teams. If everything goes well, in a few years I'll be able to release you all completely unharmed.

"When our work here is through, when the scientists have perfected our *microbotic* systems, and when the President's staff have drafted a new platform to help ensure the President's re-election, we will be well on our way to making the world a much better place. We will all look back with pride and satisfaction on the contributions we made together to that end.

"But in the meantime, let's everyone here make themselves comfortable. *Mi casa es su casa,*" he said, motioning around the room. "Family members," he continued, "be sure to knock yourselves out at the bowling alley, skeet range, movie theater, swimming pool, tennis courts, or whatever. We're here on serious business, but let's also be sure to have some fun. Life's too short to do otherwise."

Those present exchanged puzzled glances.

CHAPTER 13

Maddox did his best to walk into his office on Monday morning as if it were any other Monday and he had been through any other weekend. Over the weekend, he had been able to trace Lewis' erstwhile "girlfriend" Vera Draganovich to Reno, Nevada, where she was employed as Assistant Professor of Mechanical Engineering at the University of Nevada. After leaving Lewis in Livermore, he had gone straight to Nevada to enlist her much-needed support in constructing Lewis' cover. He then had made the long drive to Phoenix, Arizona to arrange with an ex-Marine buddy, now serving in the Phoenix Police Department, a plausible cover for the disappearance of the ranking members of Lewis' lab.

As he entered the FBI office in Los Angeles, if anyone noticed the lingering stiffness in his neck brought about by sleeping three consecutive nights in the Audi, they would have assumed he'd earned the stiffness catamaraning on his Hobie 18. Sailing catamarans was his passion, and a picture on his desk of him hiking out on the trapeze of his Hobie-cat in four-foot swells now replaced the old picture of his wife Helen. He looked at the picture of himself sailing and recalled wryly that he'd capsized in a twenty-five-knot gust of wind a moment after the picture was taken.

Pushing aside his heavy narcotics caseload, Maddox left his desk and walked down the hallway to find Randall Ricks in the Communications Center. Like Maddox, Randall was an ex-Marine, and the two had a bond going back to Lebanon. Also like Maddox, Randall was a surfer — one of just a handful of African-American surfers Maddox knew. The two often surfed Playa Del Rey together, and were usually the two oldest surfers on the beach. If there were anyone in the Bureau Maddox felt he could trust, it was Randall.

"Wass' goin' on, Dawg?" Randall said with a wide smile as Maddox came into the room. In his Marine days, *Maddox* had become '*Mad Dogs,*' and then just *Dawg.*

"Let me get right to the point, Rando." Between them *Randall* was *Rando*, and occasionally, just as a joke, *Rambo.* "I need you to help me track law enforcement channels. Listen for a dude named Dr. Bernard Lewis," Maddox said quietly to avoid others overhearing. "That's LIMA-ECHO-WHISKEY-INDIA-SIERRA: Lewis. Copy?"

"Ten-four," Ricks replied.

"He could be a material witness, then again maybe not. Anything about Lewis comes over the wire, you let me know. We cool, bro?"

"Roger that."

"You call my cell. Anything goes down, you ask me, 'you good for a beer after work?' Nothing in the clear, got it?" he added in a hushed voice.

Ricks gave a slightly quizzical look, then a faint nod.

"Dig, bro. Done."

* * *

The rest of the day moved forward like a slow-drip coffee percolator filling a coffee cup. The morning briefing lasted twenty minutes longer than it needed to, thanks to several unnecessary questions from a rookie hoping to impress the office director. A wiretap warrant Maddox had requested was two hours late and the judge unapologetic, but at least the wiretap was approved without too much fuss in the end. A search of a warehouse in South Central Los Angeles, thought to be a hub for a cocaine smuggling operation, turned up nothing. Maddox also used a bit of downtime to review his case file in preparation for an upcoming interrogation he had scheduled for later in the afternoon. Interrogations were usually at the end of the day, because you never knew how long they would last.

At two forty-two p.m. exactly, just as Maddox was finishing his review of his case files, his cellphone rang. Maddox could see that it was Ricks calling.

"Hey Chief. You good for a beer after work?" came Ricks' deep voice. Maddox paused for a moment. *That was fast! The APB on Lewis has come through already!*

"Thanks man. Love to, but got a heavy backlog. Take a rain check?"

"Countin' on it."

Maddox poked his head out of his office and asked Janice to hold all calls. He then went straight to the Communications Center, took the APB from Ricks, and studied the document without saying a word. *Wanted for questioning under Patriot Act in connection with suspected biological weapons plot.*

Maddox went back to his office to steady himself and take stock of the situation. *They're after Lewis already. Didn't take much time! Shit's really hitting the fan now . . .* Up until now, despite Lewis' affirmation, he had still harbored doubts about the credibility of the mysterious letter, and even suspected that the entire plot could somehow still be an elaborate hoax. But with the APB out on Lewis, there was now no way to deny the gravity of the situation.

This is seriously not funny. Patriot Act? Biological weapons? Maddox's head spun. He gathered all the composure he could muster, winked at Janice, and then went outside the Federal Building to the lobby of the office building across the street. He dialed Lewis' number, and after Lewis answered he held a digital tape player to the phone speaker and played a tape which said in a woman's heavy Yugoslav accent, "Bernie. It's me, Vera. I miss you. I'm in trouble and I need you a lot . . . right now."

After Maddox hung up the phone, he placed another call to Lewis' number two in the lab, Mike Zimmerman, and played a different tape containing Maddox's voice disguised as a younger man. "Yo, Zim. What's up, dude? It's been way too long. Come down to Phoenix and party with us and the guys. I gotta show you some cool stuff."

The message to Zimmerman indicated that he and the other ranking members of Lewis' team should go immediately to Phoenix, Arizona. There, they would be arrested on drug charges by Maddox's friend in the Phoenix Police Department. Released on bail, they would regroup at a secret safe house about which only they and Maddox had knowledge. To the casual observer, it would simply appear that the lab team had skipped bail.

* * *

Seven hours later at home in his pajamas, at a little after ten p.m., Maddox answered his cellphone.

"Bill? Sunee here," a voice said in a soft Thai accent. "I have a friend of yours here who says he wants to see you."

Maddox dressed himself, quickly holstered his Smith & Wesson .38 caliber service revolver, put on a black leather jacket, and ran out into the night. He dashed through a light drizzle the two blocks to *Thais that Bind*, pushed open the heavy oak door, and entered the establishment. The clientele was mostly Asian, with a smattering of Anglos and African-Americans. Most of the patrons were dressed in tight black leather. A few looked up at Maddox with suspicion.

Maddox quickly spotted Sunee, who nodded to a rear hallway next to the bar. He followed her to the back of the building, where she opened a door to a small dark room and bade Maddox enter. Maddox walked inside the room, shook hands with a tired Dr. Bernard Lewis, and double-bolted the door shut behind him.

"Boy, am I glad to see you in one piece," Maddox said. "You alone? Notice anyone following you?"

Lewis shook his head. "Not that I could tell," he said.

"Whose car'd you take?"

"Just like you told me. One of my office assistants. I swapped keys with him. He's got a four-wheeler. I told him I was going to a friend's cabin near Yosemite and needed a four-wheel drive for a little stretch of road that washed out a couple of weeks ago."

"OK, good thinking. That's why you made it here in one piece. In fact, congratulations are seriously in order: there's an APB out for you. It went out around eight hours ago or so, and you're now one of the most wanted men in America. Something about biological weapons and the Patriot Act."

"But our lab doesn't do any research in biological weapons. Never has."

"Well, there's someone out there — I'm willing to bet who — who wants America's finest to think otherwise."

Lewis nodded gravely.

"So, how's the lab work coming?" Maddox asked.

"Luckily, I had time to describe to my number two at the lab, Mike Zimmerman, in fairly detailed terms the nature and urgency of the changes in our research program over the next several weeks. He is already starting work to implement the *bot* and *elint* devices I mentioned to you in our last conversation."

"OK, fantastic. That's a start. By the way, I've seen to it that Mike and two of his colleagues are hidden from view."

Lewis nodded his approbation.

"Now let's think ahead," Maddox continued. "So we get the *bot* and the *elint* device, then what? Any suggestions on the guinea pigs?"

Lewis paused. Maddox waited tensely.

"I'm the first guinea pig. I have to turn myself in to Maury," Lewis said, "and see what I can find out from the inside."

"You know it will be dangerous to turn yourself in," Maddox warned.

"What other choice do I have? Live like a fugitive indefinitely? We have to try to get close enough to Maury to stop him, and you have to admit, unless you have a better idea, I'm our best hope to do so. And furthermore, while the recent direction of his research concerns me considerably, I still trust him not to be vicious. Unless he's completely flipped out, I just can't imagine he'd intentionally harm me."

"OK. Great," Maddox said, unable to contain a note of sarcasm. "He's holding the President of the United States hostage, and you trust him. Fantastic.

"But just one problem," Maddox continued. "You said it would take up to eight weeks to get your devices ready for testing. If I remember correctly, you said the listening device would be ready in days or weeks, but not the *bot*, that it would take longer to, to . . . to 'tape-out,' I think was the term you used. So if you allow Carpenter to capture you in a week, you'll only have the listening device with you."

"Yes, I'm the first of the two guinea pigs. I don't capture Maury's *bot*. I learn as much as I can about how Maury's *bots* work, then I communicate as much as I can to my teammates. Using that information, the next guinea pig will actually capture one of Maury's *bots*. If at that point my team can actually get its hands on one of Maury's working *bots*, then we may be able to figure out a way to neutralize his plans."

"That's a lot of *ifs*," Maddox shot back. "And you expect us to just deliver you to Maury and let him stick one of his *microbots* up your nose? According to the letter, you're the one main hope we have to stop Carpenter, and you want me to let you go right into his arms? Presumably he wants you for a reason. You're an expert in the field. If you become his hostage and he manages to co-opt you, then you'll just add to his capabilities. How can we possibly even think about letting you go over to him?" Maddox continued as Lewis took in a deep breath of resignation.

"Not to mention the danger you'll be placing yourself in. Are you really prepared for that? The FBI most likely is already under Carpenter's control. Take it from me, if the FBI ever wants to extract information from you, especially in a case ostensibly involving biological weapons and Patriot Act provisions, our boys aren't likely to play gentle."

"But what other choice do we have?" Lewis pleaded. "And to answer your question: yes, I'm prepared to take the chance. It's the last chance we have. The clock is ticking. It's probably not too great an exaggeration to say that if we don't stop Maury soon, human freedom as we know it could become a quaint footnote in the history books."

Maddox paused to weigh Lewis' words.

"OK, suppose you're right? You say you're going to communicate Carpenter's *modus operandi* to me? How do you plan to do that? And what makes you think I'll even know where you are?"

"You work for the FBI. Presumably you'll have a way to figure out where I am?"

"Maybe, but if I ask too many questions, then I potentially expose myself. Then where does that put us?"

"I'm willing to take the risk, aren't you?"

"Fair enough," Maddox replied thoughtfully. "But let's say I find out where you're being held, then how do we communicate? It's not like you'll be easy to contact. Under the Patriot Act, you won't even have the right to talk to your lawyer."

"The *elint* device, which by the way will be disguised as a hearing aid, is waterproof."

"Waterproof? So what?"

"So I'll flush it down the toilet. Using a miniature built-in homing beacon, you can track it coming through the sewage system."

* * *

At nearly midnight, Maddox and Lewis exited the bar through the back door into a dark alley. They walked quickly in the shadows to Maddox's home. Approaching from the alley in back of the house, Maddox went over a wall into his backyard, momentarily alarming his Great Dane, Rufus. Maddox then opened the rear swing-door in his backyard to allow Lewis onto the property. Inside the house, with lights dimmed, they continued the remainder of their discussion at Maddox's small breakfast table.

Nearly two hours of planning and strategizing and several cups of coffee later, they had wrought the outline of a plan. The plan was simple and fraught with risk, but in the end, both agreed that it was the only strategy that had any chance of success.

Once Lewis via the false hearing-aid had provided details on Carpenter's *microbots*, Maddox would then try either to 'turn' or insert someone close to Carpenter. Someone who would have or could gain Carpenter's trust. The status and loyalties of the members of the doctor's research team were an open question. Any direct approach was too risky, and because there was no guarantee of reaching the source of the mysterious letter, Maddox and Lewis agreed that in the end, insertion would be the only viable option. But whom to *embed* with Carpenter? *Who is the second guinea pig?*

* * *

"At least when he was younger," Lewis said, "Maury had a particular fondness for women. At conferences, he always seemed to have a beautiful woman in tow. He actually attracted *groupies*. Each time it was a different woman, and quite an unusual collection. As I recall, while some seemed the very epitome of class and style, many were prone to adorning themselves rather unconventionally, even to the point that some favored minimal adornment. I suppose they were all helplessly attracted to one of the greatest minds in our generation.

"His first girlfriend, they used to call her *Über Alice*. We used to joke that her beauty could only be measured on the Richter scale. Maury was completely smitten with her, almost to the point of obsession. I only saw her a few times. Absolutely stunning! The other scientists were always jealous of Maury. We were just a bunch of nerds, completely helpless with women. Most of the wives wanted nothing to do with Maury, they were so put off by his entourage, but the wives of one or two of our colleagues succumbed to him."

"So Carpenter's a coxman. The point of all this being?" Maddox interjected.

"The point of all this being that at least in his earlier days, Maury clearly had a great weakness for women. I must say that after he and Alice split up, his interest in women seemed to decline gradually, until at last he was completely alone. It was as if he threw all his energies into his work to the exclusion of just about everything else. Some say it's as if he found religion or something — but the relevance of this is that if it was there once, it must still be there. Unless he's become a eunuch, I'd have thought deep down he must still have his old weakness for women."

"This *Über Alice*? Does she have a full name?"

Lewis paused to think. "I'm drawing a blank, but she was in Maury's undergraduate class at Harvard. She was a sociology major, if I'm not mistaken. If you get your hands on a yearbook, you can't miss her. Just flip through until you find the most mind-bogglingly beautiful blonde, and if her name is Alice, that's her. "

As Lewis was discussing Carpenter's love life, Maddox was reflecting on his training at Quantico. He remembered that the most successful agents, the ones willing to make the highest sacrifices, were those motivated not by money or patriotism, but by love. Pure, romantic, erotic love. *Enter Bill Maddox . . .* For the first time since he received the letter, he was beginning to take a real warming to the case.

* * *

That night as he lay in bed, Maddox mulled the best way to proceed. He knew well that the recruiting of an agent can be a simple or a complex process, depending on the circumstances involved. Throughout his career, Maddox had recruited dozens of agents and informants. Most of the recruitments were simple. Arrest someone on charges. Offer a plea bargain in return for cooperation.

Occasionally he was not able or willing to make an arrest, and instead had to win over an informant from inside the targeted organization. Those cases required more complex recruitment procedures. Typically, he would motivate the target through greed, fear of arrest, or fear of harm to the target or to a family member. His role was to offer money or protection, or often both.

In two cases throughout his career, however, and only two, he'd used *love* as the hook. Both occurred after his marriage with Helen had gone sour; he'd offered up himself, his own body, as the lure. He thought of Bianca, his agent in Colombia, and felt a tingling of arousal in his groin.

The first of the two cases, targeting a Mafia narcotics smuggling ring in Italy and involving the recruitment of a porn actress, was one of the most successful operations of his career. The second, in Colombia with Bianca, came close to success before ending in disaster.

Humint, he thought to himself with a mixture of trepidation and excitement as he began to nod off to sleep, *but most importantly, where to find the bait?*

CHAPTER 14

Carpenter brushed the dandruff off his lapel, and looked at his watch. *He should be here any minute,* he thought, with expectation mixed with a tinge of dread. *On this next meeting — with Bernie, of all people — hinges the success or failure of my entire plan.*

The knock at the heavy wooden door of his office in the Aspen Lodge came sooner than Carpenter had been expecting. An FBI agent entered, escorting Dr. Bernard R. Lewis by the arm.

"Why, Bernie, what a pleasant surprise," Carpenter said, rising from his seat. "Are you feeling well?" he asked.

Lewis glared at Carpenter and remained stone silent.

"Take a seat on the sofa," Carpenter said, smiling. He nodded to the FBI agent, who then withdrew from the room.

Lewis sat down cautiously, watching Carpenter. After a moment, he spoke, adding just the right amount of sternness. "You mind telling me what this is all about?"

Carpenter took a deep breath. "Bernie, Bernie, Bernie," he began. "This isn't easy for me, so let me just cut to the chase. Oh, but before I do, just one thing."

He removed the *microbotic* kit, including the release pen and remote control. After watching Lewis flinch as the *microbot* entered his nose, Carpenter explained about the oncoming brief but strong headache that would subside immediately. Carpenter punched a few keys on his control unit, and then a moment later, Lewis was cradling his head in pain for exactly three seconds. When it was over, Lewis looked up, stunned.

Carpenter continued. "See, just like I told you. You're feeling peachy already, right, Bernie?" Lewis continued to stare malevolently at Carpenter, but Carpenter ignored his displeasure and continued.

"In case you haven't guessed by now, I've finally done it." Lewis remained impassive.

Carpenter paused, then explained with pride and excitement, "I've found the *Holy Grail*: a flight-capable, radio-controlled, bio-penetrating, *microbotic*, MEMS-based weapon system. Bio-static. Digestive bio-battery. Inert *in-situ* until radio-activated. Capable of inflicting variable damage on the host, up to and including the level of *lethality*."

Lewis watched Carpenter and remained silent.

"The least you could say is 'congratulations.'"

Lewis said nothing.

"Any questions so far?"

No response.

"OK, well. Oh, and by the way, really sorry about that just now. The headache and all. I hope it wasn't too uncomfortable. I just needed to demonstrate the system's capabilities. I'm sure you of all people can appreciate that."

Lewis spoke after an awkward silence. "Do you mind telling me why I'm here? Presumably the FBI didn't bring me all the way here just so you can try out your new invention on me. And why was I detained by the FBI in connection with some kind of bio-terrorism plot?"

"Well, actually the funny thing is, yes, they did. I mean, yes, they did bring you all the way here so that I could try out the new invention on you. Because you see, this time I've really done it. I just couldn't leave well enough alone, and, well, guess what?"

"What?"

"I went off and, well . . . I sort of implanted my little toy here in the President and a lot of other very senior government officials. And you know what that makes me?"

"A dead man?"

"Well, maybe that too, but until that time — until I expire — I guess it actually makes me, J. Maurice Carpenter, the most powerful man on the planet. Kinda cool, huh?"

"You've completely lost it, Maury," Lewis said, shaking his head. After a moment he added: "So where do I fit into all of this utter insanity?"

"To your first point, i.e. that I've 'completely lost it,' I actually beg to differ." The earlier glint in Carpenter's eyes had now hardened into determination.

"To your second point about where you fit in, I'll get to that in a minute. But before I do, on the subject of me being a 'dead man,' there's one little additional tidbit you should know: I've got a *really, really* good life insurance policy. See, if I die, so does everyone else. I mean everyone else that I've implanted with the *microbot*. So that's my life insurance policy. Foolproof. Unbreakable RSA encryption algorithms. The whole nine yards.

"So not only am I the most powerful person on the planet, I'm also one of the most protected. So many people here in Washington caring deeply about my well-being: kind of touching, don't you think?"

Bernie shook his head again. "You've gone completely mad, Maury. Just tell me what it is that you're going to do now with your newfound power. I mean, yes, congratulations to you, I guess. So you're the most powerful man on the planet; now what?"

"Now what? Well you know the old saw about what people with power want?"

Bernie offered cautiously, "They want more power?"

Carpenter nodded. "Well there's actually a lot of truth in that saying. And since you were kind enough to ask, my next goal is actually to become much more powerful than the President, because when you think about it, the President is really not that powerful, not powerful *enough*.

"See, he has to answer to Congress and to the Supreme Court, and he has foreign allies to appease, and foreign and domestic adversaries to check him, and the press to hound him and ask annoying questions of him. So in the end, if you pause to consider, apart from being able to incinerate the entire planet at a moment's notice, the President really is not very *powerful* at all." Carpenter paused for effect.

"But I, on the other hand, or I should really say '*we*,' Bernie, if you'll join me," he said, zeroing in on Lewis' guarded expression, "*we* will control the Congress, and the Supreme Court, and our allies, and our adversaries, and the press, and *we* will truly rule the world.

"A lot of people have tried — no one's ever succeeded. Not Alexander the Great, not Julius Caesar, not Genghis Khan, not Napoleon, not Hitler, not even Alexander Haig or Donald Trump. Those guys are rank amateurs compared to what we can achieve."

"You still have your sense of humor, Maury. But then what? So you rule the world. So *we* rule the world. What are you after?"

"*And then what?* What am I *after?*" Carpenter paused, a glint of soft afternoon light in his eye. "Here's the great thing, Bernie, I'm not *after* a lot. Not a lot at all. All I want is global peace and prosperity and an end to injustice, suffering, despair, and environmental degradation," he said matter-of-factly.

"And here's the kicker," he continued. "Aside from those aims, I want nothing else. Nothing for myself. Absolutely nothing. Not riches, not fame, not glory, not dominion over others, not even the company of women, though I have to admit I'm aware that power does tend to attract women, and I'm prepared to see my vow of celibacy tested in the course of the current exercise."

"Celibacy?"

"We can go into that later. The point here is — and I hate to sound like a Hallmark greeting card — the sole reason I want to take over the world is so that I can make it a better place . . . so that *we* can make it a better place. I'm fed up. I'm angry as hell, Bernie."

Lewis expelled a breath of exasperation.

"A lot of people are angry, Maury. A lot of people are dissatisfied. *Very* dissatisfied. But they don't necessarily go around inventing incredibly dangerous weapons which if used improperly have the potential to turn the entire human race into a mass of mindless automatons.

"A lot of people are angry, Maury," Lewis continued, his voice rising, "but they don't necessarily take those incredibly dangerous weapons and subsequently start *implanting* them in a bunch of people's nasal and cranial cavities! *Especially not the nasal and cranial cavities of the goddamn President of the goddamn United States of America!*" Lewis shouted.

"Stop shouting, Bernie. Get a grip, will you?" Carpenter said with a sudden firmness. "Anyone who has the ability but lacks the willingness to do those things you just said, then you know what? They don't have *cojones*. And besides, somebody's got to implant something into the President's cranial cavity. It's a shame to let all that unused space go to waste."

"Bravo, Maury. Very funny. Very noble. Hysterical stuff. But what's this '*we*' stuff all about anyway? Where do I come in?"

"You say 'bravo,' Bernie. I hope you aren't mocking me. I'm perfectly serious about everything I've said here to you."

"Sorry, Maury. My apologies. Of course I didn't mean to mock you. It's just that this whole thing is so, so . . . so profoundly overwhelming. I'm still trying to get my mind around it all."

Carpenter furled his eyebrows.

"OK, apology accepted," he said, after a moment of silent deliberation. "Now, then, as to where you fit in. That's quite simple. You see, I need a bigger canvas."

"A bigger *canvas*?" Lewis asked, incredulous. "You already have effective control of the world's only superpower. Isn't that enough?"

"Let me explain using an example from the business world. You see, Bernie, you're my Bill Gates. Without you, I'm just a few lines of code sitting at Pacific Resources in Scott's Valley, California. Just a few thousand dollars' worth of code. But with you, I become MS DOS and Windows. I become Microsoft. You take me global. You put me on desktops around the world, and I'm worth billions and billions, metaphorically speaking, of course."

Lewis nodded his head slowly. "I think I'm beginning to see what you're getting at."

"See, right now, my *microbot* is only a localized solution. The people I've implanted? They're tethered to me. They have to remain in my vicinity, or come back to me periodically for a refresh code. The end effect is that they can't travel freely, and I can't control them over large distances."

"By control you mean . . . ?"

"Right, I can't zap them. Give 'em a headache, or drop 'em cold, whatever. And that means the number of people I can control is inherently limited. There are only so many camp followers I can accommodate in my immediate vicinity. Only so many travel schedules I can manage."

Bernie nodded.

"I'm not a communications expert," Carpenter continued. "I know math. I know biochemistry. I know physics, mechanics, thermodynamics, medicine, a bit of electrical engineering, and robotics and the bare minimum in radio communications. But I'm not an expert in telecommunications. I don't know about IP, 802.11, Zigbee, WiFi and WiMax, traffic routing, packetization, signal processing, compression/decompression, encryption, A-to-D, D-to-A conversion, waveform modulation. To make it short, I have a localized solution, but I don't have the glue to put it altogether. You're the *glue*, Bernie.

"You make me, make *us*, global," Carpenter continued, his voice rising in intensity. "With *your talent*, before long, sitting at a single desktop computer or even using a single handheld device, we can gain control over every government, every political party, every army, every police force, every judiciary, every labor union, every insurgent group, every terrorist organization, every religious leader, every newspaper editor, every book club and every knitting circle in the entire world."

"And then?" Lewis asked.

"And then," Carpenter explained, his voice growing distant, "and then, we outlaw war. We disarm everyone. Nuclear weapons, conventional weapons, the works. And all that money, all those billions and trillions of dollars wasted every year on weapons will go to ending poverty, curing disease, improving the environment."

Lewis rubbed his chin. "Crazy, Maury. Definitely crazy. But intriguing, nonetheless. I'll have to admit."

"I'm glad you think so."

"But how do you manage it all? Ruling the entire world is quite a tall order, isn't it?"

"Precisely. I'm glad you mentioned that. Again, that's where you come in. Management is not really my *forte*. I'm doing my best. But you were always a much better manager than I was. It's hard work, you know, quite overwhelming actually, trying to run the whole world.

"I need a close advisor. A counselor. Someone I can trust. Someone who can help me keep the troops in line. Someone who can help me build an organization and properly monitor the infrastructure, the key players in the chain of command. One thing I've come to learn is that organization is key, Bernie. *Organization is everything.*" Carpenter continued, "And beyond all that, I need someone who I can bounce ideas off of, to keep me sane throughout this exercise."

"Sane?" Bernie echoed. "Interesting choice of words."

"There you go patronizing me again, Bernie. I guarantee you I'm perfectly sane. Or as sane as anyone else is around here, which is not necessarily saying much. So what do you think? Join me?"

"Am I really free to say? What if I say no?"

"'No' is not an option, Bernie. I've come too far, and the stakes are too high. I'd consider you unpardonably selfish if you were to say no after everything I've told you thus far, especially given how selfless my own aims are."

"Then I guess I don't really have any other choice."

"I guess not."

"But you promise me one thing," Lewis said, his voice hardening.

"What's that?"

"While you're busy using your *flies* to try to save the world . . . " Lewis said, scrutinizing Carpenter carefully and tapping on his right nostril.

"Yes . . . ?" Carpenter asked after a moment, prodding Lewis to finish his thought.

"Just make darn sure you don't become *Lord of the Flies*," Lewis said, pointing his finger inside the nostril where Carpenter's mechanical fly had entered minutes before.

"Now, Bernie. There's no need to worry about me. I'm no Beelzebub," Carpenter said with a note of sadness. "Now, I want you to call your wife and invite her and your daughter to the White House. Some nice fellows from the FBI will be waiting for them tomorrow morning at your home, and will escort them here. Welcome aboard. You won't regret it."

Then he added, "And one more thing, Bernie?"

"What's that?"

"Try to relax a little. Don't take everything so seriously."

Lewis shook his head in disbelief, and let out a sharp breath of air.

"Just one final question," Carpenter added, almost as an afterthought.

"What is it?"

"You mind telling me where you've been hiding out these last few days? My friends in the FBI tell me you've been awfully hard to reach. Not to mention, it seems as though just about half your entire team has disappeared. You wouldn't happen to have any idea what they're up to?"

Lewis did his best to conceal a gulp of anxiety as he replied as innocently as he was able, "Hard to reach? What do you mean, Maury?"

CHAPTER 15

One of the benefits of Maddox's job was that he could go just about anywhere he wanted in short order. All he needed was the minimum level of evidence that a drop might be going down, or that someone on the inside wanted to cooperate, possibly a tip-off from one of his coterie of informants, and he usually could manage to be on a plane at a moment's notice. The required "minimum level of evidence" and the "tip-off" weren't too difficult to manufacture, provided he used his creative leads sparingly. Warrants weren't a problem. He knew judges that handed them out like candy. And given that Maddox's specialty was the Mexican Mafia, and that *La Eme's* tentacles extended across the country, and even globally, Bill's range of movement was broad and nearly unrestricted. He could arrange to be nearly anywhere in the world he wanted without much difficulty.

At this particular moment he wanted to be in Austin, Texas, where a quick search of the Bureau's computer systems indicated one Alice Van Houten was currently residing. He had called the previous day to arrange an interview at her house, and though he suspected the odds were slim, if somehow he could enlist her help to track and neutralize Carpenter, then it would have been worth the risk to approach her. Besides, he had discovered early on in his career that all manner of leads and unforeseen breakthroughs could be produced simply by getting out and talking to people.

He knew he couldn't afford to let word that an FBI agent was tracking Carpenter get back to the renegade scientist. Compounding matters, the FBI files on Alice had revealed links in earlier years to the Weather Underground, as well as intimate liaisons with several wanted Black Panthers. More ominous still, she had even been arrested at a demonstration in support of Leonard Peltier, the Native American jailed for life for killing two FBI agents in a stand-off at the Pine Ridge Indian Reservation in nineteen seventy-five. Maddox thus treaded very cautiously on the phone.

Posing as a member of the MacArthur Foundation, the charitable organization that awards million-dollar genius grants, Maddox claimed sudden difficulty in locating Carpenter as the excuse for wanting to see her. She was very reluctant to see Maddox, and from his training Maddox sensed in her reticence a tinge of paranoia. Despite her protestations that she hadn't had contact with Carpenter in over thirty years, and therefore could be of no help, through sheer persistence he was able coax her into allowing him a brief visit. He won her consent, however, only by playing his trump card: promising her that he had an important message for her from Carpenter. *I hope I can figure out before I meet her what that message is.*

Stepping up the walkway to her ramshackle house in a seedier part of East Austin, he still hadn't made up his mind exactly how to play the interview. In his line of work, there were no scripts or playbooks. You felt your way along and dealt with matters as they developed.

He rang the doorbell, and was greeted by a tall lady in her sixties. Her long blonde hair was mixed with gray and pulled into a braid at the back. Though the years hadn't been gentle on her complexion, she was still quite attractive, and would have been even more so had she been able to manage a smile.

"Ms. Van Houten I presume? It's Fletcher. Scott Fletcher. Please call me Scott," Maddox said, extending a hand.

"You can call me Alice," she said, taking his hand warily. She was barefoot, and wore a red t-shirt that read: "Keep Austin Weird." She motioned to a threadbare couch in the small living room and shooed away two cats. "Scat Trotsky! Scoot Lenin," she said curtly. When the cats had left, she bade Carpenter sit down.

"So," she challenged, inviting him to talk. "Maury has a message for me?"

"As I mentioned, I'm with the MacArthur Foundation," he said, sidestepping her question. "We'd been in touch with Dr. Carpenter briefly, then suddenly he's gone and we can't reach him. So we're trying to locate Dr. Carpenter. We've checked all his friends, but none seem to know where he is. Someone mentioned you and he were close once?"

"That was a long time ago. As I told you on the phone, I haven't seen him in over thirty years. So what's the message?"

"If it's okay with you, can I just ask you a few questions first? When we're done, I'll be glad to pass you the message."

She looked dubious, but assented. "If you're having so much trouble finding him, why don't you just try the cops?" she challenged.

He paused.

"The reason for that is . . . I *am* 'the cops,' Ma'am."

"Say what?"

"Ma'am, given some elements of your background, I had a strong hunch that you might not necessarily be enamored of our nation's law enforcement officials, so I had to be a bit *inventive*."

She regarded him with barely concealed skepticism mixed with a measure of contempt.

"Ma'am, it's very simple," he explained. "Doctor Carpenter is in very serious trouble, and we really need your help to get him and a lot of other people out of that trouble and home safe," he said, producing his badge.

"Hang on a minute. You're a Fed?"

"Yes, Ma'am."

"Do you have a warrant to be here?"

"No ma'am. I'm acting unofficially."

"So why should I cooperate?"

"As I said, a lot of people are in serious danger, including Doctor Carpenter."

"Danger? What kind of danger?"

"The dangerous kind."

"Ummm. Can you possibly be a little bit more specific?"

"Before I tell you more, I need to know if you'll help me."

"Look. Since you already alluded to it, you know my record when it comes to the Law. That said, there's been plenty of water under the bridge and I've made my peace over the years. My more recent mellowing notwithstanding, however, I need to know exactly what you want from me before I can tell you whether or not I can help."

"Ma'am, this is obviously highly confidential," he said, meeting her gaze squarely and lowering his voice, "but Doctor Carpenter has taken a number of key government officials hostage."

"Hot damn!" she exclaimed with a faint smile. "Never knew the bastard had it in him. Sorry, go on," she added, regaining a measure of seriousness.

"That's it, Ma'am."

"He's taken some government officials hostage? What does he want?" She began to appear amused again, and this bothered him.

"Ma'am, we don't know."

"What kind of officials?"

"Very senior officials."

"How senior?"

"Very, very senior."

"Maury!" She appeared genuinely pleased.

"Look, Ma'am. I've been straight with you. This is not a laughing matter. Many innocent lives are at stake. Now, will you help me?"

"Just exactly what do you want me to do?"

He paused for a moment, reconsidering. The thought of her anywhere near Carpenter was beginning to frighten him.

"I'm going to have to think about that one for a minute."

Bill looked around the room, hoping to find something useful, anything to turn the tide of the conversation. The décor was sparse. The far wall had an unframed poster of Spiro Agnew dressed as a hippie. At last his eyes came on a collection of photographs on a side table next to the couch.

"Nice pictures," Maddox said, changing the subject. "Is that you?"

There was a picture of a much younger Alice, stunningly beautiful. She had a flower in her long blonde hair, and was dancing with a long-haired, shirtless hippie, a joint jangling from his mouth.

"Yeah. Summer of Love."

"And that one there? Is that your daughter?" he asked, pointing to a picture of a young girl, also stunning, blowing bubbles in the face of a thirty-something Alice. It stood next to another picture, presumably of the same girl as a teenager posing stiffly with a forty-something Alice. A third photograph showed the girl, a few years older, playing cello. Maddox took note that the girl looked remarkably like her mother, even down to the dimple each had on the right cheek.

"Yeah."

"Beautiful pictures. Beautiful girl. You must be proud."

"That's my girl, Heather," she said, smiling imperceptibly. "Haven't seen her in what, two, three years now. She's a doctor somewhere. With some guy. Complete turkey. Anyway, Heather and I, we're not really that close."

"I'm sorry to hear that. I'm estranged from my son too," Maddox said, taking very large liberties with the truth in a bid to win her confidence.

"Really? Yeah, I mean, I guess I wasn't much of a mother for her," she said, loosening her tone slightly. "In and out of rehab and all."

Maddox used his eyes to coax her to continue.

"I met her father on a commune in New Mexico. We split when she was young. She grew up with her dad and a stepmom in Minnesota."

"And you were saying it's been a couple of years since you saw her."

"Yeah. She brought her boyfriend to see me a few years back. For dinner. The guy's a total square. Says he wants to be a doctor. I saw right through him. He's just in it for the money and the status," she said, loosening her tone still further. "You know, the whole *Doctor trip*. As soon as he pays off his loans, he'll be tooling around in a *Merc* or a *Caddy*, playing golf every Wednesday. He'll have his secretary return every other call a week late. I had him nailed."

"Doesn't sound like you hit it off too well."

"Nah. One of my faults. I'm too direct. Never had the soft touch, and never much for diplomacy. I just say what's on my mind. Especially when I have a bit too much to drink, which that night I definitely did. I mean, I can't really blame her for being mad at me. I guess I'm just not the maternal type."

She shook her head in disbelief at her own clumsiness, then continued.

"So I don't fault her a bit. I haven't seen her in years, and she comes all the way to see me to introduce me to her boyfriend, and I end up yelling at her and telling her to dump the fool," she laughed, simultaneously amused and appalled at her own behavior. "Right in front of him! We didn't even finish the meal. They ended up leaving before dessert. Haven't heard from her since."

"Sometimes a parent has to be direct. She'll probably appreciate your candor later," Maddox offered lamely. He spied an angle, and the gears in his mind started to turn.

"Sorry, I hope I'm not prying here. You mentioned she's a doctor? The boyfriend's clearly a loser, but how about her? Is she in it for the right reasons? Stop me any time if I'm being too nosy. I'm just curious is all. This is totally unofficial. I'm just asking person-to-person, parent-to-parent."

Alice paused for a moment, seeming to weigh whether she should continue. Maddox urged her again with his eyes.

"Heather's not just a doctor, she's a brain surgeon. She's got her head on straight. We may not see eye to eye on everything, but she has ideals. She threw me a curve ball once in high school when she entered a beauty pageant."

Beauty pageant? He waited for her to go on.

"I mean, as a parent, you try your best right? Anyway, she told me that she *got* the whole exploitation angle, but the reason

109

she was doing it was for charity. To promote important causes. So I gave her a pass on that account. Told her I could handle it."

"Beauty pageant? Doctor? Quite a combination there. My kids don't excel at anything," Maddox offered humbly, wishing he had kids, even ones that didn't excel at anything. "What'd you say her name was again? Heather?"

"Yes, Heather Anderson."

"Interesting. Sounds like she could be in line for a MacArthur award some day," he said, smiling. "I'll have to look her up some time."

"You stay away from her," she challenged. "But if you do happen to meet her, be sure to tell her to dump the guy, if she hasn't already," she said, returning his smile.

"I certainly will."

"And so, about that message from Maury?" she asked. "That was a ruse too?" She sounded disappointed.

"I'm afraid so, Ma'am," he said.

CHAPTER 16

"I'm almost positive he's evading." Carpenter was briefing FBI Director Peter Hutchison after the conversation with Lewis. Carpenter remained vexed by the still unexplained disappearance of Lewis and several of Lewis' team members just before the FBI had brought in Lewis.

Six-foot-two, trim, with dark hair silvered at the sides, Hutchison had risen through the ranks of the FBI partly through his good casework, which was attributable to a calm, businesslike, and unrelenting demeanor, and also to his ability to navigate safely the political currents that routinely buffeted the Bureau. He seemed to have a knack for reading political tea leaves, and for falling on exactly the right side of every important issue that challenged his ascendance.

"Would you like us to get a better read on that?" Hutchison asked.

"What would you suggest?" Carpenter replied.

"Well, I'd have to say, based on everything you say, his story does raise a number of troubling questions.

"Maybe there is a good explanation for the fact that he and several members of his team disappeared just as an APB was issued for their arrest. But *if*, in the worst case, he and his team were somehow informed in advance about what we're doing, then it is imperative we find out the source of the leak, and also determine who else might have knowledge of your activities. What I'm advocating here is just sound operational protocol."

"So how should we proceed?"

"We start with a routine interrogation to establish his version of the facts, and then we escalate from there as needed. First, we see if we can identify inconsistencies in his story, and present him with these in hopes of persuading him to confess what we need voluntarily."

"And let's say that doesn't get us anywhere?"

"Then we will need to enhance the degree of coercion we employ."

Degree of coercion? "Easy, chief! Whatever you do, treat him with kid gloves. That's an order. Not only is he my friend, but his full cooperation is also critically important for our mission."

I can't kick the program into high gear until Bernie's generalized solution is ready.

"Understood, Sir. You're calling the shots. We'll play it as gentle or as rough as you deem appropriate."

"Make no mistake. We must and we *will* find out what he's covering up, but we can't let the inquiry get in the way of the overall mission. So keep it slow and steady for now, and let's continue to monitor how cooperative he is in the development efforts. In that respect, at least, he's already off to a good start."

"Understood, Sir."

* * *

As Hutchison left the room, Carpenter allowed himself a moment to collect his thoughts. With Lewis' arrival, a key milestone had now been attained; if all proceeded on schedule, in a matter of months his grand plan would come to fruition. Ever attentive to detail, he also jumped immediately to several potential pitfalls. *First and foremost is the question of Bernie's loyalty, and the delicate question of how much carrot and how much stick we need to ascertain and secure that loyalty. The second problem is that the election is only two and a half months away, and if the President loses, it would have a grievously negative impact on my plans. And the polls are not going in the right direction!*

CHAPTER 17

With Lewis in FBI custody, Maddox estimated he now had at most a few weeks to move to the next phase of the plan. It was in all the media that the President and his advisors were at Camp David. Maddox thus assumed that Carpenter and Lewis must also be there. A cursory analysis of Camp David, however, revealed that it was pointless to plan any attempt to stop Carpenter at that venue. Not only did the Camp's remoteness argue against it as a target, the level of security was thoroughly daunting.

In fact, Maddox's briefing materials indicated Camp David to be one of the most secure facilities in the world. His research showed that the camp was guarded by one of the United States Marine Corps' most elite units, MSC-CD (Marine Security Company, Camp David), with each and every Marine guard hand-picked from a Marine infantry unit and subjected to a battery of psychological and physical tests. Those that passed the tests then underwent specialized security training at the Marine Corps Security Forces School in Chesapeake, Virginia. Upon successful completion of all required schooling and duties, the candidate Marine was then subjected to the "Yankee White" background check, the highest level of background scrutiny in the military. Only after obtaining Yankee White clearance was the candidate eligible for assignment to Camp David.

Maddox surmised that with political pressure building, the President couldn't remain sequestered at Camp David for an extended period. The press pegged his stay there at no more than four weeks. *Not that the White House itself is an easy target, but I have a much better chance to target Carpenter there after he returns from Camp David in a few weeks. So now the problem is how to get to them once they are back in the White House ...*

The plan Maddox eventually settled on with Lewis was simple. He was to find a doctor to plant in the White House staff, hopefully to infiltrate Carpenter's operation. *This is where the* humint *comes in. And she has to be a beautiful doctor, because she's the bait to hook Carpenter.*

Ideally, the doctor in question would be a neurosurgeon or neurologist, and then the task would be to insert her into the Walter Reed Medical Center in Bethesda, Maryland, from whence she would be summoned to the White House to look after the President when, at Lewis' behest, the President complained of headaches.

Once at the White House her mission would be to use her feminine charms to insinuate herself into Carpenter's circle of trust, ideally seducing him, and from there somehow find a way to terminate or at least set back his plans. Maddox knew, based on his reading of Carpenter's background, that to be all the more attractive to Carpenter the female doctor would need to have a strong social conscience. Preferably too, she'd be unattached.

The meeting with Alice and her mention of her daughter Heather had intrigued Maddox. Distrustful of authority and carrying too many ambiguous emotional links to Carpenter, Alice seemed too dangerous and unlikely a choice. Heather, on the other hand, was in certain respects close to an ideal candidate. Certainly her mother's past intimacy with Carpenter had the potential to complicate the equation in unforeseeable ways.

But in her favor, she seemed to have all the requirements and attributes needed both to lure Carpenter and to serve in the role of White House doctor. Her beauty, uncanny similarity in appearance to Alice, and professional qualifications all recommended her highly for the job. Still, while he recognized that the relationship between Alice and Carpenter could serve as a motivating factor for Heather, assuming she wanted to learn more about her mother's past, the unforeseen complications that relationship might present also gave Maddox pause.

At the same time, just calculating the odds of success in finding another doctor who could fill the role was enough to utterly dishearten Maddox. *Where would I even start to find such a woman? And under such a tight time limit!* Nonetheless, for completeness' sake, try he did.

The research team brought Maddox files of all the FBI doctors on staff, but none could be described as beautiful. Discouraged, Maddox deduced that he had two simple options for conducting the search. The first would be to sift through all of the doctors in North America, and try to find which ones were beautiful. The second would be to sift through all of the beautiful women in North America, and find out which ones were doctors. He chose the latter approach.

Stealing some free time, he decided to try his luck surfing the web to see if anything easy turned up. What he discovered in under two hours of Googling amazed him.

He was able to find three qualified M.D.'s who were previously state, national or international beauty pageant contestants: one from Florida, one from Delaware, and one from Vancouver, Canada. As beauty contestants, photos for all three were readily available on the web, and all were strikingly beautiful. *Not just beautiful, but also talented.* Miss Delaware played flute, while Miss Canada was a modern dancer and Miss Florida was a singer. Miss Delaware advocated prevention of child abuse, while Miss Florida advocated protection of manatees and Miss Canada, protection of harp seals. *They've all got the social conscience box ticked. Best of all, as beauty contestants, that automatically means that all were not married as of the time of the contest.*

A quick routing through the research department later in the evening produced addresses and phone numbers for the two Americans. Data on the Canadian was expected back from the RCMP in Ottawa first thing in the morning.

* * *

The Mantovani music on the telephone was becoming too much for Maddox to bear. *It's easier to win the lottery than to get a doctor to return your call!* Despite countless tries over a two-day period, and endless minutes of elevator music on hold, Maddox had still not been able to reach Miss Florida.

A hard-won call with Miss Delaware produced the disappointing revelation that she was engaged to be married in weeks. *Not likely she'll want to drop everything to attempt a romantic attachment to Carpenter.* In a conversation with Miss Canada's receptionist, Maddox was able to learn that Miss Canada had days earlier broken her ankle in a skydiving accident, and it was expected the ankle would require several months to heal. *Too impractical to even consider.* In the end, this left Heather as Maddox's last and only hope, a prospect which left him both relieved and anxious at the same time.

* * *

"Hello, Doctor Anderson?"
"Yes, this is she."

"Thank you so much for taking my call. I hope I'm not bothering you at a bad time.

"My name is Todd Whittier. I'm with the American Journal of Organ Donation and Transplantation. We're aware of the excellent work you're doing to promote organ donation, and we were hoping to write a feature article on you in our upcoming publication."

Maddox's research on the internet had revealed a number of useful details on Heather's background, including her Directorship in the American Organ Donation and Transplantation Society.

"Um, sure . . . Uh, Todd, is it? That would be fine, I guess. Always delighted to help."

"You've no idea how much this means to us. To start, I was just hoping to get a little bit of background. I saw on the web that you grew up in Minnetonka, Minnesota?"

"That's right."

"And you're a physician?"

"I completed my internship last year."

"And now you have a practice?"

"That's right. I'm a neurosurgeon."

Perfect!

"Fantastic, and I understand you're a cellist as well?"

"That's right."

"Where do you find the time?"

"It hasn't been easy, but you make the time."

"And you went to medical school right after you graduated university?"

"No, I was in the Peace Corps for two years before medical school."

Peace Corps! She's the adventurous sort. Excellent!

"Ah, hah. So let's see . . . that would make you around . . . thirty years old, if I may be so impertinent?"

"Actually, thirty-one, but I'll be happy to go with thirty if you want to write that."

"Do you mind if I ask where you served in the Peace Corps?"

"In West Africa. Equatorial Guinea."

"That must have been quite an experience."

"It was marvelous."

Maddox cleared his throat.

"Well, now, onto the subject at hand. I hope this isn't too personal, Doctor Anderson, but would you mind sharing how it is that you became interested in the topic of organ donation and transplantation?"

"Sure. My younger brother was hurt in a traffic accident when I was in high school. A drunk driver hit him and ruptured his kidneys. He required a kidney transplant, but unfortunately he died before a donor came forward. My tissue type was incompatible with his. If I could have, I would have gladly donated one of my kidneys. So now, I do my best to raise awareness about the topic of organ donation."

"That's very noble of you, and all of us at the Foundation are extremely grateful for your efforts. Sixty thousand Americans awaiting organs . . . so few people willing to donate."

Maddox paused.

"And now, may I ask for just a bit of personal background for the story?" he continued.

"Sure, I guess."

"May I ask about your parents, professionally?"

"My father is a retired building contractor. My stepmother has never done too much."

Interesting that she didn't mention Alice.

"And siblings?"

"One younger sister. She's a high school teacher."

"Which subject?"

"Mathematics."

"I guess brains run in the family."

Here comes the hard part. This is it, all or nothing!

"And just for completeness, may I ask do you have a family yourself?"

She paused before answering.

"You mean, am I married?"

"Yes."

"No."

Whew!

"Any plans along those lines I can mention? Our readers will want to know."

Maddox held his breath.

"I guess nothing too serious right now."

Excellent! He breathed a sigh of relief.

"Don't worry, I won't print that. I wouldn't want to scare the guy off."

"Don't worry. He won't be scared. He's used to it. We're both doctors. He's an intern. We hardly ever see each other anyway, the schedules we have."

"Well, Doctor. This has been fascinating indeed. Oh, I think I forgot to mention one thing. Assuming you don't mind, we were hoping to spruce up our magazine cover a bit. We were hoping you wouldn't mind if we put you on the cover of the next publication."

"Well, I don't know . . . I guess . . . Well, why not? I'm flattered. I suppose it couldn't hurt. Anything to help the cause."

"That's terrific. If you don't mind, we'll send someone out to take a few pictures — possibly myself if my schedule allows. Outdoor shots. Maybe by the lake there? A few at the clinic with you in uniform? Won't take more than a half hour tops. Would that be OK?"

There was an awkward moment of silence as she paused to consider.

"Sure. Why not? No problem."

"Wonderful, is Wednesday OK?"

"I'll have my assistant schedule Wednesday now."

I think I've finally found my agent!

CHAPTER 18

"You see, Bernie, not to detract from the tremendous efforts you've lent us so far in developing the command and control system, but I really don't like loose ends," Carpenter said in dead earnest with a cold stare aimed straight at the center of Lewis' eyeballs. "And your disappearance just before we picked you up . . . " He turned to Hutchison, seated at his right at the formica-topped interrogation table. "What was it? Around thirty-six hours he was unaccounted for?" Hutchison nodded. "Almost thirty-six hours, Bernie. That constitutes a *real big* loose end, especially when you consider the fact that all the important guys in your lab also happened to skip town at the same time. Quite a coincidence, wouldn't you agree?"

This was the first formal interrogation of Lewis, and Carpenter insisted on leading the proceedings. The unaccounted thirty-six hours that so vexed Carpenter referred to the time Lewis spent with Maddox in Los Angeles, ostensibly under the alibi Maddox had arranged of a trip to Reno to console Lewis' old "girlfriend" Vera.

"But I told you, Maury, I had to take a trip to Reno, and I couldn't let my wife or anybody else know about it," Lewis retorted.

"Ah, yes, Reno. How convenient. That explains why you say you needed to take your assistant's four-wheel drive. To get over the Sierras. Because there were reports of a washout. And lucky for you, there actually were some reports of a washout on the state highway around twenty miles south of the route you said you took. We checked.

"It's also convenient that Reno is less than a full tank's ride away from Livermore. That explains why none of the video feeds from all the gas stations on route to Reno and in Reno proper had any footage of your vehicle filling up. Mr. Hutchison's team checked each and every single gas station. We're very thorough, Bernie."

Maddox sure knows his stuff, Lewis thought to himself. *So that's why he coached me not to say I stopped at any gas stations along the way.*

Carpenter bore down on Lewis, and Lewis felt as if he were being examined by a tunneling electron microscope, exploring and rendering every detail, all the minutiae, with the sharpest, laser-like resolution.

"And because we're so thorough," Carpenter continued, "if you have anything to say to us, I suggest you say it now while everyone's still in a good mood. Because it would be a *real downer,* Bernie, if we found out later that you're *lying.* That would seriously kill the buzz."

Lewis tried to take in a lungful of fresh air, but the interrogation room was cramped and stuffy. He felt like a fish in a tank filled only with stale, oxygen-deprived water. Facing the onslaught of questions, Lewis did his best to meet Carpenter's unrelenting and highly skeptical gaze.

"Whatever, or whomever, you're trying to hide, or trying to protect . . . " Carpenter continued, with a measure of reassurance in his voice, "I respect that. In fact, I would expect no less of you.

"But you're on our team now. We're all friends. So just tell us what you were really doing during those two days we lost sight of you, and just tell us where the rest of your team is now, and then we can all get on with more important things, like saving the world.

"And don't worry, Bernie. As you can see, we're quite gentle unless provoked. Your colleagues in the lab, and whomever else you're trying to protect, they're all in good hands with us. We come in peace. We mean no harm to anyone."

"Maury, as I said before," Lewis responded, pleading, "I *am* on your side. I'm looking forward to helping you save the world. I believe in you. I believe in our project. But you're just wasting everyone's time here.

"I had to go to Reno to see my ex-girlfriend. She called me and said she was in big trouble. She was feeling suicidal. Her life had no meaning, she wanted to just end it all. She needed to see me. Obviously, I couldn't let my wife or anyone else know about this. Anyway, if you don't believe me, as I said before, just ask Vera. I've already given you her phone number."

Carpenter studied Lewis closely for a moment.

"We did ask *Vera*, or at least we tried to, but the funny thing is that she too suddenly disappeared, or at least the next best thing. You see, she hopped on a plane to Belgrade yesterday. Bought the ticket on just twenty-four hours notice. Told her colleagues there were some family issues she needed to attend to. Another one of those remarkable coincidences wouldn't you say? And you know what else is funny, Bernie?"

Lewis shook his head cautiously.

"Mr. Hutchison here informs me we don't have a friggin' extradition treaty with friggin' Serbia! Can you believe that? How *funny* is that?

"And it just gets better, Bernie. We tried to track her in Serbia, unofficially, but she's really well hidden there. None of her family knows where she is, and the really *hilarious* thing about that is that when we visited her office in Reno she had several nice pictures on her desk showing her laughing with her family in front of the St. Sava Temple in Svetosavski Square in central Belgrade. The timestamp on the picture indicated it was taken less than seven months ago. So I really don't think it's very likely she suddenly became estranged from her family during the last seven months.

"Don't you think it's strange enough that she would go back to Serbia on one day's notice, let alone to go there to 'attend to family issues' but not even bother to tell her family that she had arrived? Come on Bernie, get real!"

Stonewall . . . deny at all costs, Lewis reminded himself of Maddox's advice on how to handle the interrogation. *They can give you a polygraph and tell you that you failed miserably, you still keep denying. Just stonewall*, Maddox had said. *And whatever you do, at all costs, don't mention my name, ever! If they ever find out about me, we're all cooked.*

"Look, I don't know. She's unstable. She was suicidal. Besides, regarding the timing of the picture, sometimes people forget to set the timestamp on their camera."

"And sometimes people are totally and utterly *full of crap!*" Carpenter shot back, starting to lose his cool. He momentarily fingered the remote control device in his pocket. "Now don't *toy* with me, Bernie. You're playing with fire!"

"Look, Maury, I'm telling the truth. She was very unstable."

"But that's yet another amusing thing, Bernie! She has no record of any mental health issues. We checked all the hospital records in every city she has ever lived in the U.S., and checked all her insurance records going back over a decade. Interviewed her colleagues. No aberrant behavior. No indication of depression. And get this: according to her colleagues, no indication of alienation from her family either. Nothing! She's clean as a whistle. Except that she's disappeared. *Completely*. I just can't tell you how overwhelmed Mr. Hutchison and I are by the hilarity of this whole situation," Carpenter said, looking over at a stone-faced Hutchison. "Now tell us, Bernie, *why* is it that everyone around you we want to talk to keeps disappearing?"

Lewis shook his head.

"And you know what else? You're gonna love this! There's no trace of your DNA in her apartment. We looked for hair samples, dandruff, all over. Urine samples around the toilet. Nobody's that accurate. They always spray a little."

"We didn't stay for long. We went to a park," Lewis protested, as calmly as he could. "I never used the toilet at her place. After the park, we went to a movie. Had dinner. Drinks. As for my dandruff, maybe she had the apartment cleaned before she left the country."

Carpenter and Hutchison shook their heads with heavy doubt. After the conversation over Lewis' fabricated trip to Reno continued futilely for another ten minutes, Carpenter then turned his attention to Lewis' missing lab team.

"Like I said, Maury, if I knew where they are, I'd be the first to tell you," Lewis offered.

"Yet another incredible coincidence there. They get busted on drug charges in Phoenix, Arizona. What on God's green Earth were they doing in Phoenix anyway? No sooner had we put out an APB for their arrest, than they disappear from sight as if they've donned bifringent metamaterial invisibility cloaks. Next thing we know, the Phoenix Police have them in a holding tank . . . on *drug charges*? Under my instructions, the FBI puts out a custody order on them; but wouldn't you know, they get released just *five minutes* before the FBI arrives at the jail to take custody. Some guy in the Phoenix PD was incredibly apologetic about the 'mix up,' as he called it. Treated it like it was some sort of *petit rien*. Blamed it on an error in the paperwork."

"Look, I don't know. Sometimes life is full of coincidences," Lewis said calmly. "All I know is that you have to believe me. I'm telling you the truth . . . "

So help me God!

* * *

"So what do we do with him?" Hutchison asked Carpenter after the interrogation produced no change in Lewis' story, and Lewis had left the room. "I mean, his story is clearly too far-fetched to be believed, but at the same time, we've been unable to punch a hole in it."

"Remind me of our options," Carpenter asked testily.

"We can and should give him a polygraph, but those aren't too hard to beat if he's been coached, so I'm not sure if that will get us anywhere. History is littered with instances of spies who passed the polygraph tests we gave them — Aldrich Ames, Karl Koecher, and Ana Belen Montes, to name a few — though we have caught a few spies here and there using polygraphs, so I suppose it can't hurt to try.

"In combination with the polygraph, we can use voice and micro-expression analysis. But the problem is, all these tests will do is tell us that he's lying or covering up the truth, which we pretty much know already."

Carpenter nodded.

"The trick is to force him to tell us the truth, and for that, I'm afraid the options are not so encouraging," Hutchison continued, weighing his words.

"Remind me again," Carpenter said, gloomily.

"I'm assuming we can't buy his cooperation. You would have already offered him that option, and anyway, even if he takes the inducement we still can't be sure he's giving us good information in return.

"So that leaves us the stick," Hutchison said, eyeing Carpenter carefully. "Depending on how convincing you want us to be, we're pretty good at getting information from people reluctant to share with us. But the problem is, this process has risks and also takes time, which you've told me is at a premium."

"How much time?"

"That depends on how aggressive you want us to be. We can probably get what we want within forty-eight hours, but the more *persuasive* we want to be, the higher the risk that we could end up damaging the subject in the process."

"When you say 'damaging,' just how damaged do you mean?"

"Like *terminally* damaged. There's always a five or ten percent risk of that if we want quick results. If on the other hand we decide to be more gentle and minimize the potential for impairment, it could take us over a month before we break him. I've seen cases that took even longer than that."

"I'm not going to risk *damaging* Bernie, Mr. Hutchison. Forget about the moral issues. He's just plain too valuable. And we also can't take him out of circulation for a month. He's too important to the project."

"There is another way that I've been reluctant to recommend," Hutchison offered in a gentle, even tone, again weighing his words.

"What's that?"

"We could always place his wife in a position of, of . . . *discomfort*. We can use her condition of distress as leverage to gain his cooperation."

"You mean we torture Danielle? The Lewises are my friends!"

"You were the one that wanted to take over the world, Sir."

"If we lay a hand on Danielle, he'll flip out. I know Bernie. He might go on a hunger strike. I don't know. Do something crazy. Just forget about that one completely."

"It's your call. The alternative is to be patient and see if we get a break somewhere down the line."

CHAPTER 19

Maddox found the small brick clinic, parked his rental car, and went inside.

He smiled at the receptionist. "I'm here to see Doctor Anderson. It's Todd Whittier. American Journal of Organ Donation and Transplantation."

The receptionist asked Maddox to take a seat and made a call.

"Doctor Anderson will see you in a few minutes," the receptionist said cheerfully.

Maddox looked around the office. There was a mother with an infant. A grandfather with his grandson. The walls were decorated with photographs of children. Children smiling, children playing, children laughing. Children at the beach. Children at the park. Maddox thought of his estranged wife, Helen, and felt a pang of regret over the child they never had.

A few minutes later, the receptionist informed Maddox that the Doctor was ready. He steeled himself for the performance he was about to give. *I've probably got two minutes to win her over, or else she'll throw me out of her office and it's back to square one!* He entered the Doctor's small office, and then closed the door behind him.

"Doctor Anderson, I presume," Maddox said, offering his hand.

"That would be me. It's . . . Todd, right?" She shook his hand and produced a curt smile. The smile accentuated her dimple. Maddox was struck by the resemblance with her mother.

"Doctor Anderson, I'll come right to the point. I'm not a journalist. I'm with the FBI. My real name is Special Agent Bill Maddox," he said, producing his badge and holding it out for her for several long moments, allowing the reality to slip in. "If you give me a few minutes to explain, you'll see why I had to use an alias when I contacted you by phone."

"Well, I have to say," she said, after a momentary pause. "I did think it a bit odd. I realized after our call that The Journal usually has a very plain cover. I don't think I've seen a photograph on the cover," she said, studying him with suspicion. "So please tell me what this is all about."

"Ma'am. There is a very important criminal we've been tracking. It's vital that we find out more about his operation. Lives depend on it. Many innocent lives," he said, emphasizing the words *many* and *innocent*.

"And . . . ?"

"Well, it turns out the subject of our investigation is prone to migraine headaches. We feel that gives us the ideal opportunity to position a doctor near him, to get close to him. Get someone on the inside. We feel it's the only way we can uncover what he's really up to."

"There are lots of doctors out there."

"Well, I hope you don't mind me saying so, but very few are as attractive as you are. We understand the subject may have a weakness for attractive women," he said. He held her gaze with a penetrating stare, hoping she'd be taken in by him even as he fought the urge to stare back into her mesmerizing, deep blue eyes.

"Time is not on our side in this investigation," he continued, doing his best to stay focused on the task at hand. "In fact, time is most decidedly racing against us, *very quickly*. We need someone who can gain the subject's confidence within as short a time period as possible. As I said, many, many innocent lives may be at stake. If this weren't critically important, and if you weren't the only one we thought could help, you can rest assured we wouldn't be bothering you."

Heather looked at Maddox carefully for several moments.

"I'm sorry. I just don't know what to say. This is all so sudden," she said.

"I can appreciate that, ma'am. I can also tell you that if you cooperate with us, you'll be perfectly safe. The subject has no prior criminal record. In fact, he donates generously to charities, and nothing in his background suggests in any way that he is prone to violence. What's more, he has a Ph.D. and an M.D., graduated from Harvard summa cum laude in mathematics, and on top of it all is an accomplished violist."

"Well, Special Agent Maddox, if indeed that's your real name. Now you've really piqued my curiosity."

CHAPTER 20

"Not a single trace?" Maddox asked Ricks.

"Nothin,' man!"

"Even in this day and age of *Gitmo* and ever-so-close co-operation with various shadowy Eastern European intelligence agencies, American citizens still aren't supposed to just disappear into the night and fog, man! Enemy combatants: no big deal. Foreigners on our soil: maybe . . . but not American citizens!"

"Whatever, man . . . but I'm telling you, there isn't a single trace of the mo' fo' *anywhere* in the systems. Nothing at the Bureau. Nothing in the *Holmes*-land Security database. *Nada.*"

Having made good inroads in recruiting Heather as his agent, Maddox's next task was to ascertain Carpenter's whereabouts. Only with this information would he be able to plan and facilitate the insertion exercise.

"I gotta find the dude, Rando. It's mission critical. Nobody just completely disappears off our own radar, man. That is just not *happenin!*"

"I'm trying my best, bro. Keep ya posted. Cool?"

"Cool."

This is it. This is the weak link. If I don't find Lewis and Carpenter, then the whole mission is blown . . . Dr. Lewis' uncomfortably sarcastic remark still rang in Maddox's ear. *"You work for the FBI. Presumably you'll have a way to figure out where I am?"*

There's gotta be a way to find those guys.

CHAPTER 21

Deadlines, deadlines, deadlines. Man, I can't stand deadlines. Lionel Gottlieb glanced at the clock for the fifth time in as many minutes. *I wonder if Woodward and Bernstein had to worry about deadlines after they got the Pulitzer. Two more hours left! How am I going to finish this? Hey, I wonder how the Nationals are doing, must be around the seventh inning by now . . . OK, focus, Lionel . . . President's press conference . . . Pulitzer. Gotta get the Pulitzer . . . What do you wear when you accept the prize? A tuxedo? Just imagine yourself onstage, accepting the Pulitzer Prize. Yes, a tuxedo. Sort of a James Bond look. Think of how easy it's gotta be to score chicks after you win the Pulitzer . . . There I am, up on stage. Ladies and Gentlemen, I can't tell you what an honor . . .*

The phone rang twice, shaking Gottlieb out of his daydream. *Quit messing up my train of thought,* he said to himself as he glowered at the phone. He reached over slowly to pick it up.

"Gottlieb," he said, bored.

"Lionel Gottlieb?"

"Who's this?"

"Who it is isn't important."

"Then how can I be of help?"

"I have some information you might be interested in, information of a presidential nature."

"Go on . . . "

"You'll be receiving a package later today in the mail. It has everything you need to know. Be there three p.m. tomorrow." The line clicked dead.

The next day, as the instructions in the package indicated, Gottlieb arrived at the payphone with five minutes to spare.

"Hello," Gottlieb said, picking up the phone on the first ring.

"I'm going to get right to the point, and I won't talk long enough for the call to be traced. I'm going to give you some very interesting information, but I'll need some information in return. The more information you give me, the more I'll give you. OK?"

Gottlieb paused, then answered, "I'm listening."

"I chose you because you cover the White House."

"That's right."

"And in covering the White House, I assume you have a variety of contacts in the Administration?"

"I do. A substantial number," Gottlieb allowed himself the liberty to embellish slightly as he pictured Mandy Garcia, the President's personal aide, in a tight dress. He and Mandy had been classmates at Brown.

"Listen carefully to what I'm about to tell you. The White House has been the subject of a biological weapons attack. The attack involved a top secret strain of anthrax developed in a U.S. national laboratory. Are you with me?"

Gottlieb's breath began to quicken, and he started jotting notes furiously.

"I'm with you. Go on . . . "

"There are two people in some way linked to this attack. What role they played is not clear: a Dr. J. Maurice Carpenter, and a Dr. Bernard Lewis. Both are weapons designers in top secret national laboratories. Dr. Lewis was arrested by the FBI and is being held incommunicado. Subsequently there are no signs of his whereabouts. Nothing in the FBI or Homeland Security computer systems. No arrest warrants. Nothing in the witness protection program database. Dr. Lewis has simply disappeared. His whereabouts are completely unknown. That's not supposed to happen to American citizens. Even in a terrorism case. Do you understand?"

"Go on. I'm with you." Gottlieb was breathless.

"I must stress that the role the two good Doctors played in the attack is completely unclear. They may have been involved directly as perpetrators or accessories, or they may just be expert witnesses the government is using as part of the investigation. We know nothing about their guilt or innocence. Understood?"

"Perfectly. They may or may not be suspects. May or may not have been directly involved in the attack."

"That's it on my end for now. If you want more from me, you need to use all of your contacts at the White House to try to find out where Drs. Carpenter and Lewis are currently located. And then get back to me ASAP. Are we clear?"

"Yes, but . . . "

"Three p.m. tomorrow. Same place."

* * *

The next day at three p.m., Gottlieb dutifully picked up the phone.

"Have anything for me?" the voice asked.

"I know where they are," Gottlieb said, breathlessly.

"Where?"

"At Camp David."

"Camp David? Both of them?"

"Yes. Both have recently been placed on the payroll of the Secret Service . . . White House detail. I called in every favor I was owed . . . Anyway, there they are, at Camp David, along with just about the entire Cabinet, as we speak."

"Any idea how long they will stay at Camp David?"

"Supposedly, they'll be going back to the White House soon. Apparently the convocation at Camp David is nearly over."

"Understood. That's helpful."

"Got anything more for me? Who do you think is behind this anthrax thing? Hello? Hello? Anyone there?"

But the line was already dead, and Maddox had the confirmation he needed.

CHAPTER 22

The scientists on Carpenter's team had met Lewis' arrival in Camp David with quiet fanfare. Few had ever met him personally, but in the field of micro-robotics his name was second only to Carpenter's. His eminence was well known to all, and after a few days at work his organizational and project management skills also became evident. Through his efforts, the path to a global command and control mechanism for the *microbots* began to come into view, and this gave the project a new impetus. Carpenter noticed with satisfaction that after Lewis' admission into the group even the skeptics among them had slowly begun to acquire a bit of bounce in their gait. The few who doubted the feasibility of the enormous undertaking were quietly being won over, while those who on moral grounds had initially resisted the plot now began gradually to bend to its growing inevitability.

Of those most anxious over Lewis' arrival was Zach. For since sending the letter to Maddox warning of the need to contact Lewis before Carpenter reached him, Zach had had no word as to whether his warning had even reached its intended recipient, much less whether it had prompted any concrete action to counter Carpenter's threat. Lewis' arrival in the group thus caused Zach intense unease, and he desperately sought an opportunity to speak to Lewis in private. To Zach, Lewis remained the best and only hope for derailing Carpenter's plans, but Lewis' loyalties were also a substantial unknown. Above all, Zach knew that if Carpenter had successfully recruited Lewis to his cause, then Lewis' addition to the project would likely have frightening consequences.

To Zach's consternation, in the days since Lewis' arrival at Camp David Zach had found no opening to meet with Lewis in secret. Carpenter had compartmentalized the individual teams working on each facet of the program, and had insisted that Zach maintain a close proximity to Carpenter throughout. As Carpenter's assistant and thus one of the few team members with a bird's-eye view of the project, Zach was on constant call at Carpenter's side, and had no opportunity for unsupervised interaction with the other scientists. Zach chafed at the especially tight leash on which Carpenter maintained him.

Aside from the physical difficulty in reaching Lewis, other considerations nagged at Zach. He feared that in addition to the lethal *microbots* holding all the team members hostage on threat of pain or death, the entire laboratory and extended living space might also be secretly buzzing with nearly microscopic and difficult-to-detect surveillance *bots*, capable of listening in on private conversations and tracking movement. It couldn't be ruled out that Carpenter might even have secretly delivered highly miniaturized surveillance *bots* into the bloodstreams or subcutaneous layers of the team members. A backdrop of suspicion and resignation thus hung over the project, and further limited Zach's opportunity to initiate any contact with Lewis.

Making things worse still were the occasions when Lewis was tantalizingly close. Often Carpenter would dine with Lewis, and just as often, Zach would be invited to join in the meals. Each time Zach looked for an opening, but none presented itself.

At last, at one meal Lewis excused himself to go to the bathroom, and Zach spied an opening. Zach excused himself, leaving Carpenter alone at the table, and followed Lewis to the toilet. But the bathroom in question had an occupancy of one, and Zach was unable to join Lewis inside. Upon Lewis' exit, Zach tried to detain Lewis briefly for a private word but Lewis used his eyes to warn Zach off. It was as if Lewis knew better than to take any chance at surreptitious conversation. Though Zach chose to interpret Lewis' gesture in a positive light, he knew that until the moment for action clearly presented itself, all he could do was watch and wait. The worst thing he could do would be to arouse any premature suspicion.

CHAPTER 23

Maddox was at Arrivals to meet Dr. Heather Anderson at the Los Angeles International Airport. Standing alone in the greeting area he felt exposed, as he always did in open spaces. In this case, however, he felt more exposed than usual. *Maybe it's just the importance of the mission*, he told himself to calm his nerves.

He nervously fingered the metal-detection-proof Kevlar knife that he always kept in his front pocket, and re-checked his reflection in a glass pane across the aisle. Any number of things were weighing on him. Not only had it been difficult to win Martin's permission to recruit Heather, a struggle costly in personal integrity and currency with his boss, his feeling of apprehension was further heightened by the fact that he had only met Heather once and still hadn't secured her ironclad agreement to cooperate in the mission. She had consented to meet him in Los Angeles for further discussion, but to Maddox's trained ear she was still far from committed to the cause, and Maddox knew there was nothing preventing her from backing out on him. She was not yet *invested* enough in the case, and it was his job to make her so. In the search for investment, he hoped that he wouldn't need to make mention of her estranged mother Alice as a means to spark her interest. *Always best to keep things as simple as possible. No need to complicate matters with stray emotions and unpredictable historical relationships.* Maddox checked his reflection again, both to make sure his appearance was up to pitching the investment case, as well as to make sure he wasn't being watched.

What a doozy! He recalled with nervous bemusement and incredulousness the story he'd spun to convince his boss, Martin, to approve Heather's recruitment. The story needed to involve drugs, because Maddox was in Narcotics, and needed to involve the White House as justification for inserting Heather in with Carpenter. In the end, using fabricated tapes and doctored photos, and with the assistance of his Mexican Mafia contacts and informants, Maddox managed to convince the highly skeptical Martin of the possibility that he might have discovered a White House-based drug smuggling operation, evoking the earlier, real-life Iran-Contra scandal in which a drug smuggling operation had truly been run out of the White House. According to Maddox's "evidence," military shipments from Afghanistan and Iraq were supposedly returning stateside laden with illicit narcotics.

To bolster his argument, Maddox had further played Gottlieb to gain his unwitting corroboration of Maddox's "plot." To do so, he had fed Gottlieb with fictitious details, and then used Gottlieb's well-intentioned but completely off-base press clippings to validate and enhance his case with Martin.

In the end, Maddox marveled that he had not only managed to win over Martin, he had even successfully convinced Martin that the sensitive political nature of the allegations and still tenuous nature of the evidence dictated that Maddox's investigation be kept as small as possible, without notification of the Washington Bureau or the Secret Service, which normally would have had jurisdiction in the matter. Thus, using up twenty years of goodwill and bending Martin against all his better instincts, Maddox had secured his boss' reluctant permission to run a two-week, two-person operation targeting the White House. He'd even been able to requisition two additional support operatives downstream of the White House sewer system to collect Lewis' hearing aid when the scientist finally flushed the device down the toilet.

Maddox checked his watch, and the reflection in his watch, and then recalled Martin's uncomfortable last words on the matter. "All right, Maddox. I can't believe I'm actually hearing myself say this, but I'm going to let you run with this *quietly* for two weeks to see if you turn up anything. Nothing comes up, we're shutting it down *A-S-A-P*. And you keep me posted up-to-the-minute, and no screw-ups like down in Colombia. We clear?" *Two weeks from yesterday, and the clock is ticking.*

* * *

Maddox had nothing concrete on which to base his current feeling of vulnerability, but he'd conducted enough undercover operations in his career to have learned to trust his instincts. And his instincts were telling him that he was now being watched. He scanned the terminal as carefully and surreptitiously as possible, but amidst the throng, no one stood out as an obvious tail. In the end, Maddox decided that if anyone were following him, the most likely candidate might be a heavyset man, who looked to be a chauffeur, with thick brown sideburns and dark glasses. *Looks vaguely familiar.*

The man was standing about fifty feet from Maddox, and was holding up a sign that read: "Mr. M. Stiglitz, TKG Corporation." As far as Maddox could tell, the chauffeur didn't seem to be in contact with anyone else.

After another ten minutes uncomfortably exposed, Maddox was relieved to see Heather arrive at last, and was gratified to see that just as he'd asked, she had come in disguise. She was wearing a pair of large black sunglasses and a headscarf covering a wig of full, red hair. Maddox also was pleased to see that as he had instructed, she was wearing no jewelry — nothing that could be photographed and later used to identify her. He knew that his precautions were probably excessive, but throughout his career he had learned that it was always better to err on the side of caution.

"Safe trip, Doctor?" Maddox asked, scanning the scene around her to make sure she wasn't being followed.

"Yeah."

"Did your boyfriend buy the story?" he asked as he offered his arm to usher her out of the terminal as quickly and efficiently as possible. *I don't want to alarm her, but I don't have a wonderful feeling here, and the sooner we can get on the road the easier I'll breathe.*

"Yeah, I think he bought it. It's just four weeks anyway, right?"

"Did he want to come along?" Maddox asked, trying to make conversation, while maintaining a brisk pace.

"The three-cities-a-day part allowed him to decline chivalrously, especially given his workload now. And as I think I explained to you in our last conversation, he and I both agreed we needed some time apart anyway."

She did her best to keep pace with Maddox.

When they exited the building and rounded a corner, his anxiety began to subside and he slowed to a more moderate gait.

"Excellent. Just so you know, we've got phenomenal resources at the FBI. We'll even get you some newspaper clips you can mail back to him, detailing the progress of your 'Organ Donation and Transplantation' tour. It'll look like the clips came straight out of the Altoona Ledger, Dubuque Daily Herald, and the other illustrious publications covering the highlights of your speaking tour."

"Great, that'll help."

As they entered the parking structure, he checked in all directions, and while his sense of disquiet hadn't vanished, he felt more confident that they were now secure, at least for the moment.

"And the other doctors at the clinic? They're fine covering you for a month or so while you're away?"

"Yep. They were delighted to help. I've got the best partners in the world. I only shudder to think what they'll demand from me in return when it's their turn to go on extended leave."

* * *

In the car, after small talk about the flight and Heather's familiarity with Los Angeles, she abruptly cut in.

"So, tell me what's next on the agenda. And when are you going to give me all the details about this little escapade you've got me wrapped up in? As you can imagine, I've been dying of curiosity since our last meeting."

"Well, according to my training manuals," Maddox began, "which by the way I haven't read in at least fifteen years," he added, winking, "the first thing a handler is supposed to do when he recruits an agent is to gain the agent's confidence and bond with the agent. It's very important that the handler and agent first develop a very close working relationship based on trust, openness, and mutual respect."

To be perfectly blunt, the idea is that you want your agent to fall in love with you. That way, they'll do anything for you, Maddox recalled his instructor at Quantico saying.

She cleared her throat nervously, but also made room for a coquettish smile. "And just how do you propose to do this . . . 'bonding?'"

"Assuming you're not too tired, I was actually going to propose we do a little sailing. Good place to talk too. No one listening, of course. Sailing's my passion. And the plain truth is that this looks like fantastic weather for a sail. Shame to let it pass."

"Sailing?" she paused for a minute to consider. "OK, sure, why not? Sounds fun. Haven't been out for ages."

"Outstanding. Warm Santa Anas are blowing from the desert out of the east. Hardly a cloud in the sky. Ever been on a catamaran, Doctor?"

"Can't say that I have. And please, Special Agent Maddox, call me Heather."

"OK, Heather. Call me Bill."

"Great. Let's drop off the bags at your hotel, then I want to run you by FBI headquarters at the Federal Building. I'll introduce you to one or two people. Let you have a look around. That way you'll be sure I'm completely on the level. I did have to throw a curve ball to you about being a journalist. I don't want you having doubts at some point during the operation. A few minutes at the office, then we'll get you a wetsuit at the watersports store near the marina, and we'll have an entire afternoon together on the bounding main."

The tour of the FBI field office went quickly. Maddox steered her clear of Martin. He didn't want any record of her cooperation, and the fewer that knew of her involvement, the better. He showed her his office, and the command and communication center, and then quickly ushered her out. "To put your mind at rest, please know that we've executed dozens of similar operations, and no one came anywhere close to being in danger," he told her quietly as they were waiting for the elevator. "We do these things all the time. It's almost routine." Even he was impressed at the ease with which the words came off his tongue. He only hoped he was right.

* * *

Never before has there ever been a better day for sailing, Maddox thought to himself as he winched the jib. The wind was a steady fifteen knots from the east. The swells were challenging enough to provide a steady thrill, but stopped short of presenting real danger. The sky was a crystalline blue, and the afternoon sun a honeyed Southern California gold. The sunlight sparkled off the waves all the way from Palos Verdes to Malibu and Point Mugu, and the air was so clear that from the waters off Marina Del Rey you could even see the violet and orange speckles of the wildflowers along the Hollywood Hills on either side of the famous Hollywood sign. Farther in the distance, the purple, snow-capped San Bernardino Mountains stood watch, overseeing the broad panorama below.

The catamaran raced through the ocean spray, and high above the mast giggling gulls circled over the mainsail. But higher still, beyond the gulls, Maddox suddenly noticed a helicopter making a wide pass. *What's that helo doing there?* Maddox asked himself. *A little close for comfort*, he decided. *Especially since it's an unmarked* Huey II, he noticed after further examination. The *Huey II* or Bell UH-1H, was the helicopter the FBI used.

Maddox looked across the transom at Heather. He couldn't think of any better way to bond with his newly recruited agent than sailing a catamaran on a day like this. Aside from the sheer exhilaration of hiking out off the pontoon, crashing through the choppy waves, and racing the boat through the cool sea spray, the occasion gave Maddox a chance to make a terrific impression on his recruit. A steady hand at the rudder and practiced seaman, she would see him as her guide and a capable captain. His muscles bulged through the wetsuit, revealing his strength. More than once, he deliberately flexed his powerful biceps and calf muscles when he caught her looking his way. Of course, he tried his best to appear nonchalant in the presence of the soft, flowing curves with which she filled out her wetsuit. *No wonder they call it 'Body Glove,'* he thought, reminding himself of the brand of wetsuit he'd rented for her. Occasionally, too, he looked up to monitor the progress of the helicopter, which his instincts now convinced him was in fact tracking them. But he avoided looking up too often because he didn't want to concern her. He feared he might ruin the mood he had gone to such pains to craft.

"This is amazing!" she shouted above the roar of the wind and sea. "I never knew sailing a catamaran could be so much fun!"

"Well, when you have the right captain, and a day like this, it just doesn't get any better!" Maddox shouted back, smiling. "Watch out, I'm going to point her down a few notches. That'll make her lean."

She handles the jib well, and no fear at all, even back then when we looked about ready to capsize. That's a very good sign, Maddox thought with satisfaction. When he looked up again, the helicopter had disappeared.

* * *

"I'm glad you enjoyed yourself. I sail just about every weekend, but it's been a long time since we had conditions that good," he said to her after they had come back to the dock and were getting ready to get back in the car at the Marina. He was encouraged by the thrill which she had derived from the afternoon sail, and was overjoyed at the chemistry which he sensed developing between them. The sun was just going down by the time they had put away the boat and showered. A gust of wind gently swayed a stand of palm trees and caught her hair in the fading light.

"By the way, I never asked, what's the name of your boat?" she asked.

"Hobie Cats don't have names."

"Well, what would you call it if you could give it a name?"

He thought for a minute, then said the first thing that came to mind. "That's easy."

"What?"

"If our mission goes off well, as I know it will, I'd call her, call her . . . the 'Helpful Heather.'"

"If the mission goes well, you better call her a lot more than 'helpful,'" she laughed.

'Heavenly Heather' is more like it, he thought to himself.

* * *

"You worked up a good appetite out there?" Maddox asked. "It's hard work, especially on the trapeze."

"Good appetite? Positively famished," she said.

"Then you're in luck. You like Mexican? I happen to know a fantastic little place on Olympic Boulevard that has the best Mexican food on the planet. The enchiladas are mind blowing, and don't even get me started on the handmade tortillas." He deliberately left out mention of the velvety margaritas. "You do like Mexican food?"

"Absolutely love it."

As he drove her to the restaurant, he periodically checked the rear-view mirror, and wondered whether a White Crown Victoria he saw behind them was tailing them. Wishing to take no chances, he deliberately ran a red light, then made a sharp right turn and pulled over long enough to satisfy himself that he had shaken the car. He fended off her quizzical look with a smile. "Nothing to worry about. Routine maneuver."

* * *

The dinner went by quickly, punctuated by a few stolen glances on both sides. He did his best to appear relaxed and charming, even as through force of habit he scanned the restaurant periodically throughout the meal. The flickering candlelight helped accentuate the mood he'd wanted to cultivate, as did the margaritas and the soft scent of spices, of cumin, chili and fried corn meal. Maddox kept the talk light over the dinner. Some small talk about sailing. Life in the FBI. What's it like being a doctor? Minnesota winters.

He quickly scanned the restaurant once more, and this time he thought he saw the heavyset chauffeur from the airport in a different guise, but he couldn't be sure it was the same person. Towards the end of the meal, he quietly promised her he would discuss the important details of their mission later in the evening.

The only awkward question to come up during the meal was: "Why the Helpful Heather?" Didn't he have a wife or a daughter after whom he could name the boat?

"No on both counts. It's a long story," was his response. He regretted afterwards that he had been so curt, but there would be time later to share more personal details.

* * *

"I hope you liked the food," he asked after they were done.

"Ambrosia and nectar," she said with conviction. "I can tell you for sure they don't have Mexican food like that back in Minnetonka."

"I know one place better."

"Where's that?"

"When this is all over, I'll cook you up a meal myself. No one makes *Burrito à la Bill* like I do."

"Hmmmm . . . *Burrito à la Bill*?" she said, half smiling, "how should I interpret that?"

"No. I'm serious. Completely on the up-and-up. No innuendo intended."

To his relief, she laughed.

* * *

Back in the car, Maddox offered to discuss the details of their plan at her hotel, a small Budget Inn on Lincoln Avenue, or, "if you're amenable, I'd be delighted to have you over to my place for a little while. Might be better to talk there. And don't worry. It's safe."

She hesitated for a moment.

"Really. It's safe. Strictly professional. I am in the FBI, after all. Rufus should get over his jealousy."

"Rufus?"

"He's my dog."

She hesitated a moment longer, weighing the decision.

"Sure," she said finally, with a small shake of the head that Maddox interpreted as coyness. "Why not? We're going to be working together. I'd love to see your place."

We're going to be working together!

Maddox was pleased that the day's activities had had their intended effect. He saw as an act her studied reticence at his invitation to visit his home, and sensed she really was starting to become intrigued by him. *That's a good thing,* he thought, *because I'm sure becoming intrigued by her.*

He made sure they left the restaurant quickly. On the way to his house, he took a circuitous route, even once driving the wrong way down an alleyway to be sure they weren't being followed.

"Just a standard operational precaution," he explained to her as they emerged from the alley.

"You sure it's routine, or are you just trying to show off and enhance my sense of mystery and adventure?" she asked, with a slightly crooked smile that suggested she was a little tipsy from the margaritas.

Maybe I gave her a little too much to drink.

"Heather, I know from your time in the Peace Corps that you have a sense of adventure, and that was one of the qualities I saw in you that told me you would be a good recruit. But please understand — and I don't want to alarm you because you're in very good hands — this is no game. And everything I do, I do for a reason."

CHAPTER 24

Maybe I should just zap this Gottlieb character and shut him up for good, Carpenter thought as he switched off the television with an emphatic punch of the remote control. Gottlieb's "special report" on the Drake Presidency was nothing more than a skewering. Of all the critical voices covering the administration, Gottlieb's was the most unrelenting and most negative. The election was getting closer by the day, and Drake's standing continued to plummet. *If Drake's not re-elected, I'm sunk.*

Carpenter's found his mood increasingly influenced by the President's approval ratings, and he felt a pressure building inside his chest and stomach. He reached for his pills on the side table. *Time to unveil the "Blueprint for America" before it's too late . . .*

CHAPTER 25

Maddox ushered Heather into his home, and noted with satisfaction that she remained wobbly from the margaritas with which he had plied her earlier in the evening at the Mexican restaurant. He gave her a brief tour of the small living room. Though it was very much a bachelor's abode, he was quite proud of the way he'd decorated the house. The style was south-of-the-border, accentuated with a few potted cactus plants standing shoulder height, a brightly colored *zarape*, two brown, gray and white Navajo rugs, and an antelope trophy head on the wall. There were also a few scattered photographs of the southwestern desert, the Zapotec pyramids at Oaxaca, and the Mayan pyramids of Tikal.

Mixed among the photos were a few shots of Maddox. One of him sailing. One of him with a sombrero, playing guitar. One at the beach, standing next to Randall Ricks, each with surfboard in hand. One with a rifle, hunting. Another in his Marine uniform, on a jeep in the desert. Yet another of him with a tight-cropped military haircut, but in civilian clothes, posing with friends in front of a cache of crates and supply drums while manning a chain-fed machine gun pointed straight at the camera.

At the far end of the small living room was a guitar, prominently displayed. Countless women had fallen to the seduction of his voice and softly strumming fingers as he played his guitar. As a consequence it was no accident that Maddox displayed the guitar so prominently. Also for this reason, it was music to Maddox's ears when, just as he was lighting a fire in the fireplace, Heather asked innocently, "You play guitar?"

Maddox turned and nodded his head slowly.

"Will you play me something?" she asked, as if on cue.

"Play you something?" He considered her words. "OK. I can do that. I have to warn you, though. I've been told I'm pretty good," he said with a mischievous smile.

Indeed, his voice had been compared to many things by his friends and lovers. It was a full tenor that one friend with a penchant for the dramatic had likened to a pure fountain spring in the high desert. When he sang, he strove to convey to his audience soft echoes of the red sandstone canyons of the Southwest, the eyries of the Rocky Mountains, and the golden valleys of California.

"Pretty good, you say?" she retorted. "I'll be the judge of that."

Sassy! I like that!

"What kind of music do you like?" he asked.

"What do you like to play?"

"I like to play Country. Pop. I like Ranchero music. Love Latin guitar."

"Oooh. Latin guitar. Sounds vaguely romantic." She arched her eyebrows. The effect of the margaritas was still very much upon her.

"Possibly more than just *vaguely.*" Maddox engaged her eyes. A spark flew from the fireplace. The two stared at each other for a moment and then she broke eye contact.

"Indeed," she said, looking at him again, her pupils dilating slightly, her body moving slightly forward in her chair. From his training in interrogation, Maddox recognized her reflexes as a clear sign of attraction.

"If I'm not careful here," she continued, "I suppose next thing I know you'll be trying to debrief me. You look like you could be pretty good at debriefing," she said flirtatiously while measuring him.

"Nothing I love better. Debriefing is my specialty."

"I believe you. That's why I need to watch myself. You're a handsome gunslinger and things here could easily move faster than prudence would suggest," she said with a sudden seriousness, looking him straight in the eyes.

"Who's Prudence?" Maddox asked with a straight face.

"Oh, she's . . . just my long-lost aunt. Nothing to worry about," Heather laughed.

"Then let's hope she stays lost," he said, smiling.

"No, seriously, Bill. We need to lay down some ground rules here. I'm with someone now. I'm not sure where that's all going. He and I still have a number of unresolved issues. But regardless of all that, I want you to know, I'm used to men hitting on me. The male nurses don't bother me, but the doctors won't leave me alone. And for the sake of the task before us, I want to make sure we understand that our relationship must remain completely professional."

"Easy, Doc. No one's hitting on anyone. I'm much too professional to allow a spectacularly beautiful lady to get in the way of my mission. That's the first thing they teach you in training."

"Good, because I'm not sure I'm your type anyway, or vice versa," she said. She was looking at a photograph on the wall showing Maddox with a hunting rifle in one hand, and a boot placed firmly on the neck of a fallen deer he'd just shot.

"I'm not sure I'm your type?" What's that supposed to mean? But so as not to ruin the mood, Maddox let the comment go.

* * *

"Now *do* play," she said, changing the subject. "I love music. I'm absolutely passionate about music."

Maddox remembered that she was a cellist.

"OK, but first, can I get you anything to drink? Water, Coke, beer, wine?"

"What are you having?"

"I'll have a little red wine if you'll have some with me. I've got a very, very nice bottle . . . something foreign, Italian or something, moderately expensive. Oh, and you don't mind if I throw a few more logs in the fireplace, do you? Cozy the place up a bit more?"

* * *

She took a sip from the wine he poured her. "Divine, just as you said. Now play a song for me, Special Agent Bill Maddox, the FBI agent who plays Latin guitar."

He took the guitar down and handled it gently. He strummed a few chords. Fingered a few soft flamenco progressions. A few country pulls. He was thinking about which song would be best to play her, to sing for her. *It's always my voice that gets them in the end*, he thought. *She's seen the photos. Probably seen I'm an ex-Marine. Knows I'm an FBI agent. And her? A neurosurgeon from Minnesota. Two years in the Peace Corps. Cellist. So what to play? Hmmm . . . Let's sing her something to give her a bit more rounded impression of me. Something to show my softer side, throw her a little curve ball.*

He cleared his throat, strummed a few bars, then began to play. The song was *Guantanamera*, the Cuban folk song based on the lyrics of revolutionary poet José Martí, a song first made famous as an anthem of the nineteen-sixties. He sang each verse first in Spanish, then translated the lyrics softly into English.

Yo soy un hombre sincero,
de donde crece la palma,
y antes de morirme quiero
echar mis versos del alma.

(I am a sincere man
from where the palm tree grows,
and before I die, I want to pour out
My soul's verses.)

Mi verso es de un verde claro
y de un carmín encendido.
Mi verso es un ciervo herido
que busca en el monte amparo.

(My verse is of a clear green
and of a fiery crimson.
My verse is a wounded fawn
That seeks shelter in the mountains.)

Guantanamera, guajira Guantanamera
Guantanamera, guajira Guantanamera

When he was finished, Heather sat still, eyes wide. After a few moments of silence, she finally spoke.

"That was absolutely beautiful. I'm just stunned. I didn't know G-Men could sing like that. Where'd you learn to play like that? To sing *Spanish* like that?"

Maddox looked into the fireplace. Outside he heard Rufus bark urgently for a moment. Maddox strained to discern the cause of Rufus' outburst. So as not to alarm Heather and spoil the cozy mood that had taken hold, he quickly turned his attention back to the conversation.

"Oh, spent a little time in Central America. An old man down there taught me to strum a few chords."

"Central America? What were you doing there?"

"Long story."

"I've got time."

"I was in the Marines. Nineteen-eighties. In the foolishness of my youth, anything to get out of my posting in Lebanon, I volunteered to be seconded from the Marines to a paramilitary unit in the CIA, which was then running covert ops across Central America. El Salvador, Honduras and Nicaragua.

"When I first joined the Marines, they had sent me to Monterey language school to learn Spanish, so I was a good candidate for the job in Central America. Anyway, we were mainly running ops against the *Sandinistas*, along the Nicaraguan, Honduran border. One base we were at, that one there on the wall," he pointed at the photograph of himself and his buddies standing next to the supply drums, "down the road was a little church. The old priest there, actually a *Capucin* monk, he could sure play some guitar. I used to sneak off the base when I could. I'd go down to the church, and he'd teach me some songs. Taught me some *flamenco*." Maddox startled Heather by playing a fiery and dramatic *fandango* strum.

"*Capucin monk*," she repeated. "Are you a religious man, Special Agent Bill Maddox?"

Maddox paused. From his training, he remembered it was best to steer clear of religion when recruiting an agent.

"I guess I used to be, many moons ago. I think I must have lost it somewhere along the way. Probably somewhere between Beirut and Tegucigalpa. Beirut was my first posting in the Marines. I was just nineteen then. I was there when some Muslim fanatics ran a truck full of explosives into the barracks across from mine, and killed two hundred and forty-one Marines.

"If Beirut and Honduras and El Salvador didn't do me in, then Los Angeles definitely finished me off as far as having any faith in my life."

"*Los Angeles*? How's that?"

"Oh, I don't know. Plenty of palm trees here, but not many *hombres sinceros*," he said, referring to a verse he had just sung in *Guantanamera*. "A day like we had today, sailing in the sun, it's easy to be seduced by the city. But you live here awhile, and you get to thinking that Los Angeles is probably the loneliest place on Earth, the furthest place from God on the planet."

"Really? In what way?"

"It's just the city's so unfathomably vast, and the distance between people here is even greater. I think it must be difficult for God to take root in a place where the bonds between people are so stretched, so thin as they are in Los Angeles. Stretched and thin, just like the freeways, draining the soul out of you, little by little.

"You live in Los Angeles too long," he continued, "and if the freeways don't drain the life out of you, then the sun will. The bright hazy sun. It tans the skin, but it bleaches the conviction straight out of your soul." Maddox looked down at the carpet, then at Heather. "This is a city of *bleached souls*."

"Very poetic, Special Agent Bill Maddox. Are you a poet too?"

"Are you making fun of me, Doctor Heather Anderson?"

"Not at all. I'm just very impressed."

"And why is that? You didn't think ex-Marine, FBI narcotics agents had souls too?"

Her smile froze.

Oops. I shouldn't have said that.

Just then, Rufus barked again. This time, Maddox stood up. Though he was concerned, he smiled to diffuse the tension, and then went to the front window. Parting the blinds imperceptibly, he made a quick scan of the street in front of the house, but unable to detect anything unusual, he went back to the sofa. Her eyes followed him across the room.

"Now don't get testy. I just asked you a simple question. No ulterior motives," she said playfully, but with a hint of warning, as he sat down. "By the way, everything okay out there just now? Dog's not going to split a gut?"

"Rufus is fine," he said casually. "He's always barking at one thing or another. But to your earlier question: am I a poet?" he continued, wanting to keep the conversation moving, trying to get back to a lighter footing. "Not really. But I've written a few songs."

Oops again. Please don't ask me to sing my own songs! They might not go down nearly so well with you as Guantanamera.

"Oh! Then you *must* play one for me."

Oh God, no! Maddox recalled his training. Remembered the instructor's words at Quantico. *When you're bonding with a newly recruited agent, you definitely want to open up, let them see your human side, but you never want to open up too far. Definitely not too far, too fast. It's safest to give them only a little glimpse. Find that within yourself that you think they* want *to see in you.*

"Well, aren't you going to play?"

"Not tonight, Heather. How about another time?"

What was that sound out front a minute ago?

162

"Now come on, Bill. You're killing the mood. I want to hear your songs. If I'm going to be working with you, working for you, I want to know who *you* are. There's no better way to know a person than through his songs. His *own* songs."

I was afraid of that.

"I promise I'll play them for you after we're all done with the mission, OK? I promise."

"Not good enough, Bill. I want to hear 'em now. You've really piqued my curiosity. You can't let me down here. It will have *major* consequences." She arched her eyebrows in a threat.

Is she just being playful, or is she serious? Man, whatever else she is, she's sure persistent.

"But they're no good."

"I'll be the judge of that."

God . . . I'm an agent of over twenty years . . . The most important operation of my life . . . It's going so well, and now I have to go off and complicate everything with one stupid slip of the tongue.

"OK, fine. You win, Doctor. But you can't laugh. I was just goofing around when I wrote these. They aren't supposed to be serious."

"I promise I won't laugh, and I won't hold anything against you. Deal?"

"Deal," he said, ruefully, still trying not to appear distracted by the sound he'd heard a moment before out the front window.

He strummed a few bars, a Country Western progression, then began singing softly. His voice carried a haunting, mournful quality.

What happened to the old school house?
Don't even recognize it anymore
The windows are all boarded up
Graffiti on the door

163

Walking down the old boulevard
I strain to see the commotion
But I can't even read the signs anymore
They're all in Farsi, Urdu and Laotian

I've got those third world blues
I've got those third world blues
Feel like I'm walking in someone else's shoes
I've got those third world blues

What happened to the old American dream?
You'd save to buy your family a little house
Now the rich cat eats his cake
Leftover crumbs barely enough to feed a mouse

Where are the old streets paved smooth like glass
Where's the carpenter, who plied his craft with such devotion?
Now the streets are filled with potholes
And that old carpenter, he's just going through the motions

I've got those third world blues
I've got those third world blues
Can't even bear to watch the news
I've got those third world blues

He paused after he'd finished, keeping his eyes fixed on the floor. He had no idea how she'd take it.

"Wow," she said after a few moments. "You're just full of surprises tonight."

"'Wow' good, or 'wow' bad? 'Full of surprises' good, or 'full of surprises' bad?" he asked.

"I'm still trying to figure that out. Just a bit of a shift in tone after *Guantanamera*, Bill, you'd have to agree. That's all. You caught me a bit off guard."

Maddox sensed a dangerous turn in the mood coming.

She continued. "I'm still trying to decide if it's politically correct: not sure how our friends in the Laotian community might feel about the lyrics . . . " She went on, searching for the right words, as his chest tightened.

Man, I've really blown it now.

"Definitely strikes me as a bit naïve . . . Some might say a touch sophomoric . . . But powerful, nonetheless . . . *Very powerful*, Special Agent Bill Maddox. Not sure I agree with it entirely, but I do like it. I like it a lot."

"You like it?" he asked, intensely relieved.

"I do. Very much. Very much, indeed. I've even got goose bumps. See?" She held out her arm for him to inspect.

"Now do play on, Special Agent Bill Maddox, knight errant, defender of peace and justice, fearless sea-captain, poet, and balladeer."

"I kinda like that description," he said, giving her a playful look but also one of warning, as if to say 'but don't you now be making fun of me.'

We're definitely bonding. But what kind of bond is it?

"Well?"

"Well, what?"

"Play on!"

"Play on?"

"Let's hear another."

"That's all I've got."

"Come on, Bill. A few minutes ago, you spoke of your *compositions* in the plural. I'm not letting you off that easily."

Man, she's perceptive! I really have to watch myself with her.

"Another time, I promise."

"See, there you go again. Stop being evasive. Play another song, *now!*" she smiled, but with a strong hint of menace.

Talk about stubborn!

"OK. Just one more. Last one. Deal?"

"Deal."

"OK, here goes. But I'm warning you in advance, this next one's not very subtle at all."

She nodded, as if to say 'that's OK', and then she added, "I was never big on 'subtle.'"

Let's hope I don't lose her completely with this one.

He picked up the guitar, and strummed a few rhythm and blues chords. Just as he was about to play, he heard a faint sound that caught his attention. *A rustling of leaves? A shoe treading lightly on grass?* He looked at Heather to see if she heard the sound, but by her expression, he could see that she had heard nothing. His training in the Central American jungle had given him the ability to distinguish between the sound of rustling leaves caused by wind, by small animals, and by a human foot. Still not wanting to alarm her, he glanced briefly at the drawer where he kept his service revolver, then after a moment, went ahead with the song.

"This one's called Milkin' It," he said just before launching into the song.

Fancy Wall Street investment banker
Sells his own mother to the highest bidder
Big corporation man tosses around livelihoods
Like throwing leftover scraps into the litter

Lawyers all run the show
Got the country by the collar

Forget about what's right or wrong
Justice for whomever pays top dollar

The special interest groups
They put the lawyers all to shame
Milking the system for all they can
We only have ourselves to blame

Up on Capitol Hill
They're busy arguing about school prayer
Whole darn country's going down the tubes
No one even seems to care

They're milkin' it; They're milkin' it
We only have ourselves to blame
Everybody's milkin' it; They're milkin' it
And they're all playing a 'zero-sum' game!

Just then, he heard Rufus bark loudly for the third time, and though there were a few more lyrics to play, he decided to cut the song short. He had one ear trained outside, and one ear to the conversation at hand.

As with the previous song, he was met initially with a moment of silence from Heather. When she finally spoke, what she said surprised him.

"Wow!"

"'Wow' as in . . . ?"

"As in: so *angry*."

"Angry?"

"I couldn't put my finger on it before. I didn't see you as an *angry* person, Bill. But you *are* angry, aren't you? How did I miss that?"

"How so?"

"The lyrics. The way you sang that last song. And the previous song. You've got a lot of anger inside you, don't you, Special Agent Bill Maddox?"

He glanced at the fire in the fireplace. *What have I done now? I've gotta diffuse this somehow before it all really spins out of control. Not to mention, there's definitely something going on outside the house.*

"Well, Doctor Heather Anderson . . . I have to be honest with you, especially since you're so incredibly, annoyingly perceptive." He gave her a wink and a smile, trying to lower the tension.

"I have to admit, when you've seen what I've seen, if you've been to Beirut, Salvador, Guatemala . . . When you see what I see every day on the streets of South Central Los Angeles, when you deal with the total, unimaginable crap thrown my way, week in, week out, I suppose it's only natural that you do get a little angry. You either get angry, or else your heart turns to stone. And I'm not ashamed to say I guess I'd take anger over indifference any time."

Steady yourself, Bill. Not too strident. Keep it light. Don't go off the deep end, and remember, it's OK to open up a little, but not too much.

A log in the fireplace crackled. She paused to consider what he said.

"I like that," she said after a moment. "Anger over indifference. Very well put. I couldn't agree more. Couldn't have said it any better myself."

He breathed a sigh of relief for the second time that evening.

"Really? And the songs? You liked them? Tell me honestly."

"Well, as I said, I'm still not sure I totally agree with everything you expressed, but I have to say, I do like them. I like them *a lot.* Some might consider them a tad trite, but they definitely strike a chord. Definitely very moving, very powerful. And you sing them so beautifully. Just hearing your voice alone . . . I'd dare say if you ever stop being a G-Man, you just may have a career up on stage. Thank you Bill. Thank you very much for sharing those with me."

"You're most welcome, Heather."

She paused to take a sip of wine, then looked straight at Maddox.

"Now, shall we get down to the business at hand? Please tell me exactly what it is that I have gotten myself into."

"We shall indeed, Heather, but first, let me pour you one last glass of wine."

As he said this, he rose, collected a pen and a scrap of paper, and quietly scribbled her a note. He passed it to her and she read: "DON'T BE ALARMED. I NEED TO CHECK ON SOMETHING OUTSIDE. IN THE MEANTIME, KEEP TALKING AS IF I'M STILL HERE, AND DON'T STOP UNTIL I GET BACK."

Her face betrayed concern, but she carried on just as he had asked, and even bravely winked at him as he withdrew his service revolver from its drawer. He tucked it into his pants, and left the living room for the back of the house. As he shimmied quietly out a back window, he heard her voice from the living room ad libbing: " . . . But before we change the topic of conversation, I wanted to just tell you something . . . I was trying to think of who you sound like when you sing, and I finally figured it out . . . Your singing reminds me a lot of Don McLean. Has anyone ever told you that? You know, the guy who sang *American Pie*?"

* * *

Quietly climbing down from the back window, Maddox eased himself gently into the backyard and urged Rufus to remain quiet. Crouched low, he then quickly stole along the side of the house. When he reached the front of the house, he hid himself behind a thick stand of bushes. From his place of concealment, he first heard, then saw, two figures in black no more than fifteen feet away. One was kneeling on one knee, facing the house, and the other was standing, facing the street. Though it was dark, by the light of the lamppost down the street, Maddox was able to see that the one crouching had earphones on. He surmised that the two had the house under surveillance, and the one standing was on the lookout.

Wasting no time, and worried Heather would run out of things to say in her improvised monologue, Maddox sprang out of the bush, cocked his fist, and decked the lookout cold before he even noticed Maddox coming. In one fluid motion Maddox then withdrew his revolver and pressed the barrel violently into the neck of the startled eavesdropper, who had been intently listening for sounds inside the house. With his left hand, Maddox briskly lifted the eavesdropper, threw him hard against the side of the house, and ripped off the man's black balaclava mask.

Right hand still pressing the gun to his prisoner's neck, Maddox fished out a small pen-light from his pocket and shone it into the man's eyes.

He couldn't believe what he saw.

"McDonough? What the hell are you doing here?" Maddox asked incredulously, keeping his voice low, but still brimming with anger. His mind raced to process the fact that the offender was his fellow FBI narcotics agent, Dave McDonough.

"Buddy, you're flattening my lymph node. Think you can you ease up a little?" McDonough pleaded, moving his eyes to look down at the gun.

Maddox eased the pressure, but kept the weapon trained on McDonough.

"Allow me to repeat. What the *hell* are you doing here?" Maddox asked insistently, his voice still raw with anger.

"Martin wanted us to check up on you. Said you've been acting a little funny recently. Thought you might be in some kind of trouble. Wanted us to make sure you were OK."

"Who's *us*?"

"Just me and Weintraub. You know, Gil Weintraub, who you flattened just now."

"No one else?"

McDonough shook his head. Maddox scanned the street, but saw no one else.

"When you guys start trailing me?"

"We picked up the tail at the airport."

"Frickin' Martin! I should have figured! Can't leave well enough alone. He could have screwed up my whole mission. Could have spooked my friggin' agent!"

"Hey, buddy! Cool down. It's okay. It's just us. Just a little misunderstanding. We're all playing for the same team."

"I'll have a word with Martin tomorrow," Maddox said, still angry, but finally lowering his revolver.

"In the meantime, I want you to collect Weintraub from my lawn and get the hell out of here *NOW!* You understand!?"

McDonough nodded his assent. He kneeled down by Weintraub, and slapped his cheeks to revive him. After Weintraub came to a moment later, McDonough slung Weintraub's arm over his shoulder and walked away slowly, laboring under the burden of his partner's two-hundred-pound frame.

"That's quite a right cross you've got, Maddox," McDonough called from the curb after he'd dumped Weintraub into the white Crown Victoria parked several doors down the street. "Next time, save it for the bad guys."

"Next time Martin asks you to spy on me, you tell him to stuff it!" Maddox said, still seething.

"One more thing, Bill?"McDonough called over.

"Yes?"

"How did you know we were there?"

"How did I know? You guys were about as stealthy as a hundred-and-fifty-five millimeter howitzer."

"Really? I thought we were pretty quiet."

"That's because you've never been to Marine Recon School."

* * *

After his colleagues had driven away, Maddox dusted himself off, rubbed his bruised knuckles, concealed his gun, and knocked softly on the front door.

"Bill?" Heather called from behind the door, her voice tinged with concern.

"Yes, it's me, Heather. Everything's fine. You can open the door. It's safe."

She opened the door slowly.

"Ta da!" he said with a cheerful smile. "See, everything's fine." He was careful to keep his right hand and its raw red knuckles tucked firmly in his pocket.

"What happened?" she asked, worried.

"Oh, just the neighbor's dog. He and Rufus don't get along. The dog got out, and my neighbor needed some help to round him up."

"You needed to take your gun for that? Climb out the back window? Make me do a monologue?"

"It's a rough neighborhood out there. Can't be too careful these days."

She looked at Maddox with extreme skepticism, but he was relieved that she didn't press the inquiry.

"So, where were we?" he asked.

"We were just about to get into the specifics of the *matter at hand*."

"Ah yes, our little 'escapade,' as you call it. Since it's getting a bit late, how about if I take you to your hotel now, and I'll tell you all about it in the car? Might have more privacy there."

* * *

After he had driven less than a mile and made sure they weren't followed, he pulled the Audi over, then spoke.

"What I'm about to tell you will strain every ounce of credulity you may or may not have."

"I'm all ears."

"First I have to swear you to absolute secrecy."

"Done."

He took a deep breath and began.

"OK, it's like this . . . "

Fifteen minutes later, when Maddox had finished describing the predicament, as he called it, Heather sat in stunned silence.

"So let me get this straight," she said eventually, after finally processing the enormity of what he had just told her. "Your Dr. Carpenter has basically taken control of the President of the United States of America, and probably the entire executive branch of the government, and we don't know what his goals are, exactly how his technology works, or even what his next move might be. There's nothing in his background to suggest he's dangerous, yet there's also nothing concrete to assure us he's not dangerous. We can presume, given the lengths to which he has gone, that he is obviously after something very big — if not, why go to all the trouble and risk. Am I correct?"

Maddox nodded thoughtfully.

"And we don't have much time left. He has taken control of this, this Dr. Lewis, who possesses complementary technology, and when Dr. Lewis' technology is combined with Dr. Carpenter's technology, we think it may be possible eventually somehow to bring the entire world under Dr. Carpenter's control. Each day that goes by, more people can be infected with these, these *microbots*, and we don't know who has already been infected, who's next, and how long it will take to combine Carpenter's and Lewis' technology. But we do know that the clock is ticking against us."

"Correct." Maddox left out the part about the FBI most probably having come under Carpenter's control, and Maddox's activities constituting a rogue operation. He didn't want to alarm her even more.

"And we know all of this because of physical and human intelligence that has already proven reliable in predicting events," Heather continued.

"Correct."

"And you're saying I'm our last hope to stop Carpenter, and 'put the toothpaste back in the tube,' as you put it, before the entire world potentially falls into his grasp."

"Correct again."

She paused to weigh the gravity of the situation.

"Well, I guess that was what T.S. Eliot meant about the world ending 'not with a bang but a whimper.'"

"Come again?"

"I suppose most of us always imagined the world ending in an explosion, or through plague, or through some similarly dramatic event, something *biblical*. Fire dropping from the sky. Nuclear war. Cataclysm. Violent weather. Meteorite collisions. Volcanic eruption . . . I, for one, never imagined that civilization might end by having microchips implanted in everyone's brains."

"Good point, Heather, very good point. Although I should add that at this juncture, while we have to be prepared for the worst, we don't know what Carpenter's agenda is, so we have to be careful not to jump to hasty conclusions about his intentions. At least so far, there's nothing to suggest he's looking to destroy the world, destroy civilization."

"Well, even if we're not talking about the end of the world, it sure sounds like the end of the world as we know it. We all become slaves, beholden to one master? No thanks."

"I couldn't agree more, Heather. Not a comforting thought. And I might add that just word of the plot leaking could be enough to spark rioting, revolution, and upheaval on a national and global scale. Other nations, if they felt threatened, might consider preemptive strikes. Can't rule out the possibility that this little *imbroglio* we've got ourselves caught up in could end up provoking a nuclear preemptive response — even a third world war — if things really get out of hand."

"Not to mention, it's just not good practice to put the fate of the entire planet into one pair of fallible, mortal hands," she interjected.

"You've no idea how relieved I am that we see eye to eye on this, Heather. You've mentioned just a few of the many reasons why we have to stop this insanity, and I'm afraid when all is said and done you're the only card we have left to play. You and Dr. Lewis, that is, whom we presume remains committed to stopping Carpenter, but whose status, location and intentions we cannot at this time fully ascertain."

Heather paused, her head spinning in disbelief, unable to fully comprehend the monumental importance of the mission for which she had volunteered.

"So tell me now what the plan is, exactly?"

CHAPTER 26

"Are you ready to go over the speech one last time, Mr. President?" Carpenter asked, coming into the President's quarters after knocking. He was careful to be deferential to the President, even in private when no one else was around to judge who had the upper hand in the relationship.

"Yes . . . Doc," the President said, hesitating before pronouncing the word 'Doc.' The name 'Doc,' in its familiarity and connotation of easygoing camaraderie, still did not sit well with him. Yet at the same time, despite his entire family having been taken hostage and his position usurped, he was strangely unable to muster a substantial degree of bitterness and rage towards the madman who had set his life upside down. He himself was amazed that as hard as he tried, he found it difficult to dislike or feel enmity towards Carpenter. Throughout their short four-week tenure together, Carpenter had always been respectful and courteous. He had never made unreasonable demands and had almost bent over backwards to avoid using his power and authority in a way that would make the President feel uncomfortable.

As the President's continuing slide in the polls threatened to jeopardize Carpenter's plans, Carpenter had decided to move forward the pivotal unveiling of the "Blueprint for America." With the release of the political roadmap now close at hand,

Carpenter wanted to make sure all the preparations were unassailable, especially as he had helped handcraft the President's speech himself along with his larger plans.

Yet there were certain edits Carpenter had made to the final draft of the President's upcoming speech that irked the President, and he was determined to hash out with Carpenter the issues that were troubling him.

"So what did you think, Mr. Prez?" Carpenter asked, motioning to the speech. "Ready to go?"

"Well . . . I have to admit, I can see some attraction," the President allowed diplomatically, speaking through his wounded pride. "I definitely see the value in a number of the points you raise . . . Doc . . . But I . . . I have to say I do feel a bit aggrieved in some respects . . . "

"And how is that, Mr. President?" Carpenter said, sounding mildly amused.

The way Carpenter uttered the words and the grin on his face struck the President as demeaning, as if Carpenter were somehow addressing a petulant child.

"You wouldn't be talking down to me now, Doc, would you? Because up to now, you've been every bit the gentleman. In fact, you've been so much the gentleman, I'm itching to know why. You hold all the cards. For instance, it's late at night now, almost midnight. There's no one around. Why didn't you call me into your cabin? We could have had our meeting there. It would have been more convenient for you, and you could have made a point to show that you're in command. Instead, you came to me. Mind you, I'm not complaining. But I'm just curious as to how you came to be so well-mannered despite being an absolute jackass."

How to explain? Carpenter took a deep breath, then began.

"I believe in democracy, Mr. President. And despite its many flaws, I truly believe in this country," he started. "I guess you can say I love this country, and I respect you as the elected leader of our country."

"Do you see any contradiction between your belief in democracy," the President retorted, "and the fact that you've stuffed *microbots* up the noses of most of the top elected officials in the land," the President asked, "and their families?"

"Look, Mr. President, life is full of contradictions. Maybe if our politicians — and politicians the world over — had been doing their jobs properly these past fifty or sixty years, I wouldn't have needed to resort to my *microbots*. But hopefully we'll all look back on this someday and see the *microbots* merely as a temporary *transition* phase."

"But what if they aren't temporary? What if they become *permanent?*"

"It's up to us to make sure they don't."

"And you say you believe in this country? Don't you think you've chosen an odd way to express your patriotism?"

"Mr. President, I have no illusions. I came of age in the nineteen-sixties, and naturally I'm critical of our record on a wide range of issues. I mean, for goodness' sake, we claim to support freedom and democracy, but under none other than 'Mr. Human Rights' himself, Jimmy Carter, we actually backed *Pol Pot*, one of the most notorious, dictatorial, and genocidal mass murderers the world has ever seen.

"And look at how many innocents in Central and South America we helped kill in the name of democracy, from El Salvador to Argentina to Chile. The list can go on, and I'm not saying we're perfect by any stretch of the imagination.

"But I also recognize all the good we have done. *Selflessly. Because it's right.* We've fostered democracy across Asia, Eastern

Europe, and increasingly across Latin America. We've brought down terrible and malignant totalitarian ideologies. We've defended a system of commerce that has brought prosperity to many corners of the globe, built a system that is so fair that we've seen competing countries surpass us and beat us at our own game.

"In our own country, though the record is still imperfect, we've made enormous strides in fostering equal rights, civil rights, and in protecting the environment. We're still a land of opportunity, where people can strive and succeed on their own merits; and even if we have made mistakes, we're still the one and only beacon of hope and freedom for countless multitudes around the globe.

"So I agree that this is a good and great nation we have. I'm not saying it's better or worse than other countries, but it *is* good and it *is* great, and it's the only country we have. It's just a real crying shame to see it fall apart the way it has. So please don't lecture me or question me on my patriotism.

"And so now, Mr. President," Carpenter continued, "it's quite late, and you have an important speech to give in a few days. If the speech is successful it will mark the beginning of a reversal in your own political fortunes. It has the power to launch the renovation of our own badly damaged country, and even an entire world in desperate need of healing. Now, are you with me?"

The President scratched his head, and, after a moment of consideration, responded. "OK . . . I'm with you. Now, where was I?"

"You were saying you felt aggrieved . . . "

CHAPTER 27

Maddox felt a queasiness grow in his stomach. This was by far the most delicate moment in the operation to date, and whereas the previous evening he had felt a positive momentum lift him as he attempted to sail, wine, dine and croon his way into Heather's heart, he could now sense the tide starting to shift the other way. After Maddox had left her at her hotel following the visit to his house, she had reflected on his plans to stop Carpenter, and now, meeting him the next day, she was having second thoughts about her involvement in the mission.

Ideally, if all had gone as scripted, he would have managed to seduce her first before attempting to put the final sell on her. If events had transpired as he had intended, they would be having the conversation in a warm bed, between soft cotton sheets, in whispered intervals separating sweet nothings and tender embraces. But though the prior evening had commenced on an auspicious note, including easily won success in inebriating her, inviting her back to his house, and serenading her with his guitar, she had proved a more elusive romantic quarry than he had hoped. That was even before the commotion outside the house destroyed the mood he had tried so hard to achieve.

So now he was parked in his Audi on a quiet tree-shaded street near her hotel, trying not to grip the steering wheel too hard, or let the impatience in his gut seep through into his voice. Though he was doing his best to seal the deal, she was proving a very tough sell. *Don't back out on me now, Heather!*

"Bill, I'm so sorry. I'm in complete sympathy with your plans, and I want to do everything I can to help you, but the more I think about it the more I think I'm just not cut out for this."

"I know how difficult this must be for you, but you have to understand that you're our only hope. Speaking from decades of experience, I know a successful agent when I see one, and I'm absolutely confident that you'll pull us through. I'm giving you my word that you'll be completely safe. We'll have you covered, totally covered."

He watched her closely to see if his words had taken effect, but she remained unconvinced.

"But you never told me before what we were up against. I was guessing all along this might be some kind of hostage situation. I had no idea that it was the entire *world* that was the hostage. No idea that I was signing on to go up against a completely new and insidious form of weaponry. No idea that I might have to deliberately allow myself to be infected through the nostrils by a mysterious, deadly, mechanical insect."

"Believe me, if we had any other choice ... "

"For heaven's sake, Bill, I'm a neurosurgeon from Minnetonka, Minnesota. I'm not *Wonder Woman*."

Could have fooled me!

"I'm more the bookish type. For me, water skiing is a big adventure. I just don't think I have what it takes to be some kind of secret agent."

He felt the urgency build within his gut.

"Look, Heather, I'm really uncomfortable trying to convince you to do this. If there were *any* other way ... Truth be told, I don't want to be here either. If it weren't for some quaint notion of duty, honor, and country, mixed in with a good dose of simple common sense, I wouldn't be here myself." Left unsaid was the fact that he knew this case also represented his last chance at personal redemption: an opportunity to put right the debacle in Colombia, and one last shot to save his career.

"But can either of us really walk away now? We just wash our hands and *bail*? Call it a day?" he prodded. "Can we just sit by and let a deranged madman take over the entire world? Because that is exactly what will happen unless you and I agree right here and *right now* to stop him."

He fixed his unrelenting stare straight into her eyes.

"Look, Bill. I know Carpenter has to be stopped. He stands for everything I oppose. I mean, politically, just so you know, I waver between anarchism — foolishly hoping that through education, advocacy, and awareness, people might somehow become morally upright enough and emotionally mature enough to govern themselves without need for a government bureaucracy to regulate society — and socialism — foolishly hoping that people will place enough faith in their government institutions to allow the government to provide an even playing field for all members of society.

"So whichever way I'm wavering, be it anarchism or socialism, Carpenter is an anathema to me. But I'm telling you, you've got to find someone else to help you, someone better qualified. I'm just going to end up screwing you up."

Maddox successfully repressed an urge to roll his eyes during the short discourse on anarchism and socialism, and by displaying his most earnest concurrence, even managed to feign interest in her political views.

"Heather, we've been down this road before. I've tried everyone. There is no one else. It's that simple. It's you and me. And I know with one hundred percent certainty that you can pull this off. And I'm telling you . . . No, I'm *promising* you, you'll be *completely* safe."

Did I convey the right amount of confidence when I said that?

"But Bill, I'm too honest. My thespian skills are quite limited."

"Your what?"

"You know, *thespian*. I'm not that good an actress."

"Oh, sorry. I'm a simple guy — I have trouble with anything over two syllables. Anyway, don't underestimate yourself — you're a great actress. You already fooled your boyfriend, right? You entered a beauty pageant in high school, right? That must have involved a lot of stage work. They must have taught you how to put on the charm even if you don't always mean it. Am I right?"

She nodded gently.

"And besides, you don't need to act. You just need to be yourself, and if you do, I guarantee you — *guarantee you*," he added for emphasis, "that Carpenter will fall head-over-heels for you. And once he does, then he's putty in your hands.

"I've handled a lot of tough cases, been on dozens of difficult operations, and I'm telling you that — stakes aside — this mission is just not that complicated. And I know — *absolutely know in the bottom of my heart* — that you're perfectly capable of pulling it off."

He beamed at her with his most confident smile.

Heather looked out the window at the quiet empty street, and let out a deep sigh. He sensed he was moving her in the right direction, but knew he had yet to convince her fully.

"There's one more thing I need to tell you, Heather," he said. "If you agree to help then you'll find this out sooner or later." She studied him carefully, her curiosity piqued.

"Am I right that you and your mother are somewhat estranged?"

"What's that got to do with anything?" she asked, taken aback.

"I met your mother. That's how I found out about you."

"Come again?"

"I met Alice. She's quite proud of you."

"Thanks for telling me!" she responded with sarcasm.

"Heather, I couldn't just mention this when we first met. You hardly knew me. I wasn't sure how you'd react."

"So you withheld it from me? And now you expect me to trust you?"

Women!

"I didn't withhold anything from you," he pleaded. "I told you just now, didn't I? I needed to find the right time."

She regarded him with skepticism.

"I don't blame you for your reaction, but please let's move forward," he entreated.

"So get to the point," she demanded impatiently.

"Carpenter and your mother Alice were once intimate. Quite intimate."

"Pardon?"

"They lived together for seven years. Almost married."

She appeared incredulous. He continued. "If you want to learn more about her, who she was, who she is, there's no better way than through Carpenter."

"Carpenter and my mother? Together?"

"That's right."

"When was this?"

"Work with me and you'll find out. Find out everything. Now are you with me?"

She stared out the window.

"Work with me, Heather. We can do it. We *will* do it. And I've got your back all the way."

She drew in a deep breath.

"I sure hope you're right, Bill," she said after a moment, shaking her head slowly. "I can only hope for everyone's sake that you're right."

CHAPTER 28

Carpenter woke up to a glorious Indian summer morning. The birds were chirping in the woods outside his suite in the Aspen Lodge at Camp David. He hadn't had such a good night's sleep in weeks. Everything seemed to be going to plan. Unbelievably so, especially in terms of technical progress. Even the President's poll numbers had stabilized on expectation of the upcoming revelation of the "Blueprint for America." The fact that the plan was working so smoothly was actually becoming a mild source of worry because in his vast scientific experience, of all the laws in science with which he was familiar, the most immutable of all was Murphy's law: *anything that can go wrong, will go wrong.*

So Carpenter spent hours each day going over in his own mind and with Lewis, and with Zach, all the things that could possibly go awry. He concocted multiple contingencies to address each potential obstacle that might arise. He contended with problems of electromagnetic interference, allergic reactions to the *microbots*, and possible psychological reactions the targets might present upon being infected through the nose with a lethal foreign object. Though he was unable to completely shake his sense of vulnerability to latent threats to his plan, he surmised that his doubts must be a normal accompaniment to any undertaking as grand as he had conceived.

Most comforting to him was the realization that as his plan gained momentum, the balance of power would tilt increasingly in his favor. His resources, growing by the day, would soon become so vast that he would be able to manage handily any unexpected problems that might emerge as his plot unfolded. It was thus in a largely cheerful and confident frame of mind that he sat down for his daily breakfast with Lewis. Nothing had prepared him, however, for what he saw when he read the morning newspaper.

He put down the newspaper, his face turning red with anger. Everything had been on track. He was certain the President's upcoming address to the nation would shape up to be a blockbuster. Lewis and his team were making good progress on the networking extension to the *microbot* control platform, and if all went well, the new long-range system would be ready to "go global" not long after the President's re-election.

And then this! This Gottlieb character. First he pipes in at the news conference, asking about "anthrax at the White House." Up to that point, each and every one of the questions from the press corps had been on the new Domestic Recovery Initiative, as the President's "Blueprint" program was now being called. *All of a sudden, that little schmuck's gotta go asking about anthrax, and you can just feel the atmosphere in the room shift, and then suddenly it's all about anthrax — all the questions — and then this morning . . . In the paper! Unbelievable! My name! and Bernie's name! We're in the papers . . . By name! Part of a new bio-weapons detail in the Secret Service — that was supposed to be Top Secret. Now Congress is calling for an investigation. Outrage that they weren't notified, blah, blah, blah. Of course they weren't notified. There was no goddamn anthrax to begin with! Somebody's gonna catch hell for this.*

Carpenter put down his newspaper and summoned a meeting for all the *true believers*, his name for the tethered souls initiated by mechanical infection into his closest circle. As he addressed the assembled group, his eyes were filled with a rage that Zach had never seen before.

"Ladies and gentlemen. I call your attention to the front page of today's paper. In case you hadn't noticed, there is an article discussing a plot to infect the President with anthrax in the White House. The article mentions me and Dr. Lewis here by name. I remind you that I swore each and every one of you to absolute secrecy.

"My plans, *our* plans, have come too far, and are too important to allow anyone to derail them. *Anyone.*

"Our goal is simple: we are trying to save the world. We seek no personal gain for ourselves. If all goes well, we will achieve a good measure of global salvation without harming anyone, not a single soul.

"What goal, what plan, what design could be nobler than that which I have just described? What could possibly be more important than ushering in — *without bloodshed or destruction* — a new era of peace, prosperity, liberty and equality?

"This is a plan for which I have selected each and every one of you personally, for which destiny has chosen you, and in which each of you has the *deep privilege* to participate. How could any person of good conscience find fault with such a plan ... such a goal ... such a design?" Carpenter looked around the room, his voice trembling with righteous anger, and he paused before he spoke next.

"One or more among you is a *Judas*, and I will find him. And I say to him, 'enjoy your 30 talents of silver now,' because when I find you, so great will be your torment that you'll most certainly wish you had never been born. This meeting is over.

Mr. Hutchison, you will please stay behind," he said, speaking to the FBI Director.

* * *

After everyone except Hutchison had left the room, Carpenter seated himself at his desk and took a deep breath. His mind was now swimming as he contemplated his options. *I shouldn't have made that threat. A threat, once made, must always be carried through. If I appear weak, unwilling even in the face of a clear challenge to use the power I possess, then my sway dissipates immediately. I've threatened them with pain and punishment if they don't cooperate with me, and if, in the absence of their cooperation, or worse still in the face of open opposition, I don't carry through with my threat, then my threat becomes meaningless. The entire plan falls apart.*

"Sir? Sir?" the FBI director awakened Carpenter from his thoughts. "You wanted me to stay behind?"

Carpenter looked at the Director. The Director was someone on whom Carpenter increasingly felt he could rely. Carpenter recognized that the Director possessed in abundance all the "three P's" necessary to the proper functioning of any bureaucracy: an interest in power, personal advancement, and patriotism. Without prodding, the Director had already confirmed his trustworthiness by personally taking it upon himself to monitor and shut down two recent initiatives from underlings at the FBI that could indirectly have compromised Carpenter's operations at Camp David.

Carpenter looked over his desk at the Director. Six-foot-two, fit, expensive tailoring, he cut a fine figure. Carpenter was pleased at the zeal with which the Director was pursuing his assignments, but at the same time that zeal also made him suspicious.

"Mr. Director. I'd like to ask you a question."

"Go right ahead, Sir."

"I'll get right to the point. I've effectively taken you and your entire family hostage. Some of the others, I can palpably feel the resentment they harbor towards me. Not saying that I blame them, but anyway, the point is that the animosity they hold against me is intense and apparent. In your case, not only do I feel no animosity, I'm amazed at the enthusiasm you continue to bring to the assignments I've given you. You've displayed tremendous initiative, and have assisted me greatly of your own volition more than once."

"And . . . ?"

"Why is that? Why no animosity, and why such ready cooperation?"

The Director took no time in answering. "Simple, Sir. I *believe*. I believe in *you,* Sir, and I believe in your cause. *Our* cause. Of course, I'm not happy that my family has been taken hostage, as you put it. But placing myself in your shoes, I see the necessity. I understand the need for sacrifice."

"You do?"

"Yes, Sir."

"And just so that we can be absolutely clear, what is it that you believe my cause to be?"

"You're trying to rebuild America. Make her stronger. Rebuild the world too, of course. Make it a better place too. From where I sit, the two goals go hand in hand."

Carpenter pondered the Director's response, but the Director continued without pause.

"And the methods you've brought to bear, they're a lawman's dream," he added enthusiastically. "Pervasive surveillance. Ability to achieve total penetration of enemy cell and combat groups. We've been shackled for too long. Too many restrictions. You're taking all that away. Finally someone steps up with some *guts*. We've been in need of a man like you for a long time. And lastly, Sir, I heard the Protector of the Nation award was your idea. For that, I deeply thank you. The award means a lot to me."

Carpenter inhaled, then released a long, deep breath.

"Mr. Hutchison. Thank you for your service. Now let me get straight to the point. As you saw from today's newspaper, there is a traitor amongst us. A *leak*.

"Obviously, suspicion would fall on Dr. Lewis, given the obvious weaknesses in the alibi he offered to justify his initial disappearance, not to mention half his entire lab team disappearing.

"I'll be the first to take blame for not following your recommendation to 'employ more robust coercion tactics' on Dr. Lewis, as you put it. But as he has been cooperating nicely — and, by the way, I've checked his work thoroughly and I can vouch that he is doing good work, free of hidden Trojans, bugs, or delaying tactics — I felt it best to leave him alone, especially given how crucial his efforts are to our overall project. Clearly, I may have been a bit too lax.

"I'm happy to say, however, that Dr. Lewis' development work is progressing to a stage where we should soon be able to take him out of circulation without compromising the project."

Carpenter looked Hutchison in the eye, then turned his gaze out the window to the bucolic scene outside.

"Then again, we can't jump to any conclusions. Maybe Lewis isn't the leak, after all. Your job is to find the leak, the traitor. You have two weeks. If within those two weeks you've not found him, I'll then assume *you're* the source of the leak, and I'll have no choice but to turn your brain into something resembling a lump of anthracite coal. Do we understand each other?"

"Yessir." The Director nodded his assent, excused himself, and then quickly left the room. Carpenter sighed, as a teardrop gathered in the corner of his eye.

CHAPTER 29

As Maddox was seated at the desk in his office, the phone rang and he picked up the receiver anxiously. He was still steaming from events at his house the previous night. He'd been trying to reach his boss Martin all day, left several messages, but had been told that Martin was in meetings "upstairs" and couldn't be reached. It was now late afternoon.

"Sir, he's back in his office now," his secretary Janice said. "You can go over and see him."

As Maddox stormed out of his office and passed her desk, Janice said, "Remember, Sir. Keep your cool."

Maddox responded with a taut smile.

At Martin's office, he knocked loudly and entered.

"You wanna tell me what that was all about last night, Sir?" he asked. "Sending McDonough and Weintraub to *spy* on me? At my house? You could have cost me my agent. She was scared stiff thanks to all the noise those clowns made," he added, only partly embellishing for dramatic effect. "Thanks to those goofballs she almost backed out! I had to spend the whole morning trying to get her back on board."

I have to get Martin off my tail. The good news is, if he's already been co-opted and knows about my mission, then I probably wouldn't be standing here a free man right now.

"Now just calm down, Billy-boy."

Don't call me "Billy-boy!" I can't tell you how much I hate it when you call me that.

"Look, be realistic, Maddox. No one spins a story about drug smuggling in the White House and gets *carte blanche* to go off gallivanting completely on their own. I'm already going way, way, *way* beyond procedure to let you run this operation in secret, but you can't expect me not to keep a close eye on you, if only for your own protection."

"Come on, Sir. Don't expect me to believe you're motivated by concern for my personal safety."

"Partly, yes, and partly I just need to make sure you don't screw things up. Is that so hard to comprehend?"

At the thinly veiled reference to Maddox's mishap in Colombia, Maddox did his best to contain his seething frustration.

"I understand your position, Sir, but I'm at a very sensitive stage of my investigation and am working with a newly recruited, untested agent. On day one, she's already getting spooked big time. If she decides to back out now, then we're really up a creek.

"So please, I'm begging you, just give me one week alone to bond with her. Get her onside, trained and properly briefed for the mission — without frightening the daylights out of her!"

He watched Martin to see if his words were taking effect, then continued.

"After one week's up, you can have me tailed to your heart's content. You and I have worked together for almost twenty years, Sir. I give you my word: during this week I won't do anything that will even remotely make you look bad."

I hope!

Martin paused to consider.

"OK, Maddox. You have my word. One week. And no funny business."

"Yes, Sir!"

Whew! That was a close one!

CHAPTER 30

In the end, it didn't take Hutchison the two weeks Carpenter had allowed him to find the leak. After the meeting with Carpenter, Hutchison immediately ordered a massive, stepped-up search of Lewis' premises, his laboratory at Lawrence Livermore, and his safe deposit boxes. "I want you to tear everything apart inch by inch. Examine each and every item in his home, lab and bank vault inside out," he told the agent in charge of the investigation. "Leave absolutely nothing unturned." Three days later, the agent excitedly phoned Hutchison.

"Sir, we've found a letter sandwiched inside one of Lewis' textbooks," he said, almost out of breath. "You're never going to believe what the letter says. Something about a 'microbotic plague,' and the President being in danger. The letter also has a signature at the bottom, which we're studying now. It's hard to read, but it looks like it was signed by somebody named 'Madden' or 'Maddox' or something like that. There are also some fingerprint samples on the document. We're running tests now."

CHAPTER 31

"Heather, it's time to move. I've gotten wind of their whereabouts. According to my sources, they've just left Camp David for the White House. We need to move into high gear. First we're going to take a trip up to Northern California for you to meet some people, then we need to get you straight to Washington."

Even though it added additional hours to the journey, Maddox opted to take Highway 1, the coastal route. Firstly, monitoring traffic conditions on the FBI online system, Maddox learned that Highway 5, the direct route, was heavily backed up by construction on the Grapevine near Tehachapi. More importantly, concerned by Heather's continued reticence, Maddox felt he needed more time to bond with his charge. This would be his last opportunity to spend quiet time alone with Heather before the demands of the operation threw them both into a rushing and tumultuous torrent of events most likely beyond the control of either.

The coastal route provided the ideal opportunity for one last bonding session. More scenic than Highway 5, it was outright romantic. Highway 5 passed monotonously on a straight line through the stockyards and lettuce fields of California's inland San Joaquin Valley, charging past towns with dreary names such as Bakersfield, Kettleman City, and Stockton. By contrast, Highway 1 wound along California's long, majestic coastline, passing gracefully through a string of enchanting and legendary haunts: Santa Barbara, Morro Bay, Pismo Beach, San Simeon, Big Sur, Monterey and Carmel. But right now, leaving Santa Barbara, it wasn't the scenery or his conversation with Heather that had Maddox's attention. It was the dark blue Chevy Impala in his rear-view mirror.

Seated in the front seat, Heather was making conversation. "That other night," she asked, "at the Mexican restaurant, we started talking about your family life. So why no wife or kids?"

"Nothing much to tell," Maddox said quickly, casting a glance in the mirror.

"Usually stories that start off with 'nothing much to tell' are the ones with the most to tell."

"Why do I get the feeling you're not going to let this one go, just like the other night at my house when you insisted I play those songs I wrote?" Maddox said, a half smile on his face as he glanced again in the mirror. *Still there.*

"I don't mean to pry. You don't have to tell me if you don't want to. But I mean, we're both on a dangerous mission together. I sort of figured we could open up a little."

"You want me to 'open up?'" He paused. "OK, well, here goes . . . "

She laid her hand gently on his arm. "No, really Bill. If you'd rather not talk about it, I completely understand. I was making conversation more than anything. Although I have to admit you're a pretty interesting character, and I don't feel as though I have you fully figured out."

"Fair enough. I'm just worried that when you do fully 'figure me out,' as you put it, you may not find me so interesting." *Man, why do you always have to go saying these things, Dawg? You're trying to make her like you! Don't scare her off!*

"As you like. I was just curious."

"OK," he said after a pause. "It was like this: I had a wife, we're separated now. Never had any kids."

"See, that wasn't so bad."

Maddox floored the Audi and overtook a truck in front. One of the Channel Islands, Anacapa, was just offshore in the Pacific. The Impala was by now out of sight. *Must have been a false alarm.*

He resumed the conversation.

"We split up a few years ago. It was never going to work to begin with, but I probably could have been a better husband."

Heather prodded him to continue.

"She was Australian. Nice girl. Beautiful. We were so young when we met. I was just twenty-one then. She was nineteen."

"What was her name?"

"Helen."

"The face that launched a thousand ships?"

"Not sure how many it launched, but it sure launched mine."

"How'd you meet?"

"I met her right after I'd been pulled out of Beirut, after the debacle. Just as I was getting ready to be shipped off to Central America. My unit was in the Western Pacific at the time, doing joint exercises with the Aussies. I hit it off with my counterpart in the Aussie regiment we were paired with. We had some R&R, and he invited me to his hometown, Coolangatta, to party with him and his buddies for a few days. Surfing, drinking from sundown to sunup. We even took a trip diving — ever been to the Great Barrier Reef?"

Heather shook her head.

"It's just fantastic, you gotta go some day."

"Sign me up," Heather said enthusiastically.

"Anyway, my Aussie buddy and I were having a great time."

"Sounds like fun."

"Fun? It was completely insane! Anyway, make a long story short: there was some kind of function he took me to at his base not far from his hometown. Free flow of drinks all around.

"I'll never forget . . . My buddy turns to me and says, 'You know, Bill, giving out free drinks to an Aussie is like handing out free explosives to a Muslim terrorist.' Man, was he ever right. The place was just totally, fantastically chaotic. I was hammered beyond belief. Next thing I know, I'm talking up this beautiful girl. It was Helen. In those days everyone liked Americans, and just speaking with an American accent was enough to get you laid in most places around the world."

"Don't sell yourself short, Bill. I'm sure it didn't hurt that you look like the Marlboro Man, sing like Placido Domingo, and sail a catamaran like Captain Cook himself. But go on . . . " She gave him a knowing glance that put a pang in his stomach for brief moment.

Wow, sounds like she might have a thing for me after all . . .

"Anyway, Helen was hammered to the same extent I was, if not more so, and the next thing I know," he continued, "she's leading me by the hand. We're stumbling through the darkness in the back of the function hall. We're in a closet, making out."

Maddox paused. He wasn't sure he wanted to go on.

"Do continue. Don't be shy. We're friends," Heather said.

"You have to understand my state of mind back then. I was still pretty shaken up by the fiasco in Beirut. Two hundred and forty-one of my marine comrades dead. For nothing. I was shipping out to Central America in a few days. I was having dreams, nightmares, of dying in a jungle somewhere in Honduras, Nicaragua or El Salvador, shot by a bullet from an assailant I never saw. No one even knows I'm dying. No one knows what happened to Bill Maddox. Just gone. So along with my normal post-pubescent hormone levels, I'd also been thinking I didn't want to die without leaving something behind. In other words, Bill Jr. You see where this is going? . . . Pretty bad, huh?"

"You don't have to apologize to me, Bill," Heather said. "I pass no judgment."

OK . . . Well, here goes nothing.

"One thing leads to another. Our clothes are half off, and she seems pretty game. Both our motors are running pretty hard, and she asks if I have a condom. And I lied. I consciously lied to her. I told her: 'Sorry, I usually carry around a condom, but the Aussie girls are just so *hot*, I ran completely out these last few days.' She laughs. She thinks that's the funniest thing she's ever heard. And the next thing I know, she's pulling me inside her anyway."

Maddox looked at Heather.

"I hope I'm not scaring you off here. I was a fink. A complete jerk. Like all guys. If you want me to shut up, just let me know. I'm probably sharing a little too much *intelligence* with you here, but I just felt as though we were friends. That we could open up. Nothing to hide, right?"

"Right on, Bill. Don't worry. I already know from both firsthand experience and careful research of the literature that *all* guys are jerks. And don't forget, I'm also a doctor. I've seen plenty of male genitalia in my day, and I'm well acquainted with the intricacies of human sexual and reproductive behavior. You don't have to feel self-conscious."

Sounds a bit clinical, but still, she's pretty cool . . .

"Not much more to tell," Maddox continued. "We did it. We hung out for another day. Did it again a couple more times. Again, no condom. We exchange phone numbers, addresses. Then I have to ship out for Tegucigalpa. I made a quick call to her once from the *Goose*. But I didn't have a lot of money then, and I was treating it pretty much as a little fling. Was thinking sometime in the future I'd go back to Australia and look her up. But I wasn't going to have a long-distance affair. Wasn't going to run up a big phone bill trying to stay in touch. Didn't have the time, money or inclination. Not with me about to get stuck in a nasty guerilla war. Jumping out of airplanes into the jungle. People shooting at me left and right. I had other things on my mind. I was just a stupid kid then."

"Don't beat yourself up. Sounds pretty normal, pretty understandable under the circumstances."

"I'm in theater for two months. I'd written her a quick letter a few weeks after I got to the *Goose*. She never wrote me back. And then, one day out of the blue, I get this letter from her, and in it she tells me she's pregnant."

"How did you feel when you got that letter?"

"To be honest, I remember feeling pretty good. Don't forget, I wanted to have Bill Jr. I liked Helen. She was definitely very attractive. For the one-and-a-half days we spent together, we had a fantastic time, body surfing, dune-buggying, swimming, partying. But I'm also thinking, how do I know it's mine?"

"How did you know?"

"I call her up. We're both really awkward at first. We don't know how we're supposed to act, and how the other feels. I asked a stupid question, but I had to ask it: 'How do you know I'm the father?' And what does she say?"

Heather shook her head.

"'Because I haven't slept with anyone else, you idiot. Have you slept with anyone else?' she says, and we both start laughing.

"Then there's an awkward pause, and she says, 'So what are we going to do about all this?' And I, twelve thousand miles away, having known her for all of thirty-six hours, say, 'Well . . .

I guess we have to get married.' Just kinda blurted it out without really thinking."

"Did you want to marry her, or was it only out of obligation?"

"Oh, I guess at the time I very much wanted to marry her. Like I said, she was very attractive, and we got on great, the little time we spent together. I liked the idea of starting a family. The idea of Bill Jr.

"So next thing I know, in between firefights . . . in between trips to the Capuchin monk down from our firebase learning to play guitar, I'm planning a trip to Australia to tie the knot. My CO gets me a week's leave and says we'll figure out where Helen's going to live later on. Helen wants to have the wedding as soon as possible, before she starts showing.

"My mom thinks it's all a crazy idea. My dad had passed away a few years earlier. He would have thought I was nuts. My Mom, she's distraught enough I'm in Beirut, Central America, wherever, in the line of fire. Now she thinks I'm throwing my life away marrying some girl I don't even know. Apparently Helen's family is even more distraught. Helen's only nineteen.

"I didn't know it until I actually went to Australia for the wedding, but Helen's also a little bit unstable. Not clinically bi-polar, but just a little more tightly wound than your average girl. No way the family's gonna let her go off to Camp Pendleton, or whatever, to live on her own on a U.S. Marine base, much less, Tegucigalpa.

"So we have the wedding, very quickly. My mom flew in, not looking too happy. Helen's parents are there, looking none too happy either. Everyone's sullen and uptight, doing their best to smile, but it's all an act. I don't even have a best man. Her brother does the honors. I use up my entire savings to buy a ring, and it isn't much of a ring. We have a three-day honey-moon on the Gold Coast, but because of the pregnancy, Helen's not feeling very well, so we didn't do much for those three days. And we're both feeling pretty overwhelmed and awkward. We realized we're married but we hardly know each other. Like, I still don't even know her favorite color, or the name of the pet dog she had when she was growing up.

"We still don't even have all the post-nuptial arrangements tied down, like where is she going to live? And the strain I was going through in the theater pretty damn near meant I just couldn't focus on anything but shooting at shadows in the jungle, and getting back with my unit. So just before I leave, we decide she'll stay on in Australia with her family until my tour of duty ends. Then we have a quick goodbye, and next thing I know I'm back in Honduras."

Maddox looked out the window at the rolling sage and scrub oak California hillsides gliding past outside the window, golden in the midday sun. The rear-view mirror was clear.

"So I'm back in theater. Got shot in the leg. Lucky. Just grazed. I took lives, even civilian lives once or twice by accident. Felt terrible about that. Truly horrible. One of my buddies took a bullet in the head.

"And amidst all the fighting and savagery, I can't say I'm being the best correspondent with my wife. Back in Australia, Helen's not having the easiest pregnancy. My mom bought her a book on pregnancy, and it turns out Helen's got every symptom in the book, no matter how rare. Some of the symptoms a woman gets like one-in-ten-million pregnancies. Well, Helen's got 'em: excessive salivation, swollen joints, you name it.

"And I'm not present at all. I'm not there for her. I'm trying to be, but I'm living mission-to-mission. She sends me an ultrasound of the baby. Our baby. But it just doesn't look real. I just can't focus on anything. I'm feeling depressed. Lonely. I forget to call Helen once or twice. Other times, I deliberately tell my buddies to tell her I'm not there when she calls. I'm just overwhelmed. I can't deal with the stress of combat. The pressures of marriage and fatherhood. It's not even real to me that I'm married. That I'm going to be a father."

Heather nodded understandingly, or at least trying to understand.

"And then one day, I get a letter. Helen miscarried. She'd been trying to call me, but could never reach me by phone, so she put it down in a letter. She told me in graphic detail how hard the pregnancy had been, and how she wished I could have been there with her. Especially when she miscarried. How she understood why I wasn't with her and she wasn't angry, but she still wished I could be there with her like any normal husband would be. She told me how she felt when she heard the baby's heart stop on the machine the doctor was using, and the next thing she knows they're putting her under. How she wakes up on sedatives and the weight in her belly is gone, and the doctor is saying how sorry he was to tell her that she lost this one."

Maddox's voiced choked momentarily with emotion. He stopped and looked out on the vast blue Pacific, twinkling in the sunlight to his left.

"And then?" Heather asked.

"And then a year later, I got out of the service and brought Helen over to the States to live with me. It took many years to repair the damage to our relationship that my earlier inattention had caused. And even then, the marriage was quite rocky. But still somehow we managed, though I can't say it was easy for her being married to an FBI narcotics agent. I travel a lot. Always on the road. I mentioned before that she was a bit high-strung. She had a nasty falling out with the wives of a couple of my FBI buddies. So we didn't have too many friends. We became a bit isolated within the FBI fraternity, and it gets pretty incestuous in the Bureau. The isolation didn't help my career prospects.

"In terms of family, we just had my younger sister. We weren't that close, especially after my mother passed away. So it was really just me and Helen, the two of us. We tried again to have kids, but she had trouble getting pregnant. We tried treatments, everything. We'd been married for close to twenty years when finally one day, I come home and she hugs me, tells me she's pregnant. A miracle. We were both so overjoyed."

Heather shrank back in her seat, knowing there wouldn't be a happy ending.

"At least I do a better job of taking care of her this pregnancy than in the first. But I'm on a really busy schedule now. And I'm tracking down a notorious narcotics kingpin in Colombia. The biggest case of my life. Even suggestions of Russian mafia involvement. Helen's eight months pregnant. If she'd been nine months, I'm sure I wouldn't have gone down to Colombia, would have stayed close to home. But I can't control when a drop is going to occur, and this was my best chance to nail the cartel. I wasn't going to leave it for someone else to mess up.

"On a stakeout, one of my agents had been shot and paralyzed a year earlier by someone in the cartel. Great guy. Father of three. Always smiling. Now he's a quadriplegic. So yes, I wanted to nail the bastards. Nail them bad."

Maddox deliberately left out mention of the postmortem report. "*Maddox took more risks with his agents than otherwise would have been warranted . . .* " *I can't afford to have Heather question her confidence in me.*

"So along with some DEA agents I take a trip to Colombia, where we had tracked down the traffickers dealing with the Estradas. We've got a stakeout going. The drop's supposed to happen the next day. And then I get a call from Helen. She's frantic. She's bleeding. She needs to go to the hospital."

Maddox's voice choked up again, but he recovered quickly.

"You don't have to go on if you don't want to," Heather said, putting her hand on Maddox's shoulder.

"No, that's OK. Haven't talked about this with anyone. Good to get it out."

Heather nodded.

"I rush back to the U.S. Land at LAX. Call the hospital right away. Nurse on call says there have been some complications. That I need to go straight to the hospital, which I was going to do anyway. I get to the hospital. Helen's in a coma. She was suicidal after she lost the second baby. She somehow got a hold of some pills that should have been beyond her reach, and tried to overdose. She came out of the coma three weeks later, but was just hollow after that. Just a hollow shell. She'd completely come apart. I tried treatment. Medicine by the truckloads. Nothing worked. I don't know if me being there would have made a difference, but anyway, she was completely gone."

Heather shook her head.

"I had to have her committed. Her family took her back to Australia. She's in a hospital there. I pay for her care. Never divorced. Just separated. I felt so guilty about not being there for her."

"I'm so sorry," Heather said.

"Hey, that's life. Sometimes things go your way, sometimes they don't," Maddox said, winking at Heather, trying his best to put on a brave face.

"I'm glad you're able to be philosophical about it."

"How else *can* I be? But that's not the half of it. It gets worse."

"You poor guy." She shook her head in sympathy.

"After the coma, my sister . . . she's a paralegal. She talks me into suing the hospital. I get a low-budget lawyer on contingency. Hospital offers to settle for twenty thousand dollars. Helen's life is ruined, mine too, and they're offering twenty thousand dollars. I got so angry at the paltry offer. Even though the offer of settlement wasn't admissible, the low-budget lawyer tells me if they're willing to settle, that must mean they know they are in some way negligent. When I say I won't settle, the lawyer says he can't keep going on contingency alone. Needs a retainer.

"I talk to a more high-powered guy, says he thinks we can get at least *five hundred K*. At least enough to cover Helen's on-going expenses. I hire him. Next thing I know it's four years later. I've already spent all my savings, close to a hundred and fifty thousand, on legal bills, and now I'm so stuck in I can't afford to back out. Not to mention the cost of caring for Helen. So here I am. Second mortgage on the home. No wife. No kids. Career not going anywhere. Hospital case still stuck in the legal system somewhere.

"And at the Bureau, they're like, 'Bill, we like you, but you have to admit you seem to have lost a bit of the edge, the enthusiasm you used to bring to the job. Maybe you're burnt out. Maybe you need a little time to yourself. Just say the word. We can arrange it.'

"Oh, and get this. You'll love this. The drug traffickers? They walk. *Walk!* Two trials. Get off both times. The last trial, around a month ago, one of the lieutenants gets five to ten. Probably be out in three. Hung jury for the kingpin. Judge declares a mistrial. The kingpin's long gone. Free as a bird. We think he's somewhere in the Caribbean now, but we've lost track. So there I am, biding my time, thinking about packing it in . . . Trying to figure out my next move after the Bureau, and then I get that crazy letter on my desk a few weeks ago, and here we are now . . . Just you and me."

Heather paused for a moment.

"Are you burnt out, Bill?" she asked after gathering her thoughts.

"From your perspective, the answer is a firm 'no.' I'm every bit on top of my game, and I'm absolutely committed to solving this case. But I guess in a larger sense, if I'm going to be perfectly and totally honest with you, I have to say that if you're an FBI narcotics agent and you're doing your job half well, it's probably impossible not to become burnt out in the end."

"Why's that?"

"Because at the most basic level you're fighting a war of attrition that you can't possibly win. The drug problem. The crime problem. Yes, crime's down eight percent this year, but then it's up seven percent the next, and it's at way damned too high a level anyway. And who knows if the reported figures are in any way accurate to begin with. You can't keep morale up in a war of attrition. That's why everyone gets burnt out."

"I'm not sure I follow," Heather said.

"Here's an example. World War I. Incredibly brutal. Terrible hardship. Appalling bloodshed. Trench warfare. Four years of fighting, and no one's winning: absolute stalemate. Morale plummets on all sides. Russia falls apart in revolution. Germany collapses. That's what I call getting burnt out."

Heather nodded.

"Fast forward twenty-five years later. World War II, Eastern Front. Incredibly brutal. Terrible hardship. Appalling bloodshed. Russians completely outgunned. Underfed. Freezing. Dying in droves. But somehow they're winning. Through sheer guts, determination, and a good dose of ruthlessness on the part of the Red Army generals and commissars, they push back the Nazi invaders. Red Army's got *momentum*. Russian morale's high. No one's burnt out. Red Army *actually prevails. Victory.*"

"And . . . ?" Heather asked.

"Moral of the story? A man, a person, can take unbelievable hardship, make incredible sacrifices, as long as there's some momentum, some progress, some *hope* for an eventual victory. But in the war on drugs, the war on crime we're fighting today, what hope is there?"

He went on.

"Let me tell you what it's like in the real world. The way it feels out on the beat, out on the *street*. It feels like we're applying a band-aid, and maybe just barely stopping the patient from bleeding to death. But we have no real momentum. We're definitely not winning the war. The bad guys are still out there. The streets are still not safe.

"The gangbangers get shot, stabbed, and they don't die: they're, like, indestructible . . . They go to jail or get deported, and then they're back on the streets in no time . . . The courts and prisons are so crowded that if the subject is a foreigner he just gets deported — it's quicker and easier that way. And after they get deported, what do you think happens?"

She shook her head.

"They just slip on back into the U.S. through our ridiculously lax and porous borders, and the innocents — the kids, the old ladies that were just in the wrong place at the wrong time — they just barely get grazed in the cross-fire and they die in a heartbeat."

The intensity rose in Maddox's voice.

"Lives shattered. Lives erased. Families destroyed," Bill paused. "Does it have to be like this? Wasn't there something in the Constitution about ensuring 'domestic tranquility?' Come along with me sometime to El Monte, to Compton, to South

Central, to Hollenbeck. You won't see a lot of *domestic tranquil-ity* out there . . . "

Heather nodded, then spoke.

"You're not burnt out, Bill."

"I'm not?"

"Anger over indifference. That's what you said the other night, right?"

He recalled their previous conversation and nodded.

"You're still too angry to be burnt out. There's hope for you yet, Special Agent Bill Maddox."

"Amen to that, Dr. Heather Anderson. Don't you count me out just yet," he said with a faint smile, already starting to feel better.

CHAPTER 32

"Sir, we've confirmed the source of the fingerprints on Lewis' letter," Hutchison said to Carpenter over the phone.

"The name's Maddox. William Alexander Maddox. FBI Los Angeles. No idea how he got the letter, or what his involvement is."

"Pull him in right away," Carpenter commanded.

"Yessir. We've got assets tracking him now. Consider it done."

CHAPTER 33

Maddox and Heather stopped at the restaurant of a vineyard inn near San Luis Obispo for lunch, the *Auberge de la Faune Blessée*, and washed down the meal with a half-bottle of red wine. A few minutes into the meal, he was apologizing for "getting so melodramatic back there in the car. I hope I didn't give you a *bad trip*," he said playfully.

The mood between them had already grown much lighter.

"No need to apologize," she said, sampling the Roquefort salad she had ordered.

She caught him grimacing a moment later at the pungent aroma a passing cheese cart gave off. She chided him matter-of-factly: "Now, now, don't be so judgmental, Bill. As Hamlet himself said, 'Everyone knows *there's no cheese either good or bad but stinking makes it so*,'" which elicited from him a hearty guffaw.

"I never read Hamlet, so I have no idea what you're talking about," he said, "but your delivery was fantastic."

Then within minutes they were laughing about the bells on the cows in the fields outside the restaurant.

"Can you imagine one of those heifers going to the veterinarian?" she said. "Doc, I've got, like, this constant ringing in my ears. It won't go away, and I just can't figure it out . . . " By this point, Maddox almost spit out his wine, he was laughing so hard.

A few minutes later he told her, "So let me get this straight, Heather. You're a *brain surgeon*, a *cellist*. You like water skiing. You've got a fantastic sense of humor, even if your sense of humor is fairly offensive to the bovine community. Anything else I left out?"

"You forgot to mention I was captain of the high school chess team and Minnesota State runner-up in chess my junior year."

"And a *geek* too? Wow! Now I'm really impressed," at which point she hit him playfully. He'd have loved to take her right then into a dark closet at the back of the restaurant. He'd start his life all over with her as if he were twenty-one again, and do it all the right way this time around.

Darn it, Dawg. Now you've really screwed up big time. You've gone off and fallen in love with your agent.

Aware of his growing attraction for Heather but unsure of her feelings for him, an operational concern now arose. He thought back to his training at Quantico. *Your agent falls in love with you: that's great, that's the objective. You fall in love with him or her: not so great, but possibly manageable. You fall in love with him or her, and he or she does not return the affection: not good at all. He or she falls in love with your intended target: total disaster.*

Just as he was reflecting on the subtleties of his relationship with Heather, he was brought back to reality by the arrival of a couple who sat down two tables away. The man was dressed in a tan suit, and the woman in a white skirt and navy blouse. Something in their gait, in the way they wore their clothes, and in the way the man glanced over at him put Maddox on his guard.

And then, yanking him to full attention, Maddox felt his cellphone buzz to indicate delivery of a message. Maddox looked down, but didn't recognize the number of the sending party. He opened the message, then read. It said simply, "Dude, evade . . . Now! — Rambo."

Rando! Holy crap!

Immediately, Maddox's operational instincts took over. He first removed the batteries from his cellphone, so his location couldn't be traced. Then he began to scan the room deliberately. He removed his pen, and holding one of his business cards under the table, scribbled a note surreptitiously. Next, concealing the card in his palm, he extended his hand and took Heather's hand in his, caressing it while gazing longingly into her eyes.

His actions startled her and she instinctively began to recoil, but he held her hand firm and she read the look of urgency in his eyes. Just then, she also felt the card in his hand and understood that he had a secret message for her. Catching on, she locked eyes with Maddox as if they were a pair of smitten lovers, and then she quietly withdrew the note from Maddox's hand while giving the hand a tender kiss.

Quick study! Maddox thought with a mixture of satisfaction and teacher's pride as he savored the tingling her kiss imparted to his hand, along his arm, and into his midriff.

The note simply said, "We might have trouble. Act natural. Don't look around. When I get up, do exactly as I say."

He scribbled another note under the table on another business card, and then called for the check. As he raised his hand to call the waiter, he noticed the man and woman two tables away take interest. A moment later, they too called for their bill, and Maddox saw the man speak quickly into his cellphone.

Definitely spooks. Takes one to know one.

When Maddox's waiter arrived with the check, Maddox pretended to examine the charges. Then he handed over his credit card, and inserted a crisp hundred-dollar bill along with the note he had just scribbled on his business card. He used his pen to call the note to the waiter's attention. The waiter's eyes widened when he noticed the crisp bill and the title on the business card — *Special Agent Bill Maddox, FBI.* He studied Maddox's scribbled note for a moment, then quickly left the table to do as the note asked.

The waiter returned a few minutes later and quietly produced two pillow cases borrowed from housekeeping at the inn. As instructed, he had also delayed the delivery of the bill to the other table. Maddox immediately secreted the pillow cases out of sight under the table. Using his knife, he worked holes in the ends of the cases. He then calmly signed the chit, smiled at the waiter, and put away his credit card.

After he had restored his wallet to his pocket, he waited until the check was presented at the other table. Just as the man in the tan suit was reaching for his wallet, hand in pocket, Maddox sprang up and rushed the other table. He quickly placed one pillow case over the man, allowing the man's head to protrude through the hole in the end of the case, and thereby trapping the man's arms. Before the man's startled companion could act, Maddox had trapped her in the other pillow case. As they helplessly struggled to free themselves, Maddox grabbed his rucksack and pulled Heather by the hand to the entrance.

They reached the front of the inn just as a golfer was exiting his Cadillac *CTS Portfolio,* and a valet was attending to the man. Maddox flashed his badge and service revolver, then brusquely pushed aside the valet and the man. He yelled for Heather to get in, then gunned the car and screeched out of the parking lot.

He turned right onto a country road, then a half-mile later slipped onto Highway 1 heading north to Livermore. Driving at top speed, he overtook the first truck he encountered, flashed his badge and revolver, and forced it to the side of the road at a scenic turnout on a cliff overlooking the ocean.

Once in the turnout, he told Heather to leave the car. He then gunned the car and threw it into neutral just before he reached the edge of the cliff at the far corner of the turnout, where the guardrail failed to extend. Just as the car was about to go over the edge of the cliff, Maddox threw himself from the vehicle, was able to take two running steps, and then rolled on the pavement judo-style, ripping his elbows but suffering nothing more grievous. The car plunged over the cliff.

After gathering himself off the ground, he ran back to the truck and pressed the driver to hide him and Heather in the rear. He told the driver to head straight for Livermore, California without stopping. "And let us off at the first gas station you see once we hit Livermore," he added.

* * *

As the truck lurched off, Maddox settled himself and Heather in the narrow space between the produce crates in the back of the truck. Shell-shocked, Heather wore a blank expression, and not long after she had seated herself she cradled her head in her hands.

"Heather, I'm so sorry about that. So sorry I got you into this. Are you okay?" he asked.

He wanted to offer her an 'out' from the mission, but given her state of apprehension, he was afraid she might accept the offer. He said nothing.

"What just happened back there?" she asked, dazed.

"To be perfectly honest, I don't really know. But I sure as heck am going to find out.

"In the meantime, please try not to worry. You're safe with me," he said with as much confidence as he could project. She let out a half-smile that only thinly masked her considerable worry.

They passed the remainder of the journey in quiet contemplation as Maddox focused on the next steps in their mission. It was cold in the trailer, and seeing her nipples hard and goose bumps on her arms, Maddox took off his jacket and placed it over her shoulders. Eventually, she fell asleep with her head resting on his shoulder.

* * *

The driver let them out at a gas station in Livermore three hours later. With Heather out of earshot, Maddox went straight to a payphone and placed a collect call to his secretary Janice on the all-hours secure line.

"Hi Janice, it's Bill. I'm in a hurry here. Please put me through to Martin."

"Are you okay, Sir?" she asked.

How did she know I was in trouble?

"Yes, I'm okay, thanks. Please just put me through to Martin, a.s.a.p."

The line went quiet, then a moment later Martin picked up.

"Bill, Martin here. Where on Earth are you?"

"No time to explain, Chief. Now what about you? You gave me your word, remember?" Maddox had never once known Martin to fail to live up to his word. *Comes with being Mormon, I guess.*

"Sorry Billy-boy. I've always been a man of my word, and I still am. What happened today wasn't on my authorization. It's way beyond me now. The Director is involved personally, and matters are completely out of my hands.

"I've been instructed to tell you to surrender yourself as quickly as possible for your own sake. I promise I'll do my best to protect you. I don't know what you've done, but whatever it is, you've got the entire law enforcement apparatus of the United States of America looking for you now."

Holy crap! "Listen, Sir. Please. You've known me for twenty years. I haven't done *anything* wrong. You *have* to believe me.

"The entire chain of command is compromised. Please just give me two weeks. I promise I'll surrender myself, and then I'll explain everything. You have my word.

"But until then . . . you gave me your word last time, and I expect you to continue to honor it, please." Maddox knew the line was bugged, but needed to take a chance anyway with his next request. He held his breath, and then pleaded.

"Not a word to anyone about our recent discussions. I'm begging you, Sir" He looked at his watch to check the elapsed time of his call. "Just two weeks, then I turn myself in. Please, Sir!" Seeing that time was up, he hung up at once to avoid the call being traced.

After replacing the receiver, he went into the mini-mart at the gas station. He did his best to conceal his raw elbows as he bought a map and two bottles of water. He then led Heather out into the cool autumn night.

The moon was already high in the nighttime sky as they set out from the gas station. They walked quickly. He kept their conversation to a minimum, careful to remain in the shadows and take residential streets as much as possible on the two-mile walk. Heather asked Maddox about the phone conversation with Martin, which she had partially overheard, but he was taciturn and told her not to be concerned. At last, they arrived at a plain two-story house on a quiet, tree-lined suburban street, whereupon Maddox said: "This, I believe, is where our destiny awaits us." Leading Heather to the doorstep, he peered in through a crack in the window, and finding nothing amiss, pressed the doorbell.

"Who's there?" came a voice behind the door after Maddox had rung.

"Special Agent Bill Maddox, and a very important guest," Maddox replied. To be safe, he kept his right hand on his concealed service revolver. He smiled tersely at Heather when she shot him a look of concern.

The door opened, and destiny revealed itself in the form of a scraggly-bearded man in a t-shirt. He instantly waved Maddox and Heather in. Maddox scanned the interior immediately. Finding it satisfactory, he ushered Heather inside and withdrew his hand from his service revolver.

"At last we meet, Special Agent Maddox. Dr. Lewis spoke very highly of you, as did your friend in the Phoenix Police Department. Make yourselves at home," the bearded man said, after taking note of the badge Maddox produced as he walked inside the house. As he offered the two a limp handshake, he reminded Heather of a fluffy, oversized mouse. "Take a seat. Don't mind the mess."

Maddox surveyed the room. *Early 'Brady Bunch,'* he thought to himself as he noted the décor. Two others were sitting on a threadbare couch.

The bearded man introduced himself as Mike Zimmerman, and explained that he was Lewis' second-in-command at Lawrence Livermore. "Call me Zim," he said.

"I notice you're admiring the décor," Zim said to Maddox. "Don't blame me. It's my cousin's house.

"What you see here is all that's left of our lab. There were seven of us originally. The FBI has grabbed everyone from our lab except me, Xiaohong and Moussavadi," he said, motioning to the two on the couch. "Luckily, we've managed to hide out undetected, so far, here at my cousin's, and we've been able to continue working out of the basement."

After the formalities were over, Zim led Maddox and Heather down to the basement laboratory. The dusty room was crowded with electronic equipment and a workbench, on which were scattered several soldering irons, rolls of solder, a small blue plastic tool chest, a wire-wound board, a miniature drill press, an enormous magnifying glass, a microscope, an oscilloscope, a computer, and other assorted equipment. He pointed to the corner of the basement at two small cots. "You guys'll be sleeping there. I hope you don't mind. The toilet's just there," he pointed to a door at the far end of the room. "Please feel free to take a shower in my bathroom upstairs. Towels are in the hall closet."

* * *

The next day, Maddox slipped out early, and returned with a package. "You may be interested in this," he said to Zim, as he opened the package and removed a Ziploc bag housing the hearing aid that Lewis had flushed down the toilet at the White House. "Don't worry, I had it sanitized," he added. Zim took the device quickly from Maddox and studied it in the light while Heather gave a puzzled look.

"Fantastic. That finally gives us something concrete to work with," Zim responded. "So let me tell you how this is all supposed to play out," he continued. "After I've analyzed the device's recordings, I'll outfit Heather with the appropriate defensive *microbot*. With Heather protected by the defensive *microbot*, you're somehow going to place her in proximity with Doctor Carpenter, and then . . . we all pray a lot, say *kumbaya*, and wait for divine intervention. Sound good?"

* * *

Zim spent the next day down in the lab, analyzing the hearing aid. The device contained a fifteen-minute recording of radio signals and comments from Lewis, explaining everything he knew or could surmise about Carpenter's *microbot* and detailing the next stages of the plan to disarm Carpenter. Meanwhile, Heather spent her free time trying to relax by lounging on the sofa and reading a lowbrow paperback. Maddox tried his best to relax in front of the TV, but occasionally found himself pacing the room.

The following day, after he had finished analyzing the device, Zim explained at breakneck speed what he was able to glean from Lewis' recording. "Ever get a really bad ice-cream headache? You know, when you eat an ice-cream cone too fast?" Maddox and Heather nodded in the affirmative.

"Well, apparently that's what Carpenter's *microbot* headache is like. If Dr. Lewis' calculations are correct, the *bot* uses an electrical stimulus on the glossopharyngeal nerve to produce a debilitating headache in the target. That nerve is the same nerve that's at the root of the ice-cream headache.

"Now for a bit of good news," he said. "The most important point here is that Lewis believes the *microbot* resides in the nasal cavity, remaining there *in situ* after invading the host. This approach minimizes the risk of microbial infection to the host, and also offers the ideal location from which to produce the headache or to terminate the host once the command is given.

"For us, the good news is that Lewis is convinced the *micro-bot* simply remains on standby in the nasal cavity: if it unloaded its payload into the blood stream from the start, for instance, or tried immediately to penetrate from the nasal cavity into the brain, the chance of infection would be too high.

"To sum up, then, Dr. Lewis is fairly certain that the device resides *inert* in the nasal passages until activated to terminate the host, and that means our defensive *microbots* will probably have a reasonable window to try to intercept and neutralize the intruder."

Maddox let out a small sigh of relief at hearing the first real dose of good news in some time.

"And do we know yet exactly how to stop it?" Maddox asked. "Override it? Jam it? In other words, how easy will it be to put together a defense against it?" he prodded.

"Unfortunately, Dr. Lewis doesn't know much more at this stage, and none of us will know more until we recover one of Carpenter's actual *microbots* from Heather's nose," Zim said, looking at Heather. Her face grew pale.

"But there are two additional positive items to note," Zim added. "Firstly, the device does *not* seem to emit an all-clear signal when it is inserted. If there had been a radio signal, the hearing aid would have picked up the signal when Dr. Lewis was infected.

"That means Carpenter must use the headache mechanism as a manual check to be sure the *microbot* is seated correctly and working properly after he infects his target. This is key, because it means that as long as the recipient puts on a good show of pretending to have a really bad headache, we should have the chance to intercept the intruding *microbot* without Carpenter realizing it has been incapacitated."

"And the second piece of positive news?" Maddox asked anxiously.

"Dr. Lewis was able to learn that the microprocessor core is very similar to the one we use for our own *microbots*. This means that once we obtain one of Carpenter's actual *bots* — and that's up to you two," Zim said, shooting a penetrating glance at Maddox and Heather that forced in Maddox an involuntary gulp, "we should have a pretty good chance to decode its workings.

"Once we have decoded a working *bot*, we should then be in position to craft our countermeasures. So, assuming you can get Carpenter to send a *bot* up your agent's nose, and assuming our defensive *bot* can neutralize that *bot*, then after we retrieve said *bot* from said nose, we'll have it sent off for a full analysis.

"Now, this may take several weeks, but then hopefully if all goes well, once we have our data we'll finally be in position to go on the offensive." Zim paused, then spoke again. "So how to get the *bot*?" he asked, engaging Maddox directly in the eyes.

Maddox paused, then nodded at Heather, who cleared her throat and excused herself to go to the bathroom. A minute later, Maddox heard a vomiting sound from inside the bathroom where she had gone.

* * *

Later that night, Maddox took Heather aside.

"Look, I've been thinking about this. I should never have gotten you into this mess. This whole thing is becoming trickier than I was expecting. If you don't want to go ahead, I won't blame you at all."

"What? You don't think I'm going to let you have all the fun," she said, doing her best to shoot him a brave smile.

CHAPTER 34

Gottlieb's revelatory article on anthrax, even if off-base, and the discovery of the warning letter at Lewis' house signed by FBI Agent Bill Maddox spurred Carpenter on with a new urgency. He was anxious to moves his plans forward as fast as possible.

President Drake thus found himself seated in the Oval Office before the television camera, making a last minute adjustment to his tie. He was conscious of the fact that this would be the most important speech of his career, indeed his entire life. With the speech highly awaited like nothing before on television, his staffers had told the President that the night's viewership was forecast to dwarf handily all prior records. "Believe it or not," his aide Mandy had told him excitedly, "that includes last season's hotly contested finale of American Idol!"

The camera man called out: "And taping in Five . . . Four . . . Three . . . Two . . . One . . . " Drake rubbed a bead of sweat from his temple, looked over at Carpenter, who was seated to his right just off camera, and then launched into the speech. "My fellow Americans, good evening . . . "

* * *

To Drake, though it actually lasted seventy minutes, the speech seemed simply to fly by. Before he was aware, he found himself saying, "And to all, good night and God Bless, and God Bless this great country of ours," and then the light on the camera shut off, and all was quiet.

"Well?" he said, looking at Carpenter. "How was my Möbius strip?"

"Just perfect," Carpenter said quietly, with a gentle smile. "Just perfect."

* * *

After the speech, the talking heads went frenetic and the airwaves were abuzz with analysis. One commentator marveled at the President's *"chutzpah,"* as he put it, "to propose such a dramatic and revolutionary initiative aimed at re-engineering the very fundamentals of our government and our economy." Another was left "breathless," as he admitted, by the President's willingness to take head-on "heretofore highly divisive social issues, and in doing so make a serious attempt to heal the spiritual rift that has divided our country for so long."

* * *

"Phil, you're not going to believe this!" Gottlieb shouted excitedly into the receiver of his cellphone, addressing his editor. "I just got a peek at the initial polling data, and guess what? It looks like Drake actually managed to knock the ball out of the park!

"I've never seen anything like this before," Gottlieb continued. "He's already bounced *fifteen* points, and his ratings are still climbing. If this continues, the election could be anyone's bet!

"What to my mind were the salient points we should go with?" Gottlieb continued. "Well, I know it sounds like a stretch, but I've already heard mention that the tax restructuring initiative the President led off with could promise to launch an entirely new evolution of capitalism.

"He's talking about dramatically *lowering* income tax rates — while still maintaining the progressive tax system — by funding the reductions largely from *increased inheritance taxes*. He started by quoting Carnegie on the evils of inherited wealth, and said something to the effect that everyone should have a level playing field. No one, regardless of station or social status, should have an advantage from birth in education or in healthcare or in securing justice or obtaining political influence. But apart from those four areas,' he went on, 'let's pull out all the stops,' I believe were the actual words he used.

"'What you earn by the sweat of your brow or by the fruits of your imagination, you keep,' he said. "And when it's time for you at last to bequeath your worldly gains onto succeeding generations, then and only then do you return your full due back to society.'

"On the other side of the equation, he wants to lower spending by pushing not only for nuclear arms reductions, but also across-the-board reductions in *conventional* weapons. 'There's no reason the U.S. should incur such a heavy tax burden to defend the global peace, while so many of the countries we defend convert into lower tax rates the very protection we provide them, and then use those lower tax rates to compete against us in the global economy,' were his exact words. As he pointed out: 'To put it simply, we're funding our own economic demise.'

"Of course, he also talked about funding the reduction in income taxes by significantly reducing the 'nearly two hundred billion dollars we waste each year in agricultural subsidies,' and by modifying those subsidies to encourage production of biofuels, and by increasing taxes on imported fuels.

"By this point in the speech, he was gathering steam, because the next and last part of his economic plan was even more radical. He talked foremost about 'using our greatest weakness as our greatest strength,' and admitted that some might find it hard to accept what he was about to propose. But he said: 'unfortunately, we can ill afford to be squeamish at this critical juncture, because we must recognize that we face desperate challenges which require extraordinary measures in response.'

"When he talked about using our greatest weakness as our greatest strength, he meant we should use our prison population, 'the largest in the developed world,' to 'power our economy, and — in a humane way that's in keeping with our fundamental principles — provide the cheap source of labor that we will use only to replace the torrent of low-cost imports that are flooding our shores.' In doing so, he said, 'we will not only help to train and rehabilitate our woefully and unacceptably large prison population, but we will actually save entire industries that we have already exported abroad lock, stock, and barrel. And as we save those industries and bring them back onshore, so we will restore our great manufacturing base and create hundreds of thousands if not millions of new jobs at home, outside the prison sector. By focusing on sectors which have already moved completely offshore, my solemn pledge to the American people is that we will create and not lose jobs through this initiative,' he said. He concluded his point with a quote from the Bible, saying: 'Let him who stole steal no more: but rather let him labor, *working with his hands the thing which is good, that he may have to give to him that needeth.'*

"A little wild, Phil, I'll grant you, but if you listened to the speech you'd have to say, he carried it off incredibly well.

"Next up was education, 'the lifeblood of our economy, our society, and our nation,' as he put it, and our 'only hope for the future.' He really brought down the house on this one, citing figure after figure to show how we have slipped so badly, so shamefully, especially in math and science. 'This country is on a sugar high,' he said, 'having relied for so long on imported scientific and technical talent. By many estimates, nearly fifty percent of the engineers and entrepreneurs and scientists in Silicon Valley are from overseas, and while they have contributed enormously to our growth, the day may come when many of them will want to return home. And where will that leave us?

"'China alone,' he said, 'produces *tens* of thousands of concert pianists per year, while the world probably only requires no more than a few thousand. The world is becoming more competitive, and in response we have no choice but to raise our game to the highest level.'

"'The reality is that even if we resolve to spend more money on our schools, on better facilities, that alone will not produce the results we, as a nation, need. We already spend a lot on our schools, as well we should. But what's critically missing in our efforts is a deep *commitment*, a deep cultural commitment, and, yes, a deep *spiritual* commitment to promoting education, to setting the bar as high as possible,' as he put it.

"He mentioned several ways to help achieve that level of commitment, then when he was finished with education, he went on to offer some very hard-hitting prescriptions for healthcare, energy and the environment. The amazing thing here was that he directly blasted the big special interest groups,

Pharisees and *Sadducees* I believe he called them, that had been 'controlling the debate for so long,' and pledged to 'eliminate their influence in the *Temple of Government.*' I mean, it was riveting. Even I was excited, and you know how cynical I am.

"At this point, it *really* gets interesting. He shifts gears, and starts to address what he calls 'the spiritual divide' in America.

"He begins this new thread by saying, 'Normally, when our political leaders ask us to consider difficult social questions, they begin by asking us all to agree to *disagree*. Well I'm going to do something different tonight. I'm going to ask us to agree to *agree,*' and then he lobs in this bombshell: 'Let's start by *agreeing* that you can't be *pro-Life* and *pro-Death* at the same time.' He says flatly, 'Let's agree that it's high time we get rid of the death penalty.'

"'No, I'm not soft on crime,' he explains. 'Let's lock 'em up and throw away the keys, if necessary. Let's resolve to reform our prisons into institutions that will actually deter crime rather than serve as universities offering advanced degrees in criminal behavior.

"'But let's agree to do away with the death penalty, because the simple odds are that in applying the death penalty, we have in the past and will continue to put *innocent* people to death.

"'Let's face it,' he continued, 'the death penalty is terrific except for one small problem: it's too *permanent*. Too permanent to put into the hands of fallible humans, and into a fallible justice system that has as its basis the judgments of fallible humans.'

"His voice gains momentum again, and he says 'And just as we reaffirm our commitment to Life by eliminating the death penalty, let's also reaffirm our commitment to Life in other ways.

"'Whether you use the term 'murder,' 'choice,' or something else, is it really best for us as a society to treat the human fetus as a disposable object, to be thrown away when it becomes an inconvenience to us? So, yes, let us redouble our efforts in family planning, in all forms of birth control, but at the same time let us not enshrine in the laws of our land any concession that detracts from the miracle that is Life.'

"Phil, I'm telling you, by this point even *I* was starting to get goose bumps. Me, *goose bumps!*

"There was nothing in his speech that he was afraid to tackle head-on. On gun control he strongly reaffirmed the constitutional guarantee of the right to keep and bear arms, but also called attention to the fact that just as the second amendment begins by saying '*a well-regulated Militia being necessary to the security of a free State*, thus do we need a well-regulated way to make sure that guns don't fall into the hands of criminals and the mentally ill, and these well-regulated ways should include the mandatory and well-regulated locking and securing of weapons, accompanied by a mandatory and well-regulated method for tracking the distribution and sale of weapons.'"

Gottlieb paused to catch his breath.

"Finally, after dealing — and I have to say even if you didn't agree one hundred percent with all his points — dealing pretty darn well with all those thorny social issues, he concluded his speech with a pledge to restructure the *very fabric* of government. He talked about the pernicious effects of money and special interests on the political process, how the revolving door of public office stifles the chance for true reform.

"For a while it even seemed as though he might propose dramatically restructuring the three-branch form of government. 'Why do we have judicial review only *after* a law is passed?' he asked. 'Why not have judicial review *before* the laws are passed, so that we don't go to all the trouble of passing laws, only to have them struck down, or modified, or rescinded. Is this any way to run a country? No wonder we have gotten our-selves into such a mess!'

"Even I found myself nodding in agreement with him on most of his points, can you imagine?

"But the really amazing thing was, at the very end of his speech, you'll never believe what he does. He actually holds up a strip of paper, twists it around, brings the ends together and says. 'My fellow Americans, I hold in my hands a Möbius strip. For those unfamiliar with this object,' he says, 'what makes it remarkable is that it looks like it has two sides, but it really only has one.' Then he looks straight into the camera and concludes: 'The same is true of our beloved country. Please join me as I show you how this is possible.'

"At that, my jaw just dropped, as I'm sure must have hap-pened to almost every jaw across the country.

"Phil, I'm completely out of breath here, so I'm going to wrap it up if it's OK. I'll have my piece ready for you in a couple hours.

"Oh, and one more thing . . . remember how I mentioned a few minutes ago that the President was up fifteen points in the polls after the speech? Well I just checked the monitor and it looks as though he's actually bounced back seventeen points already. If he can continue the momentum, he just may be able to win this election after all!"

* * *

After the speech, the President huddled with his advisors in his study to celebrate the speech's success, and to plan the next steps in its aftermath. The immediate reversal in the polls left the President elated, and his staff was positively ecstatic. A festive atmosphere infected the White House, punctuated by high-fiving and backslapping. There were only four weeks left until the election and a lot of ground to cover, including the need to resume campaign stops in key battleground states.

The President looked at Carpenter for a moment.

"Didn't I tell you you could do it?" Carpenter said to the President, checking himself just as he was about to give the President a pat on the back. The scientist had a gentle smile, and appeared serene.

The President nodded in acknowledgment.

A moment later, a young man in suit and tie ran into the room and shouted excitedly, "*nineteen* points and rising! If the election were held today, we'd win!"

Carpenter pulled the President aside and quietly gave him and the First Lady leave for several quick two-day campaign swings, provided that the President's children remain with Carpenter at all times. After each two-day swing, the President would need to return to the White House.

As the festivities continued, Carpenter excused himself. He went to his study to plan the next phase of his project. *Everything completely on schedule!* he thought with satisfaction. *Except for that Maddox character . . . But how much damage can he do, anyway? In a few short weeks, the final victory will be ours!*

CHAPTER 35

"Hi Bernie. Thanks for coming by," Carpenter beamed cheerfully as he swiveled his chair around to welcome Lewis into his office at the White House. Director Hutchison was seated on the end of Carpenter's bureau. In contrast with Carpenter, he bore a stern expression and his arms were folded to convey displeasure.

"No problem, Maury. What's cooking?" Lewis asked, glancing at Hutchison. He had expected the meeting to be focused on engineering details, possibly even to convey a congratulatory "well done." Aside from the general high spirits infecting the White House following the President's ascendance in the polls, earlier that day Lewis had, with only a few minor glitches, successfully simulated a large scale, highly distributed *microbot* infection governed by a remote centralized command and control system. In weeks, a system for controlling up to one hundred thousand people around the globe would be ready for deployment. At the push of a button Carpenter would be able to give a headache to, or even kill at any spot around the world, anyone who had been infected with one of his *bots*.

"You'll never guess what Mr. Hutchison's folks came across at your house," Carpenter said in an even voice, his face bearing a pleasant but menacing grin.

"What's that?" Lewis asked. His heart began to race as he suddenly understood the purpose of the meeting.

"Oh, just this," Carpenter said, motioning to Hutchison, who produced the finger-printed copy of Maddox's transcript of Zach's original warning letter.

"Ring any bells?"

Stonewall? Admit everything? His mind swirled, and sweat began to accumulate around Lewis' temples. He took a big breath, then blew it out, deflated. He weighed his options. There was nothing left to say but the truth, while still admitting as little as possible.

"Look, Maury. He came to me. He needed help. He told me the President had been infected with one of your *microbots*. Said that innocent lives were at stake.

"I knew nothing about your project then, or your aims. Didn't know if you'd gone off the deep end. What was I supposed to do? *Of course* I had to help."

"Just so we can be clear . . . *who* came to you?"

"Him," Lewis said, pointing at the paper. "Maddox." *There, I said it.* The word was difficult to pronounce, but having said the name, it felt good finally to unburden. *They've got the physical evidence. There's no way I can deny it now. I can only hope you still have a few tricks left up your sleeve, Maddox.*

"Anyone else?"

Lewis shook his head.

"I hate to say what I'm about to say, Bernie, but I've come too far and there's too much at stake. So I'm gonna come right out and tell you.

"I consider you my friend, and you've done a terrific job in helping to develop our command and control systems. At the beginning, we had our doubts about you," Carpenter continued, glancing at Hutchison. "I was half expecting you to try to sabotage the development effort, or at least delay the project, but you've been a gem. Totally cooperative.

"Everything you've done works perfectly and, most incredibly, is pretty much on schedule. In fact, I can't remember the last time I was involved in an engineering project that met a deadline.

"But all that aside . . . " Carpenter suddenly became serious, and his earlier cheerfulness had now completely disappeared.

"As much as it pains me to say this, your accurate answers to my questions and your overall truthfulness will have a *direct* bearing on your own longevity as well as the longevity of your loved ones."

Lewis gulped.

"So allow me to repeat, and please think carefully before you answer. Is there anyone else involved with you besides Maddox?"

"No, Maury. Absolutely not," Lewis replied at once. "Not to my knowledge. In fact, Maddox said that no one else must know about his plans. I was to be the only one he would tell."

Good Lord, please protect me!

Carpenter studied Lewis with a probing look, and in his stern gaze, Lewis felt like a beetle specimen pinned to a display mounting.

"Which now leads me to the next question," Carpenter stated, arching his eyebrows ominously. "Once you knew my aims, why didn't you tell me about this Maddox character? How am I supposed to think you're not still working with him to thwart our project somehow?"

"Look. Once I knew of your aims, I threw myself wholeheartedly into the project. I believe in you, in *us*. But I'm not a rat, Maury. You've known me long enough to know that.

"I didn't want to get him hurt, in trouble, infected," Lewis explained. "I didn't think there was any way he could stop us. He's just one guy. How dangerous could he be? We're too powerful, and have too many resources. For god's sake, Maury," Lewis said looking at Hutchison, "we've got the entire *flippin'* FBI on our side."

"*Almost* the entire flippin' FBI," Carpenter corrected Lewis.

"But how can just one guy possibly touch us?" Lewis asked.

"That's what I want you to tell me," Carpenter said, startling Lewis as he slammed his right hand abruptly on the table.

"But I have no idea what his plans are," Lewis offered feebly after a moment.

"That's an unfortunate answer, Bernie, because, see, right now your credibility is somewhat *in question*. So you can either tell me now, or I'm going to have to leave you and Danielle with Mr. Hutchison and his colleagues for a while and we can see what they are able to find out.

"Oh, and one other thing, Bernie?" Carpenter added.

"Yes, Maury?"

"You wouldn't happen to know who was the original source of the letter to Maddox, would you? We'd like to have a nice, friendly chat with the fellow."

* * *

"So, Mr. Hutchison," Carpenter said after Lewis had left, leaning forward in his seat and rubbing the bridge of his nose. It was now nearly the end of the day. Exhaustion seeped out through Carpenter's rumpled shirt and well-worn pants and sat heavy on his eyelids. "I understand you managed to let Maddox slip away?"

"Sir, he's a resourceful agent. He has military training on top of his law enforcement credentials. But I'm confident we'll get him before long. We've put out a nationwide APB out on him, and I've got a hundred-agent task force tracking him. He can run, but he can't hide."

"I hope for your sake you're right," Carpenter shot back. "Is there anything more I should know about Maddox?"

"Sir, he's a mid- to low-ranking agent. A twenty-plus-year veteran of the Bureau. Marine Recon before that. He works out of the Los Angeles office, in Narcotics actually. Nothing too remarkable either way in his record, but he did get a reprimand for a slip-up on an operation in Colombia a few years back. On the flip side, he's got a small claim to fame as an authority on the Mexican Mafia."

"Narcotics? How in God's name did a narcotics agent get mixed up in all of this?"

"Sir, we have no idea."

"Any indication yet that he's working with others?"

"Sir, we're unable to determine that, but based on his call records he appears to be working alone. We've also looked at his case records, and they all indicate routine activity."

"Well, Mr. Hutchison, as I said once before — I don't like loose ends. And as far as I'm concerned, Mr. Maddox represents a pretty *loose*, loose end, as loose ends go. So you need to remedy that, *lickety-split*."

"Yes, Sir. Consider it done. He's toast. We've already made that a priority."

CHAPTER 36

Heather opened the manila folder and studied one last time the briefing materials Maddox had prepared for her. The materials detailed every aspect of her assignment to the Walter Reed Medical Center, including background on superiors, subordinates, call signs and other operational details. There was even a brochure on the hospital itself, complete with a layout marked in red with escape routes. Reading the brochure, she noted with interest that Walter Reed had been an incredibly tireless, selfless and patriotic Army surgeon. At the turn of the twentieth century he led the team that confirmed the theory that Yellow Fever is transmitted by mosquitoes, rather than by direct contact.

She noted that Reed's work not only led to a cure to a problem which had been plaguing the Army for decades, but also gave rise to the new field of epidemiology. *And maybe, some day, I'll be remembered for my own pioneering work in epidemiology — robotic epidemiology*, she thought to herself wryly. Heather read further that in order to find a cure for the disease, several on Reed's heroic team had deliberately allowed themselves to be infected by Yellow Fever-bearing mosquitoes, and many died in the process. Drawing the inescapable parallel with her own predicament, Heather put down the reading materials with a sickening feeling of deep trepidation.

* * *

Just as the instructions Lewis had recorded in his hearing aid dictated, at precisely eight a.m. Maddox had a friend place a purple lilac wreath on the fortieth spike on the fence to the right of the main gate of the White House. This was the signal to Lewis that Heather had been installed successfully at Walter Reed. When Maddox received word that the signal had successfully gone out, he steeled his gut. The plan would now move to the next phase, wherein the President would act on instructions Lewis had slipped to him in secret. *The critical phase.* Maddox began to pack for Washington D.C.

* * *

The call went out at eight sixteen a.m. The President had fainted, and when he came to, he complained of severe headaches. The White House Doctor, never more than two minutes away from the President, performed a perfunctory exam, and then, as per protocol, phoned in the incident to Walter Reed. A minute later, Dr. Heather Anderson, assistant chief neurosurgeon of the Walter Reed Army Hospital, was paged and dispatched along with a team of paramedics to take the call. She arrived at the White House at eight twenty-nine a.m. *This is it,* she thought to herself. *The future of the planet rests in my hands. This has to be the best performance of my life,* she steeled herself, as the gate to the White House opened to admit the ambulance.

* * *

She followed the young man in the suit down the hallway to the President's bedroom. She couldn't believe that she was about to examine the President of the United States.

She entered the room. The President lay prone on his bed. Lewis had coached the President in advance.

"Mr. President? I'm Dr. Heather Anderson, assistant chief neurosurgeon at Walter Reed Army Hospital. I was the doctor on call when a distress signal went out from your medical staff. May we examine you, please?"

The President nodded, and the paramedics began taking his temperature and blood pressure. "Temperature one oh one," the first paramedic said, looking at the doctored thermometer pre-programmed to provide a random reading between one hundred and one and one hundred and five degrees. "Blood pressure one oh eight over sixty-three," the other said, using similarly a pre-programmed sphygmomanometer.

"Please tell me what is bothering you, Sir," Heather continued. She noticed out of the corner of her eye a figure appear at the door. *I hope that's he.*

"Well, I started coming down with headaches yesterday. Off and on, but they're getting stronger," he said, as he had been coached by Lewis, holding his head and wincing in pain.

Heather saw Carpenter in silhouette in the doorway. *He's much shorter than I was expecting.*

She examined the President's throat, eyes and ears, checked his breathing with a stethoscope, and then used a reflex hammer on his knee to test his reflexes. *It's time now.*

"You!" she said, turning to Carpenter, who was still hovering in the doorway. "What do you think you're doing there?" she said angrily, remembering Maddox's instructions. *'You have to really rattle his cage. Remember you once told me you were never big on 'subtle?' Well, you make sure this is one time you're not at all subtle. We absolutely need to provoke a response straight away.'*

Carpenter responded aggressively.

"I'm on the President's security detail," he barked. "I'm also a doctor. In fact, it should be *me* examining the President." He looked her over, once, then twice, particularly fixated on the dimple on her right cheek. His voice softened. Her resemblance to Alice had just registered, and for a brief moment he appeared mildly confused.

She continued to stare at him menacingly. Enough to make strong eye contact. To let him look her fully in the face. She also had made sure that her overcoat was loose, and that she had buttoned her blouse one button too low.

"No one treats the President but me," she said with finality. "Now if you'll please excuse me," she said, turning to the President before Carpenter could say anything. *'Carpenter will want to keep you away from the President at all costs. You can't let him succeed. Also, you need to make sure that in the end he feels so threatened and attracted by you that he zaps you, so that you become part of his entourage.'*

"Mr. President, it's probably nothing, but we need a full battery of scans," she said loudly for Carpenter's benefit.

"I want MRIs, X-rays, blood and urine samples. It's probably nothing, but we've had reports of others at Camp David coming down with similar symptoms recently," she said, embellishing, "so we just can't take any chances. I want you to come with me to Walter Reed right away."

On mention of the MRIs and X-rays and a trip to Walter Reed, Carpenter quickly pushed past the young aide in suit and tie and shoved him physically out of the room. He then slammed the door shut behind him and locked it quickly.

"Doctor, Doctor Anderson, I believe? I'm afraid I can't let you move the President. This is a matter of national security. I'll treat him here." His breathing had quickened.

"The President's health is a matter of national security, Doctor . . . Doctor . . . what did you say your name was?"

"Carpenter."

"Doctor Carpenter. Listen. We're not taking any chances here. It's probably nothing, but we need to run tests to be sure. We're taking him to Walter Reed, and neither you nor anyone else is going to stop me. Now, please, open the door. We don't have time to waste!"

"I'm afraid you don't leave me any other choice then," he said as he removed his *microbot* pen, and the cellphone-shaped remote controller.

Excellent, she thought, before steeling herself with a deep breath. *He's taking the bait.*

* * *

The fact that she didn't seem to register significant discomfort when the *microbot* flew into her nose struck Carpenter momentarily as odd. *When the President had his nose job, he practically snorted his way off the stage. But then, I suppose different people exhibit different levels of sensitivity in their nasal cavity*, he thought to himself.

In fact she felt little, having fifteen minutes earlier applied an anesthetic nose spray so that the impending "battle of the *bots*" in her sinuses wouldn't bother her. She registered a sensation of pressure as the predator *microbot* in her nose secured Carpenter's intruding *microbot*, and she heard the very faint beep signaling that the predator had successfully secured the intruder. And then she realized Carpenter was talking to her.

"I'm sorry to have had to do that just now. Please take a seat, Doctor Anderson."

"Firstly, I don't have time to take a seat, and secondly what exactly is it that you *did to me* just now?" she asked, mustering all the impatience and anger she could.

"I have inserted into your nasal cavity a *microbot* capable of causing extreme discomfort or even death."

"You did *what?*" She glared at him. "Are you *crazy?*"

As he picked up his remote control and began to explain to her that she would feel a momentary headache coming on, she remembered Lewis' instructions on the hearing aid recording. *'When he punches in the code, grab your head and double over. You need to count up to ten. He may try to give you a headache for just a few seconds, maybe five, maybe ten. It's better to take no chances and stay doubled over until ten, groaning for the first five seconds. In the unlikely event you actually do feel a headache, that will mean the predator microbot has somehow failed and it will be impossible for you to move forward with the plan.'*

After Carpenter had explained to her the mechanism of the *microbots*, he walked over to the President, and put a hand on his forehead. "See, fever's down already. By the looks of it, doesn't seem like the headache's too bad either. Nothing to worry about," he said.

"Unfortunately, Doctor Anderson," Carpenter continued, after taking Heather aside into the neighboring room, "through no fault of your own, you've managed to involve yourself in a plot to take over the world. *My* plot."

She looked at him, doing her best to appear incredulous. In actuality, she hardly needed to act, as she was having difficulty processing the dramatic stream of events that were sweeping her away towards an unknown end.

When Carpenter had finished explaining her predicament, she spoke.

"Why are you doing this? What do you want? What are you trying to achieve?"

"As I told you, I'm trying to take over the world," he said matter-of-factly. "Why I'm doing this is simple. My aim is to eliminate unnecessary suffering, poverty and injustice. In these efforts I seek nothing for myself. *Absolutely nothing.*

"I was very reluctant to involve you in this exercise, but your determination to remove the President from the White House left me no choice."

Everything is moving forward so far just as Bill has predicted, she thought to herself.

CHAPTER 37

The red sandstone cathedrals of Zion National Park floated by in the distance, but Maddox was hidden in the back of the van alongside Zim. They were dozing on and off, unable to see the striking panorama outside. Just past the Sand Creek Massacre Historic Monument in Colorado, on a deserted stretch of highway, Vicente pulled the van over. Maddox and Zim ran out briefly to relieve themselves, then resumed their place of concealment for the onward journey.

Vicente was the cousin of Maddox's informant Omar Rodriguez. At Rodriguez's behest, he was using his beat-up Ford delivery van to transport Maddox and Zim surreptitiously from California to Washington D.C. Concealed in the back of the van with Maddox and Zim were a number of crates containing sophisticated laboratory equipment. Some of these banged against Maddox's knee whenever Vicente took a hard tight turn. While Maddox and Zim were in transit, Zim's assistants Xiaohong and Moussavadi remained in Livermore, continuing to develop the technology needed to defeat Carpenter's *bots*.

Maddox spent his time in the back of the van mainly in subdued silence. He was focused on planning the upcoming phase of the mission, which he knew would be dangerous. He didn't mind so much the danger to himself, but was gravely concerned about the significant danger Heather was likely to face.

In the back of the van and in the grip of a profound and restless boredom, he often found his mind drifting back to his training in Marine Recon school. For reasons he didn't quite understand, bits of the *Recon Creed* taken as an oath emerged from his memory. He could almost hear his platoon chanting in unison in the sultry morning heat of the Naval Amphibious Base at Little Creek, Virginia:

> *"Realizing it is my choice and my choice alone to be a Reconnaissance Marine, I accept all challenges involved with this profession . . .*
>
> *"Sacrificing personal comforts and dedicating myself to the completion of the mission shall be my life . . .*
>
> *"Conquering all obstacles, both large and small, I shall never quit. To quit, to surrender, to give up is to fail. To be a Recon Marine is to surpass failure; to overcome, to adapt and to do whatever it takes to complete the mission . . .*
>
> *"Never shall I forget the principles I accepted to become a Recon Marine. Honor, Perseverance, Spirit and Heart . . . "*

Finally, after three long days on the road, Vicente at last yelled back to a dozing Maddox that the van was approaching Washington. Maddox shook off his slumber, sat himself upright, reached into his rucksack and pulled out his old dog tag. He kissed it, then fastened it around his neck. He was wearing it now for the first time in over twenty years.

CHAPTER 38

Carpenter didn't like it. Not one bit. *Not enough leverage over her.* All the others he'd infected except Zach had close family members who were also infected. *Hostages.* And none of the others who were infected had been allowed to leave Camp David or the White House grounds. Now this Doctor Anderson — who had no immediate family to infect — was claiming an urgent need to go back to Walter Reed to perform an emergency surgery on a top-ranking Army General. *And supposedly the back-up doctor had called in sick, leaving her as the only possibility.*

Making matters worse, it would raise eyebrows back at Walter Reed if she were forced to stay in the White House. The other *true believers* were part of the administration, and could always be said to be huddling with the President as part of the emergency re-election effort. They were involved with planning implementation details of the *Blueprint for America*, but Doctor Anderson? *Without raising a multitude of questions, on what pretext could she be possibly be sequestered indefinitely at the White House? It's risky to let her go, and equally risky to have her stay*, Carpenter thought, his head spinning.

* * *

He called the FBI Director into his office. "Mr. Hutchison. I need a two-man detail to escort Doctor Anderson back to Walter Reed. They are to follow her closely, stay with her at all times, and immediately intervene in the case of any suspicious activity. She performs her surgery, doesn't contact anyone, then presto! She comes right back here. Is that clear?"

* * *

Heather left the White House. She rode in an unmarked black FBI Crown Victoria to Walter Reed. Carpenter gave her a six-hour leave, telling her she'd be watched constantly and that all her conversations would be monitored. She was to go only to Walter Reed and then was come back immediately to the White House.

Maddox had given Heather two paging devices — an emergency pager to signal that she was in trouble or that complications had developed, and the other to signal that she was in the clear. When they checked her purse, Heather had told the FBI agents that one pager was for Walter Reed, and the other was for the Georgetown University Medical Center where she had just started back-up duty. When Heather reached Walter Reed, she used the emergency pager.

The two humorless FBI agents in suits watched her every move. Because of the story she'd told Carpenter, she was now supposed to be performing surgery on a high-ranking General. In reality, she was fresh out of her internship at the University of Minnesota Medical Center and felt as though she barely knew her way around the operating theater. She wondered how she had gotten herself into such an unbelievable mess. More importantly, she somehow needed to elude detection and deliver the *microbots* in her nasal cavity to Maddox and Zim, who were waiting at the hospital.

Heather paged Maddox just as she was arriving at the hospital, to let him know she was almost there. Escorted by the two FBI agents, she took the elevator to the third floor, then walked down the hallway towards Neurosurgery. She spotted Maddox, wearing a hairpiece, glasses and false mustache. Zim was waiting for her there as well. The two were dressed in white lab coats. *They almost look like they belong here*, Heather thought. *I hope I do too.*

As she approached Maddox and Zim, she gave a slight shake of the head, just enough to signify that she was being watched. Maddox and Zim stood aside and let her go down the hall to her office. The office, and everything in it, was a set-up. She had no patients. Didn't make rounds. Certainly wasn't about to perform surgery, especially not neurosurgery.

Now she had two FBI agents sitting outside her office, keeping watch over her and preventing her from rendezvousing with Maddox and Zim. Worst of all, eating away at her most urgently was the problem that, having told Carpenter she needed to be back in the hospital for surgery, she couldn't possibly produce the non-existent operation on the non-existent patient. Clearly the agents following her would report back to Carpenter, and it wouldn't be long before he discovered she was not who she had made herself out to be.

A wave of despair bordering on panic swept over Heather, and she buried her head in her hands as she hunched over her desk. *What to do?* She took a deep breath and collected her thoughts. Amidst the despair and perplexity, at last the outlines of a plan began to form. Feeble though it seemed to her, it was the only choice she had. She rose from her chair, collected a few manila folder files from her desk, and went to the nurse station at the entrance to the neurosurgery ward. The two FBI agents followed closely behind.

As she approached the reception desk, she caught a glimpse of Maddox and Zim out of the corner of her eye. *This is it!*

"How many times do I have to ask for the Williams file?" she demanded testily, angrily throwing the files down onto the desk in front of the startled nurses. "Now," she began in a loud voice, loud enough for Maddox and Zim to hear her, "I'm going to go to the powder room, and when I come back I expect to see the Williams file. Understood?"

The nurses exchanged bewildered glances.

Heather walked away from the nurses' desk and indicated to Maddox with her eyes that he was to head towards the restrooms several meters down the hall. Giving Maddox time to go first, Heather first stopped at a drinking fountain. The two FBI agents followed closely behind as Heather marched to the bathroom.

Inside the bathroom, she looked under the stall doors for men's shoes. The first two stalls were empty, but the last one was closed. A huge wave of relief swept over her as she looked down to see not one, but two pairs of men's shoes. She knocked on the stall door. The door opened, and inside were Zim and Maddox. Maddox quickly put his index finger to his mouth, indicating 'silence.'

Heather joined the two in the cramped stall. She tried to keep her distance, but it was difficult and soon she found herself rubbing up against Maddox's thigh. *He's definitely not pulling his thigh back*, she thought to herself. *In fact, the rascal is actually applying a bit of pressure if I'm not mistaken.* Some of her hair waved in his face. Such close quarters were awkward, but titillating at the same time. She didn't have time to think about her unsettled feelings for Maddox, however, because soon Zim was painfully feeling around in her nasal cavity with a long, protruding device. In a matter of moments, he had retrieved the *microbots*, which he deftly deposited into a vial before stopping the vial tight.

Using his index finger, Maddox admonished Heather to remain silent. He spoke softly and rapidly in her ear. "You're not going to be able to maintain your 'day job' at the hospital without blowing your cover. You need to go back to the White House and act hysterical, almost as if you're having a nervous breakdown. You need to stay sequestered at the White House, and try to get as close to Carpenter as possible." He handed her an envelope.

"Where are you staying in the White House? Does your room have windows?" She nodded. "Apply this clear plastic sticker to the window of your sleeping quarters. It will be visible to us using special night vision goggles. If you change rooms, take the sticker with you. If you're ever in danger, and if you're able to do so, then cut the sticker in half and re-apply it.

"Here, take this." He handed her a small mascara bottle and brush.

"Take out the brush. When dipped in the clear liquid in the mascara bottle, the brush will appear to someone with special night-vision goggles to be glowing. Use the brush to write invisible messages on your window before you go to sleep. For optimum effect, each letter should be about the size of your thumb. There is enough liquid in the bottle for around five windows' worth of messages. Use it sparingly, only to communicate important information. The morning after you place a message on the window, wipe down the window with a damp cloth without fail. Do you understand?"

She nodded.

"OK. Go back to the White House now and await further instructions."

"But how will you see the windows? What if my window is not facing the street?"

"As long as it's above ground, we'll see it. We'll use a miniature, remote-controlled blimp to monitor all the windows in the building. It was designed for the military, and can stand off two miles from the target. We'll have you covered.

"One last thing, Heather," he added. "When you sleep, try to leave your window open, at least a foot gap, OK? At some point, we might try to get something to you through the window. Check the floor in the mornings for anything that might have come in overnight. Here's a magnifying glass. We may be sending you a message, and it'll be too small to read with the naked eye."

He handed her a heart-shaped necklace, with a crystal pendant. When she peered through the crystal, she saw it functioned as a magnifying glass with a very short focal length. She nodded her assent, and Maddox replied with a wink. Her heart fluttered momentarily as she locked onto his hazel-green eyes and fingered the pendant.

* * *

In truth, Heather was taken with Maddox. She found his rugged looks irresistibly handsome. On top of this, his singing voice had melted her heart, and she also found herself attracted to the aura of vulnerability resulting from his unfortunate, semi-tragic circumstances. She treasured the time they had spent sailing, eating Mexican food, driving up the California coast. Yet at the same time, her feelings were unresolved. She still had her rap-aficionado boyfriend back in Minnetonka, in a well-worn, though frayed relationship. Attracted initially by Stan's undeniable good looks and refreshing irreverence, Heather was now more annoyed with him than anything else. Yet she still felt she owed him loyalty — at least until they could resolve things. *And Bill's an FBI narcotics agent? Ex-military? A hunter? Is he really my type?*

In the end, the task at hand was so enormous she didn't have the time or inclination to question or develop her feelings for Maddox. There will be plenty of time for that later, *if at all*, she told herself as she extricated herself from the stall.

The next thing she knew she was back in the hallway.

"So where's the file?" she demanded at the nurse station. The nurses again stared blankly.

"My God, do I have to do everything here myself?" she asked, cutting off one of the nurses just as she was about to question Heather's sanity. Heather went behind the counter and made a show of rummaging through a stack of files on the nurses' counter.

"Here it is, for Pete's sake," she said as she randomly grabbed a file and moved purposefully back to her office.

After a minute in the office she came storming out and approached the larger of the two FBI agents.

"Just got an e-mail. They canceled my surgery for today. Patient had anaphylactic shock. They've also managed to misplace all my files. I just can't take this anymore. Let's get back to the White House." She walked angrily down the hallway, leaving the two agents struggling to keep up.

* * *

"That was fast," Carpenter said, looking at his watch as Heather entered his office. He had found himself waiting anx-

255

iously for her return ever since the agents had radioed that she wanted to come back to the White House ahead of schedule.

"Look," she said impatiently to Carpenter. "I'm a complete wreck. I was fortunate today they canceled my surgery; but even if they hadn't, I don't think I could have gone through with the procedure."

Carpenter examined her quizzically as if to say, "What do you mean?"

"I'm a frickin' neurosurgeon, Doc. When I'm operating on someone, I require total, *absolute* concentration. I'm naturally uptight and high strung to begin with, but there's absolutely no way I'm going to be able to concentrate on my work knowing that I have a goddamn robot stuck up my nose, especially one that can fry my brains at a second's notice. I'm going completely insane just thinking about it." She blinked her eyes to indicate stress.

Carpenter nodded to acknowledge that he was sympathetic.

"How do I know these *microbots* are safe? We have indications of possible infection in the President and in several staff at Camp David. How thoroughly have these devices been tested?" she prodded.

"And then there's the headache mechanism," she continued. "How does that work? And what is the potential for allergic reaction? I can't take this. I'm going to have a nervous breakdown any minute just thinking about the risk of infection. It's worse than having a bug stuck in my ear. I can't live like this, with a deadly foreign object sitting in my nasal cavity."

Carpenter walked over.

"I understand how you must feel," he said, looking in her eyes. "I really do. And it pains me that I was forced to put you in such a difficult situation. Please rest assured that you're perfectly safe. The device in your nasal passages is well tested, and unless it is commanded to inflict harm, I assure you it will cause no ill effect."

"What about the fevers? The headaches?"

"Almost certainly unrelated. There is no breakage of the blood-brain barrier unless instructed; otherwise there would be too much risk of infection. The headache response is triggered by electro-stimulation of the glossopharyngeal nerve. The *bot* is coated with antiseptic nanomaterials. The possibility of infection is extremely remote, approaching zero."

"So the President's headache and fever? The guys at Camp David? Just a coincidence?"

"I don't know if we're in a position to conclude they are a coincidence yet, but they are almost certainly not related to any dysfunction of my *microbots*. Possibly psychosomatic."

She found his confidence strangely calming. *He's almost serene*, she noted.

"Dr. Anderson. If I may say so, you strike me as highly stressed out. Why not take some time off your work to enjoy yourself a bit? Hang out here with me as my guest at the White House for another few weeks, or even months. Take a leave from the hospital. Think of this as a vacation. We can have it all arranged for you very easily. Relax a little bit. You know what I do when I feel tense?"

She shook her head.

"I play chess."

She paused.

"Really? So do I," she said, genuinely surprised.

"Then how about a game?"

They sat down in the Oval Office and she played chess against Carpenter.

CHAPTER 39

Chess and music. That became their routine. Whenever Carpenter had free time or needed to unwind, he'd slip away from his work to play chess with Heather, or to play string duets, he on the viola, she on the cello. Carpenter arranged for an authentic eighteenth-century Jean Baptiste Vuillaume cello on collection at the Smithsonian to be delivered to the White House for her to use on loan. And because she had nothing else to do except read and watch television, she actually came to look forward to their chess and musical interludes. Of course, in terms of furthering her mission to make Carpenter fall in love with her, the more contact between them the better. To this end, she was always careful to show a little bit of cleavage before she sat down at the chess table.

She moved her pawn to Queen four.

"Are you sure you want to do that?" he asked.

She looked at him disapprovingly. *Stop that! I can't stand when you do that!* "Doc, you've got to stop doing that!" she said to him, frustrated. "You're driving me crazy. You can't keep asking me every other move if I'm sure I want to move here, move there."

"You're right. You're right. I'm sorry. I promise I won't do that again," he replied.

"But you've promised three times already."

"I promise this is the last time."

"Do you have any idea how daunting it is?" she said, genuinely exasperated. "I mean, I'm a decent player. Like I said, I was Minnesota State runner up in high school. But you. You're in a whole other league, another *world*.

"It's hard enough playing against you, *prima facie*. But then all your 'helpful pointers,' your constantly asking me to re-evaluate my every move, constantly causing me to question my strategy . . . I just can't take it anymore."

"I know how you feel."

"Oh really," she said, not bothering to mask her sarcasm.

"Really I do."

She looked at him skeptically.

"Do you like Bergman?" he asked. "Did you ever see 'The Seventh Seal?'"

"Remind me. Is that the movie where the guy plays chess against Death?"

"Exactly. I see you're an existentialist."

"Among other things."

"I too know what it's like to play chess against Death," he said matter-of-factly.

"What's that supposed to mean?"

"I played chess once against *Big Blue*."

"*Big Blue*? The IBM supercomputer?"

"Yes, the supercomputer," he said with a hint of contempt. "And just as you feel playing against me, it too seemed to know my every move. Seemed to question me at every turn. Made me doubt each piece I played. Made me want to resign, just like you feel now. Just as Antonius Blok tried to do in the Seventh Seal. So you see, I do truly know how you feel," he said sympathetically.

She gave him a skeptical glare.

"But don't sell yourself short," he continued. "You're quite good. Actually I'd say you're one of the better players I've encountered." He scrutinized her warily. "I have to watch myself at each and every move. If I let my guard down once, make one careless move, you just might beat me."

She did her best to maintain her *sang froid* and returned his gaze bravely.

"It's not just your prowess at chess, Heather, that keeps me on my guard," he continued. "As much as I like you, I dislike coincidences. Never believed in them. Just like Einstein, I really don't trust quantum mechanics. To me, randomness is just an excuse, a name we use when we're unable to understand a phenomenon at its fundamental level."

She locked eyes with him, unsure where the conversation was leading.

"And so you see," he pressed on, "I checked your files last night. And here's what I want to know: am I really supposed to believe that you, daughter of my ex-lover Alice Van Houten, and recently appointed assistant chief neurosurgeon at the Walter Reed Medical Center, are here in the White House playing chess with me as a matter of mere coincidence?"

She gulped softly, and stared at him blankly as he took her queen and announced, "Checkmate."

* * *

Heather had trained for this. As she had practiced many times with Maddox, she did her best to appear incredulous when Carpenter raised the connection with Alice. Genuinely curious, and just as Maddox had coached her, she pressed Carpenter for details on her mother. She told Carpenter truthfully that she had never been close to her mother and had not seen her for over three years. Regarding her recent transfer to Walter Reed, she explained matter-of-factly that she was not getting on with her boyfriend, that the opportunity arose in Washington, that she applied for the position, and given an impressive academic background and on the strength of glowing recommendations, she was fortunate to have been offered the position. As she mouthed her lines, she felt her explanations were convincing, but she was unable to determine whether or not Carpenter accepted her story.

* * *

That evening as she was curling up in bed, something Carpenter had said over chess stirred her memory. She vaguely remembered somewhere in the back of her mind hearing something about the Seventh Seal. *And when he had opened the Seventh Seal, there was silence in the heavens for half an hour,* she recalled. *That was it! Her boyfriend's diatribe on the Death of Art.*

She pulled out a copy of Gideon's Bible from the bed stand, skimmed through until she found 'Revelation,' and read. *"Only after the breaking of the Seventh Seal shall God's great secret, the secret of life, be revealed . . . "* And as she read further in 'Revelation' she quickly found herself in the midst of the Biblical text on Armageddon.

CHAPTER 40

Maddox's instructions were clear. *Get as close to Carpenter as possible. Get him to fall in love with you. Find out as much about him and his plans as possible. Then wait for an opportunity to communicate back to me everything you know.*

Even with Carpenter's lingering suspicions, getting close to him wasn't too difficult. He was clearly fascinated by her. Attractive as she was, she had been around enough men in her life to know when men were interested in her. As a doctor, she knew how to read people's eyes. The extent of pupil dilation. The rate of blinking. The speed and frequency of eye shifting. The amount and intensity of eye contact. All the signs pointed to Carpenter's high degree of physical attraction to her. Yet at the same time, she sensed a reticence. It wasn't caution or suspicion, of this she was sure. It wasn't even shyness, she knew. Everything in Carpenter's eyes told her he was powerfully drawn to her, and he made no attempt to mask his feelings. Yet at the same time, she also sensed in him a strange resistance and a dark emptiness.

They played string duets together. She found they both had an insane passion for Bach. She played the Suites for Unaccompanied Cello for him and he listened intently, almost in religious rapture, as the notes melted off her strings. Among their chess interludes, once she had even managed a draw.

They dined together, both sharing an obsession for spicy food — Thai, Indian, Korean, Chinese, Mexican. In fact, the White House chef needed to learn a whole new repertoire, as Drake's taste in food favored a much more tepid fare. She sensed Carpenter's growing delight in and craving for her company, and she felt a mutual bond begin to intertwine the two of them. But not once in their acquaintance did he show any sign of romantic intent. And not once did he come close to revealing to her any of his secrets. Once or twice, she thought he was ready to open up to her a crack, but each time just as he raised her hopes he quickly shut the door.

On one or two occasions, she tried to raise with Carpenter the subject of her mother. Her mother was a source of intense curiosity for Heather. She also wondered if her mother's past relationship with Carpenter might explain Carpenter's reticence in getting closer to her. Each time she tried to broach the subject, however, he waved her off, saying that his parting with Alice hurt him considerably, and that he still missed her a great deal. Each time, just when Heather thought he might share more, he retreated back into silence. The best she could obtain from him was a weak promise to share more with her at some unspecified time in the future.

He was busy most of the days and well into the nights, working with Lewis on the networking extension or working with the President and his staff on policy. Heather was left idle for most of the day. She practiced chess in the vain hope she might one day beat him. She practiced her cello, to keep up with him in their duets. She read books, magazines and newspapers. And mostly she waited. Waited for the chance to catch Carpenter off guard. Waited for some type of communication from Maddox.

And then there was Maddox. *Bill.* With Maddox and Carpenter now in the picture, her boyfriend Stan back in Minnetonka was completely unseated. She had come to see the relationship as one of convenience, long past the expiry date. In the grip of Carpenter's overwhelming presence, even Maddox was receding farther and farther from her mind, despite her earlier physical attraction to him.

She ran a letter by Carpenter's censors, ending her relationship with Stan by post. She felt little regret as she sent it off. In the case of Maddox, she had been captivated by him early on. His good looks, his singing voice, his strength, his prowess, his easy manner and his tragic aspect exerted a strong pull when she was physically near him. She could also tell that Maddox was taken with her. But given time and space to think, she was starting to conclude that he and she were too different to be together.

Particularly at issue was the question of firearms, specifically in hunting. With a lifelong commitment to non-violence and organ donation, she detested guns and hunting. She could never suffer the needless taking of any life. While she understood and respected Maddox's record in the military and law enforcement, she found herself unable to accept his interest in hunting. In the end, she could not imagine being with someone who would take pleasure in the killing of a defenseless creature.

As romantic attraction to Maddox gradually receded from Heather's mind, so did Carpenter and his charismatic personality loom all the larger. Certainly he was past his prime years: with stooped shoulders, round belly, and a bald pate he could not in any way be called attractive. But his blue-gray eyes had a way of delving into her soul and expressing an unmatched appreciation for who she was. He also had the most phenomenal intellect she had ever encountered, and his talents and interests almost completely meshed with hers. As her interest in Carpenter grew, she found herself probing him not only as a means to locate his weaknesses, but also out of genuine fascination.

One day, she managed to capture both his bishops and threaten his king.

"Remind me again, Doc, *how* it was you came to do all this?" By *this*, it was clear she meant his attempt to take over the world.

"I've already told you why," he responded matter-of-factly. "To make the world a better place. To eliminate injustice, poverty and oppression."

"No, I know the 'why.' I mean, you've already told me your aims," she said. "My question is more like '*why?*' as in '*what?*' *What* was it that pushed you over the edge? How did you get from the idea to the reality?

"A lot of people — myself included — would love to be able to save the world. I'm sure there are plenty of others who dream about conquering the world. But few, if any, actually act on their desires. So how did you go from the thought to the action?"

"Before I answer your question, I'll let you in on a little secret," he responded. She tilted her head in curious anticipation.

"My actual goal goes deeper than just trying to eliminate war and poverty and hunger and injustice," he continued.

She raised her brows quizzically.

"By doing those things, I'm actually hoping . . . " he paused and looked out the window pensively. A glint of light sparkled in his blue-gray eyes. "Hoping to re-cast the human soul in a better way. My ultimate aim is actually to allow good to triumph over evil."

She looked at him doubtfully and started to wonder about his sanity.

"You see, my aim is actually to remove the major negative feedback loops that plague our society. Foremost among these plagues is violence. Did you know there are Eskimo cultures that have thrived in the absence of violence and war and know only gentleness and harmony? Macbeth said 'blood will have blood.' So I say, 'wash away the blood, and the wound can finally heal.' Did you know that smiles are contagious? Good deeds spread. I believe there is one-third good, one-third evil and one-third indifference in the world. And it is an open question as to which is more powerful, good or evil — which will triumph in the end. I'm just trying to tip the odds as much as possible in favor of *Good*."

"You sound more like a priest than a scientist."

"The more I study science, the more I believe in God," he professed.

"You know, I don't believe even a savage monster like Hitler was necessarily *born* evil. While he will justifiably be reviled throughout history as the embodiment of Absolute Evil, isn't it strange to consider that at one point in his life he was merely a baby? An innocent baby. What caused him in later life to become the cruel, sadistic sociopath we now despise?"

She shook her head.

"Think for a moment about his origins. He was a Corporal in the German army in World War I. A runner and machine gunner. His job was to grind men into hamburger meat with his machine gun. By the time he was twenty, he'd seen a thousand times more death and suffering than most people will ever see in a lifetime. The death, the suffering, the insane waste of life . . . all that had to have changed him.

"War changes people, and rarely for the good," he continued.

"But not everyone who goes to war returns a genocidal mass murderer," she argued.

"But it only takes one, or just a few, to do a tremendous amount of damage. A dog born in the wild has both savagery and gentleness in its heart," he explained. "Beat it and treat it cruelly, and it will most certainly become a vicious beast. Treat it with love, and chances are very good it will become a gentle, loyal companion.

"That's what I mean about taking out the negative feedback loops in society, fostering the positive. Take away the capacity for war, for evil, for crime and dishonesty and we can finally allow the good in people to come out, to triumph."

She nodded her head thoughtfully, weighing his words.

"OK, let's go with that for a minute," she interjected at last. "Let's say I buy your argument that war is bad — not too much of a stretch — but what about other 'negative feedback loops,' as you call them? Just what else do you intend to *eliminate* from society? There are plenty of negative influences on the human soul in our society. Violent television programming and movies? Video games? Antisocial lyrics in rap music? What about boxing, or football? How far are you prepared to take this? Are you going to start censoring free speech? Freedom of expression?"

My God, she sounds just like Alice.

"Well, first of all," he retorted, "I'd say eliminating war and promoting worldwide disarmament constitutes a pretty good start. That's eighty to ninety percent of the battle right there, and I'd be quite satisfied just to have achieved that much. But since you asked, I'd have to admit I wouldn't greatly oppose taking violent, antisocial programming off the airwaves."

"Aha!" she said triumphantly, "so you *are* talking about censorship. You're talking about becoming just another tyrant, a common dictator. Don't you see you're on a slippery slope?"

"Now hold on a minute. No one's talking about censorship."

"But you just said you wanted to take offensive programming off the airwaves."

"Precisely."

"Precisely?"

"Yes. In my book, censorship and dictatorship equate to throwing people into jail, into the *gulag*, even executing them for what they wrote or said. That's not what I'm after at all. As far as I'm concerned, people should be allowed to say and write whatever they want, provided of course they don't shout 'fire' in a crowded theater, or incite others to violence."

"But how is that consistent with your other point about eliminating negative influences from the airwaves?"

"I believe that people should be allowed to think, say, write, read, sing, film whatever they want. *Whatever*. But nowhere is it written they have the right to *get rich* by doing so. No one has the right to *sell* morally damaging content for a profit. If someone feels strongly about their freedom to create violent or pornographic video games, by all means let them do so. No one should stop them, and they shouldn't be sent to jail.

"But if the content is truly socially repugnant," he explained, "then let's tax the proceeds at a rate of 100%. If someone wants to exercise his right to write and sing expletive-filled rap music advocating the raping of women, conduct of violence against homosexuals, perpetration of genocide in a concentration camp, or killing of law enforcement personnel, then I suppose we have to let them do so. But let's tax the proceeds from such '*art*' at a rate of 100%. They can post their content to the internet, can provide it to non-profit organizations dedicated to preserving freedom of expression, do whatever they want with it, but I don't see why the law has to guarantee their right to get *rich* peddling socially abhorrent material."

She seemed to be absorbing the argument, but still looked somewhat dubious.

"Look. I appreciate your concerns," he offered. "This is all beside the point, and if you don't agree with me, that's fine. The main thing I'm after is to eliminate war and the machinery for making war. We can worry about the finer points of the First Amendment later. I give you my word and an absolute solemn promise that once my plan is complete, the First Amendment stands. As long as someone doesn't shout 'fire' in a theater, he or she can say, sing or write whatever he or she wants without having to worry about going to jail."

"OK, let's say I concede all these points to you," she challenged, "the point on war, even the point on eliminating profits on socially damaging expression. But look at how you're planning to accomplish your aims. By turning people into robots? Don't you see something just a little bit, fundamentally, TOTALLY AND COMPLETELY WRONG with your approach?" she asked, her voice rising at last.

"Don't over-dramatize," he responded. "I'm not talking about turning anyone into a robot. Besides, the *microbots* are only a temporary means to an end. Once we have broken the negative feedback loops, then we don't need the *microbots* anymore. The Eskimos don't need *microbots*, do they?"

"Fine," she conceded after a moment. "But even if I allow myself to agree for a minute that your goals may somehow be noble, and make an even greater leap to accept that the means might somehow be acceptable, you have to see that you're taking enormous risks. With your own life and the lives of others. You've taken innocent women and children hostage, including myself. How can you possibly justify this? Don't you have to ask yourself which is worse, the disease or the cure? How are you able to face up to the terrible risks you've assumed?"

"The question, Heather, is not 'why' or 'how', but rather: 'how could I not?'" He paused and looked out the window at the red autumn leaves on the trees bordering the Jacqueline Kennedy Garden. "That brings us back to your original question as to *what* drove me over the edge."

She nodded, urging him to continue.

"You see, Heather," he explained, "I have always felt the world's pain deeply. I've always hated injustice to the core of my soul. It's a fundamental part of me. Even when I was a young child, I remember some 'genius' running our school district had the brilliant idea that handicapped students should go to school with 'normal' children, so that the handicapped would learn to cope in the broader world and 'normal' children would learn how to tolerate and support the handicapped.

"In practice, what this meant was that a child in our school crippled from *Spina Bifida* was the subject of constant taunting and torment from the bullies in my class. One day, I saw the boy on crutches reduced to tears as a group of 'normal' boys threw balls at him, just missing his crutches by a hair each time. I still remember their bullying laughs each time the crippled boy cringed. I and a few of my classmates stood in horror as we watched the crippled boy cry out in bewilderment, screaming for help as he tried his best not to fall off his crutches. And you know what I did?" Carpenter asked, strain in his voice.

She shook her head.

"I did nothing. *Nothing*. I just stood there watching." A tear formed in the corner of Carpenter's eye.

"Why didn't I act then?" he asked her, a note of pleading in his voice. "Why did I just stand there waiting for someone else to intervene? And worse still, even if it wasn't in me to confront his tormentors, at least after those bullies were gone couldn't

I have done something in the aftermath?" He shook his head, then continued.

"But what did I do? Did I go over to comfort the boy, when he most needed a smile, a kind word, or a friendly hand?" His voice trailed off for a moment, as if he were speaking to himself.

"No, I just turned my back and I walked away, ashamed." Carpenter's eyes had become misty.

"And then, as I grew up, my despondency at the world's inequity only grew. You know, I read the newspapers every morning, and often I cry. I actually cry.

"I cut out all the stories of injustice and despair that I read, and I keep them in a scrapbook. Let's put aside The Holocaust, Nanking, Unit 731, Armenia, Cambodia, Rwanda, Darfur. Look what's happening every day. I'll show you my scrapbook some time if you're interested."

She shook her head slowly.

"The child of twelve in Pakistan who hoped to bring himself and his cohorts out of slavery in a Persian-carpet sweatshop, gunned down in cold blood by his master.

"Little girls in Afghanistan stabbed to death simply for trying to attend school.

"The lady in Cambodia of startling beauty raped by an army Colonel, only to have her face splashed with acid by the Colonel's jealous wife. And of course neither brought to justice because of the Colonel's station," he said, voice starting to tremble.

"Of course, I could go on and on and on. Did you know there are over forty million slaves in the world today? And I don't need a newspaper to see the world's injustice. There was my own brother's senseless death in Vietnam. My older brother, James. You've no idea how much I looked up to him, how much I loved him. And then one day he's gone. From *friendly fire*!

271

And for *what?* For a war that turned out to be nothing more than a bureaucrat's miscalculation.

"So one day, I was eating breakfast, watching a fly crawl up the wall and disappear into a crack in the ceiling. And from that observation, the idea for a bio-penetrating *microbot* came to me. *Just like that.* And as I thought about it, it dawned on me that such a device might someday actually give me the power to stop the injustice, the hatred, the killing . . . That someday, if the science progressed, I might possibly have the power to help *remake* the world.

"And once I had this revelation, this *vision*, how could I put it down? Though fraught with risks, wouldn't it truly be immoral for me *not* to try to bring the vision to fruition? How could I ever go on with my life knowing that I could have prevented countless deaths, untold suffering? *'The time is out of joint, Oh Cursed Spite! That ever I was born to set it right.'*"

He looked her deeply in the eyes, then continued.

"And so I dedicated my life to developing the *microbot.* I told myself initially that I would develop the device first, and then figure out what — if anything — to do with it later. And then as my researched advanced, I came to the point where I knew the technology could work. Then I was trapped: I had to go forward. *I had no choice,*" he said sternly, the strength in his voice surprising her.

"And at last, through relentless toil and through progress in the technology at large, I finally came to a point where the technology was ready to deploy. At the same time, I felt age creeping up upon me, and I began to feel the urgency to act quickly."

At this point, Heather had to interrupt: "But why not give the technology to the government, let it use the technology?"

"Because very rare is the politician who would know how to apply the technology properly. If I had given the technology to the politicians, the odds were too high they'd screw it up. The power involved is awesome. The temptation to wield the power I have now would corrupt most men. Or others, who might not be corrupted, simply might not have the vision to use it to its fullest potential.

"Many would be tempted to shelve the power, to be used only if necessary as a defensive weapon. This is just what happened before 1949 when the U.S. had a monopoly on the atomic bomb. As cold as it sounds, the threatened use of the bomb might have prevented so many needless, innocent, tragic and senseless deaths in Russia, China and other countries around the world.

"So in the end, when I looked around — and believe me, I did look around — I was the only one that I felt I could trust with my technology. The only one I knew had the vision and integrity to use the power wisely and to its fullest."

"You would have used the atomic bomb on Russia if you were President back in nineteen forty-eight?"

"That's only an analogy. Let me put it this way. Let's say you had a magic wand, and by using it, you could wipe out all the hunger and suffering and injustice in the world. But mind you, using the wand would violate a few arcane laws against 'use of magic wands without a permit.' Would you use the wand? Or better put, why *wouldn't* you use the wand? How could you *not* use it? Wouldn't you be morally remiss if you *failed* to use the wand?"

She tilted her head, considering his argument and inviting him to continue.

"Now let's relax the analogy a bit. Instead of a magic wand, let's say it's a new technology we're discussing. Let's assume the use of the new technology is very safe, safer than a lot of other substances that are on the market and approved for use in the human body. But yes, there could be small unintended health consequences for some recipients of the technology. And of course, the technology is unpleasant, and could potentially be socially destabilizing if awareness of its use were widespread. But let's consider that its use can be kept secret and that those potential unintended health consequences are a very small price to pay in return for ending or dramatically reducing a far, far greater incidence of death, suffering and injustice on the planet. Not as palatable as using a magic wand, but wouldn't you still be morally remiss not to use that technology?"

She pondered his remarks.

"We can relax the analogy further, but at what point do we go from the weight of moral obligation shifting away from use of the wand in favor of not using it? Where is that magic line?" he asked earnestly.

"From where I stood, carefully considering all of the issues," he continued, "I strongly felt that I had reached a position whereby moral obligation *compelled* me to use the wand."

He was remarkably persuasive, but Heather remained unconvinced.

"OK, but even assuming I grant you there may be some moral legitimacy in what you're trying to achieve," she asked, "isn't it incredibly dangerous to concentrate such powerful technology into the hands of one man? All humans are fallible."

"All the more reason for me to use the technology to rid the world of weapons and armies, and then do away with the technology itself once the job is done."

"But what if you die before you reach your goal? You could drop dead from a heart attack tomorrow. Then what happens to me, and to all the others you've infected, and to the technology itself? What if your cure ends up becoming a scourge? The worst scourge the world has known?"

At this, Carpenter just smiled. But that was before she took his queen and forced a draw, and then his smile died away.

"The day is coming soon when I'll have you, Doc," she said, stroking her silky hair and thrusting her chest forward seductively.

"Not if I can help it," he said sullenly, as he put the chess pieces back into place.

CHAPTER 41

"You're sure it's him?" a dismayed Carpenter asked into the phone.

He turned to look in the mirror and noticed the dark bags under his eyes. He hadn't had a good night's sleep in days. On a personal level, his constant proximity to Heather was taking its toll. By now he ached for her whenever they were apart, and simply knowing that she was sleeping under the same roof caused in him a yearning and a restlessness that fed his insomnia. He often found himself pacing his room at night, thinking of her. Also feeding his sleeplessness, Lewis' work had hit some last minute snags. Not long ago, Carpenter's plans seemed to be coming together so well, but now the entire schedule appeared in jeopardy.

"Yessir. Positive," the Director replied.

"On what basis?"

"Sir, we gave all your scientists and all the cabinet officials polygraph tests. We also used sophisticated voice-stress and micro-expression analysis. Employed all of our latest cutting-edge techniques. Anyone who didn't pass these tests — and there were only three who didn't — we subjected to more strenuous methods."

"I don't want to know about that."

"Nothing too extreme."

"Go on, please."

"Well, he's the only one that didn't pass the tests. In the end, in fact, he confessed, and the confession appears authentic."

"How bad was the leak? Just that one letter to Maddox?"

"We still haven't been able to verify completely. Under a fair amount of duress, he admitted to writing the letter, but claimed he sent it only to a reporter at the New York Times with the instructions that the letter was to be made public on his death. I need to stress, we haven't been able to confirm anything yet.

"He says he doesn't know any Bill Maddox at the FBI, but our analysis suggests he's probably lying about some or most of the details he's given us, trying to cover up his tracks. We're still trying to refine the information, but he's been a fairly tough nut to crack."

"OK, bring him in. Oh, but first . . . "

"Yessir?"

"Anything more from Lewis yet?"

"No, Sir. Nothing. Since you said we still need his help, we haven't been able to really put him to the test yet. We're still waiting for your go-ahead."

"We're almost there. We've hit a last minute snag. Just a few more days. Once the system is ready, then I can let you take a stab at him."

"Yessir. Just say the word."

* * *

Five minutes later, hearing a knock on the door, Carpenter called, "Come in."

Through the door stepped the FBI Director followed by a bedraggled Zach in handcuffs, flanked on either side by two FBI agents.

"Zach," Carpenter began, "Zach, Zach, Zach," he repeated, shaking his head. "You, Zach. You, of all people. I can't tell you how disappointed I am."

"I could say the same about you, Doc," Zach responded defiantly.

"Now, why would you be disappointed? How can you possibly argue with what I'm trying to achieve? What *we're* trying to achieve?" he asked earnestly, but also with a hint of impatience wrought by the strain of his circumstances.

"You can't force salvation, Doc," Zach responded. "It's supposed to drop like rain from the gentle heavens. You don't ram it up people's noses."

Carpenter sighed.

"I don't have time to argue with you now. We're on a very tight schedule here, and I'm under a lot of stress. The election is in a week. Then, you recall, we have a lot of work to do to get our systems ready for the next stage, right after the inauguration. So we have less than twelve weeks to do a tremendous amount of final development work, testing, and meticulous planning," Carpenter explained, a testy edge to his voice.

"It didn't make my job any easier to have to launch this investigation into the leak you caused," he continued. "And because of this investigation, everyone on our team now knows that *you're* the leak. As I'm sure you can appreciate, all this leaves me in a tremendously awkward position."

Zach stared stonily at Carpenter.

"If I let you go," Carpenter continued, "I run the risk that discipline in our group will completely evaporate. Believe me, I wish there were another way. But unfortunately, you leave me no choice but to make an example out of you. A *stern* example," he added with menace.

At that, Zach's legs began to tremble.

CHAPTER 42

Maddox was decidedly not liking what he was witnessing, or to be precise *not witnessing*. Since coming to Washington, he had spent almost three weeks in the back of Vicente's van, and hadn't received any direct contact from Heather in over a week. Was she in trouble? If so, wouldn't she have affixed the warning sticker to the window by now? Was there a problem with the surveillance blimp he was using to check for messages from her? Time was ticking on, and the entire operation had come to a standstill. *How long would it be before Martin divulged Heather's name to the Director?*

And why no word from Heather?

Their surveillance routine was to park the van within three miles of the White House, let the blimp out through the sunroof on the van, and then watch the device fly itself. The blimp used pre-programmed GPS coordinates, with two foci defining the elliptical path to follow around the White House each night. Maintaining in memory the launch coordinates, it found its own way back to the van using a low-power homing beacon for the last hundred yards of flight. The beacon was so power-efficient that an electric toothbrush emitted more radio frequency radiation, and the blimp so stealthy that a seagull had a larger radar signature. In addition, it used advanced sound suppression technology on top of its already quiet electric motors, so if one were to hear it at all at four o'clock in the morning when it made its nightly journey, it sounded like nothing more than a very soft rush of wind.

Each morning, Maddox and Zim examined the camera's downloads, frame by frame. But despite all the effort, still no messages from Heather in almost two weeks.

Nearly at wit's end, and under the strain of an array of operational considerations, Maddox jumped when the phone rang. It was Xiaohong calling for Zim, and he used the pre-arranged code word. Zim was on the phone for several minutes. Each perfunctory "uh-huh" or nod of the head further piqued Maddox's curiosity as to the purpose of the call.

"Xiaohong and Moussavadi have been busy the past several weeks. Working round the clock," Zim explained after finishing the call. Maddox scrutinized Zim and didn't like what he saw. The bearded scientist had been working at all hours, collaborating long-distance with his colleagues in Livermore. He looked like a walking skeleton, with huge black rings around his puffy, bloodshot eyes. He hadn't washed or shaved in weeks.

"My colleagues have made good progress decoding the circuitry in the device we recovered from Heather's nose. For the sake of speed, I actually had to use back channels to send the IC to a Taiwanese-owned facility in mainland China that specializes in reverse-engineering semiconductor chips. I think within a week or so we should have it all figured out.

"Based on what we have so far, my impression is that the functionality is fairly limited. It's still too early to say for sure, but I'm guessing Carpenter may have rushed to go operational with a scaled-down version, figuring he could phase in improvements later as his team and budget grew. I'm not seeing a lot of the encoding, anti-jamming and security circuitry I would have expected. He probably figured he was racing against the clock, and wanted to save on time-to-market, power-budget, size and weight with this initial version."

That's the first good news we've had in a while, Maddox thought.

"So you think we've got a chance to disarm these things?"

"Too soon to conclude, but so far, I'm not seeing anything that suggests the presence of the doomsday feature you said was supposedly in the device. It's most certainly lethal, and will kill on Carpenter's command, but so far there's nothing to suggest the device will *automatically* kill if it doesn't receive its periodic refresh. Obviously we can't take any chances, but my take is that Carpenter may actually be bluffing about the supposed *automatic doomsday* functionality.

Bluffing? Maddox's ears perked up.

"We could be missing something of course. We'll know a lot more when we get independent verification from China in a week or so, but let's keep our fingers crossed.

Maddox crossed his fingers unconsciously.

"Some more good news," Zim continued, after he'd poured a coffee for Maddox. "Aside from developing the direct countermeasures to Carpenter's bot, our team has also been busy perfecting the technology on a few other devices which may prove enormously useful for you.

"I'm not sure if Dr. Lewis ever told you exactly what our lab was working on just before this business with Carpenter erupted."

Maddox shook his head.

"Obviously, this is highly classified," Zim said. Maddox nodded.

"We just completed a project around two months ago to create a network of self-propelled, micro-robotic listening devices. The devices can be linked by invisible infrared laser communication transceivers, similar to the remote control on a TV.

There is no detectable radio radiation, except in the line of sight. Aside from the tiny micro-circuitry the devices are all made of compound materials, with almost no metal parts. As such they can be very stealthy, quite difficult to detect unless someone conducts a very, very thorough bug sweep. The delivery devices are equipped with six wheels, and can handle difficult terrain.

"We call it the Snake," he explained. "On command, the individual vehicles self-assemble into a line, like a snake, and then decouple when prompted. When coupled into a snake that is long enough, they can climb up or down steps. They bend into an L-shape, and then the protruding portion collapses onto the upper step. The Snake can also use a disposable magnet to hitch a ride — to fix itself magnetically to the underside of a vehicle, for instance. Using this mechanism, it could potentially hitch a ride underneath a car right to the front door of the White House, and then it's just a short hop, skip and jump to deploy it inside the White House itself."

"Wow," Maddox exclaimed. "And . . . ?"

"Xiaohong was kind enough to get my cousin to FEDEX us our Snake prototype from Livermore. Vicente just needs to pick it up at the FEDEX office a few blocks from here."

* * *

"So here's the Snake," Zim said forty-five minutes later, as he opened the package that Vicente had retrieved from the FE-DEX office. Zim handed Maddox one of several small, white-colored, six-wheeled boxes contained in the package. The vehicle in Maddox's hand was around the size of a matchbox, but was much flatter than a matchbox, exhibiting the thickness only of a credit card. In the middle, a round, detachable object was seated. "That round thing is the listening device," Zim explained.

"The wheels can retract. They flip horizontally in line to give the vehicle an extremely flat profile. Here, watch." He pushed a wheel with his index finger and it flipped up, in line with the top of the body of the vehicle. He also flexed the vehicle. It was made of a very pliable plastic compound, and bent easily.

"If you link them in a line and hook up a posterior vehicle, you can retract the wheels and drive them straight under most doorjambs.

"The tiny wheeled vehicles transport the listening devices to the desired locations. Then, using a shaped charge, each vehicle launches its listening device onto the ceiling or wall. The listening devices are coated on top with a highly adhesive compound and will adhere firmly to the landing surface. They also have miniature cameras, and can relay not just audio but also low-quality visuals of the target area.

"Once the wheeled delivery vehicles have delivered the listening devices, the vehicles then serve as transceivers. They position themselves to link the listenting devices by line-of-sight infrared radiation. The wheeled vehicles have intelligence to hide in dark spots and take evasive action when they detect nearby movement. They slowly and silently move back into position when movement subsides and the audio field is clear. The wheeled delivery vehicles can also communicate with each other using very low-power, short-range radio communications. This way, even if they are they can't achieve line-of-sight linkages, such as if blocked by a doorway, they can still communicate with minimal chance of detection.

"Each vehicle is powered with a thin-film lithium-polymer battery, and the listening devices use high efficiency, miniature lithium-ion batteries. Under normal conditions, the network can run for up to two months. The system can record and buffer up to twenty-four hours of audio per channel or one hour of compressed video, and then burst download the data in as little as three minutes, depending on the range. There's even a special sleeper mode allowing it to turn on only when there is sound or movement in the field of surveillance. That way you don't waste bandwidth recording empty rooms."

"Impressive," Maddox said.

"I'm glad you think so. I'm hoping this little baby might help you get a better idea as to what's really going on over at 1600 Pennsylvania Avenue," Zim said, proudly holding the Snake up for Maddox to inspect.

Maddox breathed a sigh of relief.

"That sounds like just what I need right now. You're a flippin' genius, Zim," he responded, examining the equipment.

"Xiaohong sent us one more toy too."

"What's that?"

"It's a small radio-controlled plane about the size of a hummingbird. Actually, not really a plane, but rather an *ornithopter*. In fact, we call it the Hummingbird. It has wings that flap, just like a real hummingbird. You know the stealth blimp you're using to monitor the White House window communication?" Zim queried. Maddox nodded.

"Well you can use it to control and relay signals to and from the Hummingbird through line-of-sight laser. Basically, with a little practice we should be able to fly the Hummingbird into any open window within a two-and-half-mile radius.

"Maddox, I think we ought to get started right now. It's been ages since you've been outside. Let's drive over to a park and practice."

At a park by the Potomac, Maddox and Zim donned disguises, and in the fading late autumn twilight, practiced maneuvering the plane around and landing it in pre-specified target areas. When by accident Maddox rammed the Hummingbird at high speed into a tree trunk, the device was unharmed.

"Rugged piece of equipment," Maddox noted with satisfaction. Zim nodded.

"Now. One last item," Zim continued, "to pick up the signal from the Snake."

He opened his tote bag and handed Maddox what looked like a large video camera with a large telescopic lens, mounted on a tripod. It reminded Maddox of the kind of camera one would find in a movie studio. The farsighted Zim had brought the camera in a crate along with the other lab equipment when they drove cross-country in the van.

"To guide the Snake network into place and later to obtain the ongoing data feeds, someone's going to have to stand periodically in sight of the front lawn of the White House and use this device."

Maddox shook his head doubtfully. "With all the security at the White House, that's a big ask, especially since we're all wanted men."

"Well, I suggest you think of something. We don't have much time left."

Maddox pursed his lips.

"If it's any consolation," Zim continued, "the camera actually does take video. So if someone demands to inspect the device, you can demonstrate that it is a functioning video camera. You could say you're taking time-lapse footage of the White House for one project or another, like Michael Moore. I'll leave that to you to explain."

Maddox shook his head slowly, a feeling of trepidation brewing in his gut.

He sensed the mission hurtling to a climax, and knew the time was fast approaching when he would have to abandon his cover. The prospect did not sit well with him. As a Marine Recon sniper, Maddox knew it was his cover that had kept him alive on countless occasions. He also knew he would need more help soon, so later that evening he called Rando on Vicente's phone.

CHAPTER 43

Two days later, Randall Ricks touched down at Dulles International Airport. Vicente greeted him at arrivals, and then brought him to the van. In the back of the van, Maddox briefed Ricks during the ride to the Holiday Inn hotel on C Street, near the Capitol.

"You're lucky you get to stay in the hotel, Rando. Me, Vicente, and Zim have been camped out in the back of this van for a couple of weeks.

"Not that I'm complaining. Better than sleeping in the Nicaraguan jungle, dodging *fer-de-lance* snakes and *Sandinista* snipers," Maddox added. "Hooah!"

"Hooah!"

* * *

That night in the back of the van, as he was falling asleep, memories of Nicaragua troubled his consciousness. He remembered marching through the jungle, sweat stinging his eyes. He recalled shifting his sixty-pound pack on his back, the angry buzz of mosquitoes in his ear. He carefully checked his compass, took an azimuth with his sextant, then moved slowly towards the clearing in the dark green jungle. He looked at his watch.

"Almost there," he signaled to Caudillo with his fingers. It had been a three-day trek through the jungle.

They came to the edge of the trees and tangled overgrowth. The harsh glare of sunlight broke into the humid green light of the sanctuary.

Maddox fumbled for his sunglasses, the pack heavy on his back.

He peered out into the bright sunlight, and saw the village down a gentle slope in front of him, just where the map indicated it should be.

He and Caudillo knelt down slowly, gingerly removing their packs.

Caudillo scanned the village with his binoculars. He was looking for the mayor, a suspected *Sandinista* sympathizer. Maddox removed a drab olive case from his pack. He quietly unlatched the clip and removed the receiver of his military-issue M-40 A1 sniper rifle. He attached the barrel and the scope. He whispered to Caudillo for range and windage. Made the appropriate adjustments. Then the two placed foam mats on the ground, sank down quietly to lie prone, and scanned the village. And waited. And waited and waited.

Maddox checked his watch. Two hours had gone by. Not a hint of movement in the village. *Where are all the people?* He made a sign for Caudillo to radio to base. After a few moments, Caudillo indicated that Command had come back with orders to stay put. Keep watching. Keep waiting. *Keep waiting.*

By now, Maddox's clothes were soaked. The buzz of the mosquitoes was maddening. Two more hours gone by. No sign of anyone in the village. Strange. *Very strange. Something's not right.* Yet another two hours. No movement. No sign of life at all. It was late afternoon and the sun was starting to move behind the tall mountains on the right. Another call to base. *Stay put. Make camp overnight if necessary.*

They monitored the village at night. No lights on. No sign of movement. "This place is abandoned," Maddox whispered to Caudillo. Caudillo nodded.

Up at dawn the next morning, they scanned the scene again. Nothing. Placed another call to base. Abandon mission, return to base immediately, came the instructions. *Abandon mission?* "What's going on?" Caudillo asked. Maddox shrugged.

"Let's go check out the village," Caudillo whispered.

"You heard the orders. 'Return to base immediately,'" Maddox retorted.

"*Chingada* 'orders'! I want to know what happened down there."

"Might be booby-trapped," Maddox warned.

"Screw it, *pendejo*. I want to know what happened in the village."

The next thing Maddox knew, he was hustling after Caudillo, running down the slope into the village.

What he never forgot were the flies. The stench was bad, but it was the flies that left the most indelible impression. It wasn't so much the loud sound the flies made, like a leaf-blower three houses down, but just the mere sight of the flies. *Why do they always congregate around the eyes?* Around the eyes of two small children, hugging. Around the eyes of an old lady. *Probably their grandmother.* Around the eyes of two old men in front of a tin-roof bar, broken beer bottles still in their hands. And pools of brown blood, caked into the dirt. Pools of brown blood everywhere, covered with flies. Flies everywhere.

"Looks like the Contra death squads got here before we did," Caudillo whispered.

* * *

Maddox stirred from his half-sleep. The unsettled feeling in his stomach was still with him, the same feeling he had twenty years earlier when he was scanning the Nicaraguan village. *Something doesn't feel right. Time is ticking down, and I have no idea what's going on in the White House. But whatever it is, it can't be good.* The waiting was taking its toll.

Ten minutes later, he sent one of his six Hummingbirds into Heather's room. Attached to it was a note requesting an update, and a confirmation that everything was OK. The next morning, he waited anxiously for the readout of her window message response to the Hummingbird. It was dismayingly terse.

Everything OK, but progress difficult. Have not gleaned useful information. Not sure how to proceed, but will keep trying.

Maddox's insides churned with frustration. Above all, he chided himself for wishing from Heather at least a small show of tenderness. *Were you hoping she'd sign it 'Love, Heather,' you fool?* he asked himself. Her terseness concerned him. Was she in danger? And then the nagging, sickening doubt. *Had she somehow fallen in with Carpenter?* And as Maddox weighed the odds, the tension inside his gut mounted. *No final word yet from China on the microbot circuitry. No indication of progress from Heather. And the clock is ticking away.*

He felt the weight of inertia creep into the operation. *The art of running a stakeout is the art of weighing patience against inertia*, he could hear his instructor at Quantico say as if it were yesterday. Running a stakeout is all about waiting patiently. Waiting for an opportunity. Waiting for the appearance of weakness in your target's defenses. *But patient waiting can also be your single biggest enemy*, he recalled the instructor saying. Before long, inertia sets in. *Without an immediate pressing need for action, the tendency is to do nothing. Meanwhile, your case slips away. On a stakeout, you will often find the need to fight inertia. To create an opportunity, not wait for one. That is the true art of the stakeout.*

It's now or never, Maddox told himself. *If I sit back and do nothing, then maybe the world as we know it ends in a whimper. But, on the other hand, if I take the offensive, there's likely to be a pretty big bang . . .* He let out a large sigh. *I guess it's better to go out with a bang than a whimper.*

Maddox sensed with increasing dread the impending arrival of the moment he would finally have to abandon his cover. Unconsciously, he rubbed his thigh. Leaving the cover of a clump of bushes for the space of five seconds had cost him the injury to his leg in Nicaragua. But as he saw it now, he simply couldn't wait patiently any longer. And he knew there were two ways forward, both of which would require him to come out into the open.

* * *

"Let's go over this one more time. If — and it's a big *if* — if we're able to insert the Snake in the White House, we need to assume we will have maybe a day or two if we're lucky before someone discovers the White House has been bugged. Also, in the process of inserting the Snake, chances are high that Rando will blow his cover when he's sitting with the time-lapse camera in Lafayette Park, filming the front porch of the White House. Blow his cover *wide* off."

Ricks was supposed to be on vacation. He had still not been linked to Maddox, but the potential danger of his connection was a big concern to Maddox. Ricks was now Maddox's only meaningful resource within the Bureau.

Zim nodded thoughtfully. "I'll do my best to make sure the technology is working," was all he could offer. "The rest is up to you guys."

* * *

And so, there they were at ten at night in the back of the van, and Zim was using the Hummingbird to fly a five-foot-long Snake through the one-foot gap in Heather's window. The Snake played hell with the aerodynamics of the Hummingbird, but in the end, Zim managed to make it through the window. Using the monitor in the van, it took Zim five hours to maneuver into the proper locations throughout the White House each of the twenty individual vehicles that constituted the Snake.

"How do we get the terminal vehicle out of the White House," Maddox asked, the glare of the Hummingbird readout monitor shining in his eyes, "so that we can pick up all the communication signals from the Snake?"

"We don't," Zim replied, "get it out of the house. It stays inside, near the front door. We're also going to position a vehicle *outside* the front door, hidden in the shrubbery. The vehicle in the shrubbery will use a short-range radio link to pull the surveillance data from the network inside the White House, and then on command, it will temporarily leave the cover of the bushes to shoot the data to us. We'll be sitting in Lafayette Park, and Randall's FBI badge will come in very handy during each fifteen- minute window when he needs to 'film' the White House to retrieve the data."

* * *

Ricks scanned Lafayette Park. It was a bright, late fall morning. Birds were chirping. A light breeze was in the air. *And there are two cops over there.* Ricks gulped, before positioning the camera with a clear view of the White House. He began to film, and glanced over at the two policemen. The African-American was tall and fit, with enormous biceps. The Anglo sported a pot belly that bulged under his police shirt.

"Roll 'em," Ricks said to Vicente, as he began to film.

After a few minutes, the cops began to stroll in Ricks' direction. *Don't hassle me now!* Ricks thought.

A moment later, the cops were a few paces away.

"Hi there!" the portly cop said loudly, a false smile on his face. Police training dictated that to assert authority, any police officer arriving on scene was best served by using a decibel level significantly louder than that required to be audible.

"Hello, Officer," Ricks replied.

"You gentlemen may not be aware that it is unlawful to film the White House from here, not without a special permit."

"Sorry, it's OK ,Officer. I'm FBI," Ricks said. *There. Now I've blown my cover. This better not get me shot.*

"FBI?" the cop asked. "You have some identification I can see?"

Ricks produced his badge and ID. The cop eyed the identification suspiciously.

"You're a long way from Los Angeles, Special Agent Ricks. I'm going to have to run the badge. You don't mind, do you?"

"Not at all," Ricks said as nonchalantly as possible, cursing to himself.

As the portly cop called in Ricks' badge number, the large cop nodded in Vicente's direction. "He FBI too?"

"No. He's civilian. Technical expert. Helping me out. He's under my direction."

"You don't mind if I see some ID?" the tall cop said to Vicente. Ricks nodded to Vicente.

Vicente produced his driver's license. The cop jotted Vicente's name and license number down on a notepad.

"OK. Looks like you're clear, Special Agent Ricks," the portly cop said a moment later after finishing his call. "I'm not even gonna ask what it is you boys are up to."

"Nothing interesting. Pretty boring, routine stuff," Ricks said as cavalierly as possible.

"Well, take care then. It's always the boring, routine stuff that ends up killing you," the cop said, as he and his partner walked off.

* * *

Back in the van with Zim and Vicente, Maddox ran the speed at two times fast-forward on the feed, and took in the audio and video from the White House room by room. The receivers had cut out all the dead spots, so a full day's worth of recording in eleven different rooms and areas of the White House was condensed down to three hours of replay at two-times speed. Maddox divided the feed among himself, Zim and Vicente. Maddox took all the feed from the rooms Heather was in. Zim took the feed from Carpenter and Dr. Lewis. Vicente took everything else.

"I don't know exactly what to tell you to look for," Maddox said to Zim and Vicente. "Look and listen for anything unusual. Any hint of plans or methods. People or places. Take notes highlighting anything that strikes you as important. We'll regroup in an hour."

When they regrouped, Zim noticed Maddox looked wan. Maddox had watched Heather and Carpenter play chess. Listened carefully to their conversation. He was struck by the degree to which the chemistry between the two seemed to have progressed. At one point in the game, Carpenter had played gently with a loose strand of her hair. She'd taken his hand and kissed it gently. Maddox had run their conversation through a voice analyzer package, and he didn't like the result. The analysis indicated the chemistry was genuine.

"So whaddaya got?" Maddox asked the others.

Vicente shrugged.

Maddox looked at Zim.

"I've only got one thing," Zim said.

Maddox held his breath.

"But that one thing is a *doozy*," Zim continued.

"So what is it?" Maddox asked, perking up.

"Listen to this," Zim said, then pressed play on his monitor. "I think I know what they are up to. It sounds as though Davos and the upcoming G20 meeting are their next targets."

Maddox blanched, sizing up the information. *If they manage to infect all the political, military and business leaders at Davos and the G20, they really* will *control the entire world.*

Maddox listened to the feed.

"Bernie, look, I've decided," he could hear Carpenter saying. "Davos is just around the corner. You've made fantastic progress on a limited scale and everything seems to work well so far for the mid-range solution, but we both know there are bound to be some last-minute hiccups when the global satellite system goes live. We need more time for tests, and I'm just not completely convinced the global network is going to be fully ready for deployment in time. The advance delegations will start showing up in a matter of weeks.

"But even if we can't get the global network fully on-line in time, I still want to zap as many people as possible. We can turn on the extended network later once we're sure it's ready for full operational deployment. In the meantime, the *bots* will lay dormant in the targets until the network is in place."

"But Maury, I have to disagree. That's too risky," Lewis shot back. "These things show up as only a tiny speck in an X-ray, but they do show up. What if somehow people start discovering the devices? If they're *uninitiated* and out of range of the network, they're out of our control. They will go public and word will leak. All hell will break loose. We *have* to stick to our initial premise. No zapping without *full initiation* and *full coverage*."

"I hear you, Bernie, but we've got Generals there," Carpenter retorted. "We've got Secretaries of Defense, Secretaries of State, of Commerce. We'll have to wait another year for our next chance to get so many prime targets together at once. As we've discussed, the *big* opportunity is the G20 in Japan. How are we going to run operations in Japan without a good contingent of senior allies on the ground in Japan in advance? That means zapping people at Davos first, especially the Japanese contingent.

"Now that we're on the verge of extending our range of coverage, we've *got* to zap now quietly, and take our chances that we won't be discovered. Then we wait for the satellite coverage to be ready later."

Maddox sat stunned. *Davos. G20. It's hard enough for me to try to stop them in Washington. Forget Switzerland and Japan!* The reality hit home that he would have to act soon, or else lose any chance of stopping Carpenter. *But how to get them?* Indications were that some of Carpenter's team could be leaving for Davos in days.

Try as he might to focus on Davos, though, Maddox's thoughts kept straying back to Heather. *I'm losing her*, he admitted to himself as he gritted his teeth in helpless frustration.

He played the next recording over one more time. The tape showed Heather and Carpenter in the Blue Room, playing chess, engaged in conversation. Listening to her tone of voice, almost coquettish, he knew he should be pleased she had progressed well in her intimacy with Carpenter; but he also struggled with his feelings about her apparent progress. He wasn't sure whether her developing relationship with Carpenter satisfied or saddened him.

"You may think you've won me over to your cause, and maybe to a point you have, but there's one last thing Doc. If you really want me as your disciple, you still need to do more to convince me," Heather said in a teasing voice. "Convince me about *you*, the *man*. We've had countless conversations, chess games, musical interludes . . . but I still don't feel I really *know* you," she said seductively, fondling the top button on her blouse.

"Know me? What's to know?"

"Know you . . . " she whispered seductively, "perhaps, as in *biblically*."

Maddox couldn't believe what he was hearing. He squinted at the screen. *Is she acting, or does she mean it?* She was giving Carpenter a long, penetrating stare. Carpenter appeared to gulp, and then paused before answering. Maddox felt a stiffness in his own loins as he continued watching the tape. *Whose agent is she, mine or his?* Maddox wondered.

"Heather, you're a phenomenally attractive and desirable woman. Any man would be crazy not to want to take you. But in the end, I'm not just any man."

"But I know that. That's why I want *you* . . . want to know you better. Body and soul."

"But that's what I don't get, Heather. I have to be one of the least attractive men you've ever met."

"Don't sell yourself short, Doc. Besides, just what do you think it is about you that attracts me? '*Est is Der Geist Der Sich Den Koerper Baut*,'" she whispered.

"Ah, yes. '*It is the spirit itself which makes the body.*' Schiller?"

"Precisely."

Carpenter looked at her for a long time, then spoke softly, "Heather, Heather, Heather, don't do this to me."

Maddox felt nauseated. *I'm losing her. Is she trying to seduce him for the mission's sake? Or is she genuinely falling for him. No one could be that good an actress. Of all the things that could go wrong. Not now! Not her!*

For good measure, he ran the conversation through his voice analyzer software. The software was used as a lie detection measure. For an unaware subject, the accuracy was surprisingly high, with more than an eighty-seven percent likelihood of detecting falsehood or insincerity communicated by the subject. The test showed no indication of falseness or insincerity. *No one could be that good an actress.*

* * *

The two calls came through in rapid succession and cut through Maddox's torpor like armor-piercing rounds through a tank skin. The first was for Zim from China via a heavily encoded voice-over-IP protocol to inform the final findings regarding the remaining key features of the *microbot* circuitry. It was all good news.

Zim summed up the call for Maddox. "The main finding from China is there is no indication of any circuitry that would provide a *doomsday* feature in the event of failure to refresh the maintenance code. In other words," as Zim explained in plain English, "if Carpenter pressed the button on his control, the device could certainly kill the subject. If Carpenter were to die, however, only the headache mechanism would trigger, and there was nothing in hardware, software, or firmware to suggest any *lethal* sequence would ensue."

"How sure are you of that?" Maddox asked.

"Pretty darn sure. Nothing's ever one hundred percent, so I'd say at least ninety-eight or ninety-nine percent for sure."

Maddox gulped. *Ninety-eight percent is good, but still not good enough considering how many innocent lives could be at stake.*

Whatever fleeting sense of relief Maddox took from this first call was quickly shattered, however, when Ricks received a call on his cellphone. Maddox knew there was trouble as soon as he looked down and saw the number from which the call had originated. It was from the FBI Los Angeles office. Maddox had been dreading this call since the mission began.

"*For the love of Pete,* you mind telling me what's going on, Ricks?" Martin said, an even sharper edge than normal in his voice. Ricks could not recall ever hearing Martin use profanity: this was the closest he'd ever come.

"How so, Chief?" Ricks replied, as ingenuously as possible.

"Don't play games with me, Ricks. I just received a call from the *flipping Director* himself. He wants to know why in Heaven's name a Los Angeles-based FBI agent, supposedly on vacation, is in Washington D.C. conducting surveillance on the White House, without telling anyone including his direct superior or anyone in the Washington office."

"I'll explain later, Chief," Ricks said as he hung up, turned off his cellphone, and dumped the batteries. He knew without a doubt the call was being traced and his location pinpointed. He and Maddox looked at each other; they knew the moment of truth was at hand.

So it begins in earnest, Maddox thought with trepidation. *We've lost our cover for good.*

CHAPTER 44

"Ladies and Gentlemen, as most of you are aware by now, we have a traitor in our midst," Carpenter began, looking over all the true believers he had gathered in the main ballroom of the White House. He then pointed at Zach, seated at the opposite end of the table. Zach was flanked by the same two FBI agents who, after uncovering Zach's betrayal, had accompanied him to Carpenter's office. Carpenter directed significant looks at the President, the FBI Director, and then at Heather, but he averted his eyes quickly after she returned his stare. The concern and disapproval evident on her face troubled him greatly, but he reminded himself of the need to appear stoic and implacable as he faced the throng.

"As much as it pains me to pronounce sentence, there can only be one punishment for treason, for anyone who stands in the way of our cause." All eyes turned from Carpenter to Zach. The tension in the room was palpable.

He slowly and deliberately withdrew his remote control device from his jacket pocket, held it up for all to see, and then pressed a button. All eyes shot over to Zach. Zach immediately bent over in severe pain, then dropped to the floor. For interminable seconds he writhed to and fro in a seizure, and then lay still at last. On the FBI Director's behest, one of the two FBI agents guarding Zach bent down, took his pulse and then after a moment pronounced, "He's dead, Sir."

"Remove the body," Carpenter ordered, and the agents efficiently zipped Zach's lifeless corpse into a body bag pre-arranged for the occasion.

"Let that be a lesson to us all," Carpenter pronounced. "Lest any of us forget, may I remind everyone what the Bible tells us: '*the wages of sin is Death,*' he said for final emphasis, scanning the room.

"That will be all," he commanded. "Everyone back to work, now! We don't have any time to waste."

He strode out of the room.

* * *

Maddox watched with horror all of the proceedings on his monitor — watched Zach fall to the floor like a sack of potatoes. *We have to stop this madman, now!*

CHAPTER 45

We don't have much time — the FBI is onto us. It's now or never. D-Day in two days. The Marine in Maddox now took over.

That evening at five, just around dusk, Maddox sent a message to Heather via Hummingbird. He didn't want to over-dramatize, but he needed every possible measure of cooperation from her. She was his agent, and distant as she was, he needed to motivate her to the maximum extent possible.

"Require from you firsthand confirmation that *microbot* possesses no doomsday function. Must use all means available to obtain direct confirmation from Carpenter. Heather — I need all your commitment and talent in this endeavor. Without exaggeration, fate of entire world rests on your shoulders."

* * *

Maddox watched the monitor carefully. Carpenter and Heather were seated at dinner in the Green Room. The table was elegantly set.

"He's not dead?" she asked incredulously.

"If I didn't make an example of him, I would have lost all my authority. So I had him and the FBI agents play their parts,

302

sworn to secrecy on pain of death — and if ever they did let out that it was all a sham, I really would've killed them, gladly.

"Now that I've told you, Heather," he said locking eyes with her, "you're in my circle of trust."

Heather listened, still stunned.

"You're saying the episode with Zach was only a ruse?" she asked again, to make sure she understood. "You had me worried. When you pressed that button, I was shaken to the core. I nearly lost all faith in you."

"No, it was all play-acting. He's locked in a room in the basement of the White House."

"In that case, Doc, your secret is safe with me, and I'm all yours."

* * *

"Today's a special day," Heather was saying a few minutes later, taking a sip from her glass of white wine.

"And just how is today different from any other day?" Carpenter asked.

"It's my birthday."

"Your birthday? Really? I'll need to check the records."

"Actually, my birthday is in a week, but I want to celebrate it early. I know you're going to be busy wherever it is we're going in a day or two, so I thought it would be nicer to celebrate my birthday tonight," she said with a playful pout. *Nice range of emotion*, Maddox thought as he watched the scene. "And I'm expecting a very special gift," she said as she rose from her seat and walked over to Carpenter.

"And just what gift would you like on your birthday?"

"Something very, very wonderful," she said softly as she approached his chair from behind.

"And what's that?"

303

She stood behind his chair and put her hands tenderly on his shoulders, massaging him lightly, then kissed him softly on the crown of his bald head.

"You," she whispered seductively.

Maddox's eyes were fixed on the screen.

After a moment Carpenter spoke. "You know that's the one gift — as much as I wish otherwise — that I just can't give you Heather. I can give you most of me, but as I've told you, just not *everything*. Definitely not *now*. Not before the mission is complete."

Yours is a beauty truly too rich for use.

"Well I want everything, and I'll settle for nothing less," she said, pouting. "This isn't about my mother, is it?"

"Of course not."

Carpenter paused for a moment to think, then continued. "Actually, I have just the gift for you," he said.

"And what's that?"

"After dinner I want you to undress."

"But I thought you said . . . "

"I know what I just said . . . I'm going to paint you. A splendid watercolor."

* * *

Maddox watched Heather in the monitor, her naked form, round breasts, amply curved hips, flowing hair, and wished more than anything that he could trade places with Carpenter just for five minutes. He felt a burning in his loins, and anger and amazement, and relief too, that Carpenter could not be moved by Heather's beauty. *What a waste. The guy must be gay, or must have had his nuts removed.*

But just as Maddox was thinking this, he noticed in Carpenter's groin a protrusion. *The old goat's definitely got a hard-on.* A moment later Heather saw it too. She slowly rose and, without saying a word, noiselessly walked over to Carpenter. She put a soft hand on his right cheek and caressed it gently, He took her hand, as a father might take a child's, and kissed it softly. Maddox's stomach cringed to see the growing intimacy. He felt helpless watching the scene play out before his eyes.

He knew he should feel happy that Heather was finally landing her target. But he felt actual physical pain to think that Heather might not be acting. Her performance appeared too natural, too unforced, and Maddox was now thoroughly convinced that she had fallen for Carpenter. Jealousy overwhelmed him.

The next thing Maddox knew, Heather was leading Carpenter to the bedroom. By now, Maddox was nearly nauseated with jealousy and by the feeling of helplessness that he could not prevent what he was sure would ensue. Maddox switched the monitor over to the bedroom and saw the two sitting on the edge of the bed.

Maddox adjusted the knobs on his monitor to pick up more clearly the hushed conversation between Heather and Carpenter. After a moment, Maddox heard a quiet sobbing, and saw that it was Carpenter crying softly.

"Don't cry, Doc. Why are you so sad?"

"I'm not sad. These are tears of joy, but also of fear. I feel that in some way I've betrayed myself and forsaken my mission."

"You haven't betrayed anything, least of all yourself. And don't worry. I would never betray you. Never harm you. I love you, Doc. I love you more than I've ever loved anything or anyone before. I believe in you. I believe in what you're doing. I understand how difficult all of this is for you."

"I love you too," Carpenter replied in hushed tones, feeling her cheek with his palm, and kissing her forehead softly.

"But there's just one thing, Doc," Heather added. "I want to give myself to you utterly and completely; but how can I do this knowing I'm still your *slave*? That I'm still under your direct control? That I'm infected with your *microbot*? I need you to make me believe in you completely, please!"

At least she's trying to get the intel out of him! Maddox remarked with satisfaction. *Maybe she's still my agent after all,* he allowed himself to believe for an instant. *And she doesn't even know she's being recorded.*

"How can you know that I truly love *you* if I don't have my freedom?" she continued. "How can I truly love a man who would doom innocents to their death? Doom so many to death upon his own death? What if you die suddenly of a heart attack? They will die too? What will happen to all the innocent people you've infected?"

"Judge not lest ye be judged," he responded.

"*Pardon? My* conscience is completely clear, Doc. Is *yours?*"

"If that's your concern, then you don't have to worry," Carpenter softly replied at last, with a sigh.

"How so?" she asked.

"Heather, Heather, Heather. I've said enough. Knowing me as you do, do you really think I'm capable of hurting innocents?"

"So the doomsday feature of the microbots: that was just a bluff?" she asked. "Anything you say is safe with me, Doc. You know I would never hurt you."

"I've said enough. It's better for both of us that I say no more," he added sternly.

Maddox couldn't believe what he was hearing.

She nodded. "I promise by all that is holy to keep what you say secret."

Carpenter remained silent.

"So let me be sure I have this straight," she pressed him, trying to put words into his mouth. "The *bots* are lethal if you push the button, but they don't automatically kill their hosts if you die?"

Heather waited for his response, but none came.

"Heather, you're persistent just like your mother. But please, for everyone's sake, don't ask me any further. I've already said more than I should."

Maddox could feel his own heart stop briefly. *He's toast!* he thought to himself. *He's all but confirmed there's no doomsday function.* And though his sense of elation was mixed with a twinge of sorrow and even pity for Carpenter, he felt in his gut only a steely determination. *I'm going to take the bastard down.*

* * *

Maddox endured a restless night in the back of the van. He awaited impatiently the next message from Heather, which would confirm the important news she had extracted from Carpenter regarding the almost certain absence of the doomsday feature. It was the key piece of *intel* that had become the main focus of her mission.

Dawn was just starting to break, and it was still dark outside when Maddox got up, aching with exhaustion. Zim was still sleeping. Maddox made himself a cup of instant coffee, then went over to the monitors. Nothing new.

* * *

Maddox rapidly prepared and launched the stealth blimp. His heart pounded in expectation of the message he would hopefully find on Heather's window, to confirm the intelligence he'd gained overnight via video. A few minutes later, when he'd maneuvered the blimp into position, his heart sank. She had only left a brief message on the window: "Leaving soon for extended trip. Will travel with Carpenter and crew right after election. Will try to keep you posted."

Maddox's head began to swim. *I've lost her. I've definitely lost my agent. She's gone over to Carpenter, and now she's protecting him. She didn't know we were listening, and she completely failed to mention the probable absence of the doomsday feature. She's been turned. Heather is the enemy now.*

CHAPTER 46

"You wanted to see me, Sir?" FBI Director Hutchison asked after entering Carpenter's office.

"Yes, Mr. Hutchison," Carpenter replied. "I wanted to be the first to deliver the good news: our development work is now complete and will be ready for full operational deployment in just around two weeks. Dr. Lewis is therefore no longer essential to the mission, and as such, you and your colleagues are now free — and even encouraged — to interrogate him vigorously. It's probably nothing — just a minor detail by now, given how far along our capabilities are — but just for safety's sake, we need to know how, if at all, that Maddox character is planning to stop us. We need to know in particular whether any others are working with him. Please also keep an extra close eye on Doctor Anderson."

"Yessir. Leave that to us. We'll have a word with Dr. Lewis and his wife right away."

* * *

"Sir, we've really put the screws on Lewis, and on his wife," Hutchison reported back a few hours later. "He's not budging an inch. He's given us nothing. He's under tremendous stress, and I would say he's quite unstable right now.

"If you want us to continue we're going to have to ratchet up our tactics further. It won't be pretty, and there could be side effects. But first I thought you should know, he's requesting a word with you in private."

* * *

Carpenter entered the basement room. Lewis was tied to a chair, covered in sweat. He looked ashen and spent. There was a stench of urine and vomit in the room, though none was apparent to the eye.

"I'm really sorry about this, Bernie. Believe me, I wouldn't be doing this if I had any other choice," Carpenter said apologetically.

"You may know, I've been spending a lot of time with Dr. Anderson. In a moment of weakness, I probably told her a bit more than I should have. As a result, I'm extra antsy, Bernie. So I need to know about your plan with Maddox. Just tell me now and no one gets hurt. We can all be friends. I'll treat Maddox well."

"Maury, I want you to know," Lewis said after a moment, his voice weak. "I truly believed in you. In your plan. I wanted you to succeed. Wanted *us* to succeed.

"But at the same time, as strange and contradictory as it sounds, I still wanted you to fail, *us* to fail. I was on the fence, torn. I have been all along."

"No one ever became a hero riding a fence," Carpenter responded. "As much as we'd like to stay on the fence, there are times in life when fate forces us to choose our horse and ride it."

"I never wanted to be a hero, Maury. Just to do what's right. Initially I liked what you were trying to achieve. Even if what you were doing constituted a form of enslavement, at least I took some perverse pleasure in the fact that you were enslaving from the top down," he said, with partial sarcasm. "Throughout history," he explained with irony, "enslavement has usually occurred from the bottom up."

"Then all the more reason you should help me."

"But that's just it Maury. I agree that your goals are noble, but your means are completely wrong.

"Can't you see that nothing good will come of planting *microbots* in people's noses? We rely on Technology to improve our lot, but then in the end, slowly, imperceptibly, we surrender all our freedom to Technology. In the final analysis, I fear we will all become completely enslaved by our dependence on technology.

"You may think you've hit upon a good idea, Maury, but as the poet said, *'between the idea and the reality falls the shadow.'* And then when you executed Zach in cold blood, I saw the shadow in true clarity . . . "

"Never mind ideas and shadows, Bernie. I need information *now*. I need you to tell me about Maddox, NOW," Carpenter said angrily, "or else you're next. Or better still, Danielle."

Lewis glared at Carpenter with deep loathing. For several moments, he seethed with rage before he suddenly slumped in his seat, defeated.

"Okay, Maury, you win. Just leave Danielle alone," Lewis pleaded, his voice exhausted.

"But please, can't you untie me? These ropes are burning my wrists. I'm an old man, Maury. You've got nothing to fear from me, especially not with two FBI agents over there guarding you," he said, nodding in the direction of two agents in dark suits and sunglasses.

"Untie him," Carpenter instructed one of the agents.

No sooner had the agent untied Lewis, than Lewis lunged forward. He groped for the agent's gun, holstered under the agent's armpit. "You leave Danielle alone, you sonofabitch!" Lewis yelled at Carpenter as he wrestled with the agent.

Before Carpenter had time to react, the second agent emerged from behind and quickly placed Lewis into a stranglehold. Lewis writhed in his arms, choking, then a minute later his body suddenly went limp. After a pause, the agent eased his hold and Lewis fell to the ground. The agent bent down to check Lewis' pulse.

"We need medical attention quick!" the agent yelled into his walkie-talkie. "He might be gone," he said, looking at Carpenter.

"No! Bernie!" Carpenter yelled, tears starting to flow as he gathered Lewis' limp body in his arms. *No one was supposed to be harmed!*

CHAPTER 47

Maddox fingered his dog tag and pondered his next move. He was weighing his options, and he didn't like the odds. Losing Heather was a heavy burden to bear, all the more so because the loss came at both the personal and professional level. He had the same feeling he'd get when he was sailing his catamaran and the wind suddenly died, leaving him stuck dead in the water. He felt adrift, without direction or momentum, and despaired of the hollowness inside him. Pushing aside his melancholy, the pressure to act drove him forward.

Zim could tell that Maddox didn't want to be disturbed, and he gave him a wide berth. Maddox sat in the corner of the van, rubbing the bridge of his nose, interrupted occasionally by a shake of the head, or the expulsion of a sigh. Finally, he gathered himself together, arose listlessly, and collected the blimp as it landed on the sunroof. He then asked Vicente to proceed to the airport to retrieve his cousin, Maddox's long-time informant Rodriguez, who at Maddox's urgent request was just now flying in from Los Angeles and was scheduled to arrive in a little over an hour.

* * *

Zim was watching the monitors. With growing horror, his attention zoomed in on the scene that was playing out with Lewis in the interrogation room. "Bill, come quick, look at this!" he managed in a strangled voice.

"That's Dr. Lewis," Maddox exclaimed, as he watched Lewis lunge at the FBI agent, watched as the agent placed Lewis in a chokehold, and then watched Lewis' limp body fall to the floor.

Maddox played and replayed the scene.

"I heard Carpenter say he only staged the death of his assistant Zach, the other day. But this. This here doesn't look staged. Besides, there's no reason for them to stage it, because there's no audience on hand to stage it *for*," Maddox reasoned out loud.

"You've got to stop him now," Zim demanded, "before he hurts someone else."

* * *

Visibly grieving, Zim managed to continue to monitor events on the screens. Then a half hour later, the screens suddenly went blank, one by one. Zim checked the settings, but nothing could restore the audio or video feeds. He nudged Maddox.

"Look here. No feed." Zim checked the settings again. "They must have discovered the devices. Our eyes and ears are gone," he informed Maddox.

Maddox steeled his gut. *There's only one way to solve this now.*

* * *

Maddox, Ricks, Zim, Rodriguez and Vicente sat huddled on the floor of the van. Maddox was nearly done explaining to his team the predicament facing them.

"So, it boils down to this," he told them. "I'm completely certain that we, the five of us here, are all that stands between the world as we know it and a new age of mechanical enslavement. Just before the monitors went blank, I personally saw one of Carpenter's men choke Dr. Lewis — just dropped him in cold blood. On top of this, we've lost our eyes and ears at the White House. Worse still, our agent on the inside must now be deemed unreliable.

"The election is in two days, and immediately after the election we believe a large part of the team, including possibly Carpenter and the President, will go to Switzerland. They will go ostensibly for a ski vacation. But we think the real motive is to begin to prepare for a mass infection at the upcoming Davos conference, at which almost all the world's political and economic leaders will be in attendance. So at best, we have around twenty-four to thirty-six hours to complete our mission. If we fail, if they succeed at Davos and then at the upcoming G20 meeting in Japan, Carpenter will have the entire world tightly in his grip, *literally*. So, Gentlemen, it's no exaggeration to say it's now or never.

"I've made some preparations, but most importantly, Zim, I need you to rig up a few of these toys here," he pointed to the Hummingbirds and blimp, "with some of these M-80s, road flares and smoke bombs I've got."

"When we move in, someone will need to escort the President to safety and someone will need to take out Carpenter. Shall we draw lots?"

"That's OK, Dawg" Ricks said. "It's your mission. You pick."

* * *

The sun was high in the clear, blue sky. A flight of gulls circled high above. A black Crown Victoria pulled up at the main gate of the White House. Two guards were in position in the guardhouse, and one had his finger on the trigger of his M-16 assault rifle. Rodriguez was at the wheel of the car, Maddox in the passenger's seat, and Ricks was in the back seat. Before arriving at the gate, Maddox stuffed a cotton ball in each nostril. At the gate, Ricks flashed a badge at the guards and exited the car. The guard pointed his rifle at Ricks and ordered him to stop. Ricks slowly produced a document from his breast pocket.

"I'm an FBI agent and I have a warrant here for the arrest of the President's personal secretary, Mandy Garcia, on charges of trafficking narcotics."

He had forged the arrest warrant several days earlier.

"Whoa! Hold it right there! Step over to the side: I'm gonna need to call this in, and also run your badge. This will take some time, so you just make yourself comfortable over there where I can see you by the side of the guardhouse," the guard said, keeping his weapon trained on Ricks.

On cue, Ricks signaled to Maddox, who lowered his window, and fired a dart gun at the armed guard. The dart hit the guard squarely in the neck, and he fell to the ground instantly. The second guard rushed to train his weapon on the vehicle but before he could procure his mark, Ricks had already withdrawn his service revolver and had it trained on the guard. He quickly disarmed the guard, handcuffed him, and bound his legs with duct tape. He then used Vicente's cellphone to call Zim. "Clear to proceed."

A few moments later, a Hummingbird came whizzing out of the sky and crashed with a loud bang through a window in the front of the White House. A split second later, a burst of what sounded like gunfire erupted from within the White House. It was a string of M80s — the payload that the Hummingbird was carrying. Guards scrambled from around the White House to assess the danger. A few seconds later, a second Hummingbird came crashing into the wall on the left wing of the White House. Attached to the Hummingbird was a smoke bomb, billowing gray smoke. A third Hummingbird with a red flare alight crashed through another window on the second floor of the White House.

By now, Marine guards were running in every direction, scrambling to take up position on the front porch to the left side of the White House.

Smoke poured out of the second story window where the flare had been delivered. Onlookers in Lafayette Park began to assemble, gawking at the spectacle. A few moments later, the blimp itself darted in for a quick landing, the rising sun at its back. It was belching a huge plume of smoke from several dozen smoke flares attached to it. It circled low, downwind of the White House, and scattered five smoke flares on the lawn on the left side of the building before landing on the front lawn of the White House and releasing more smoke flares. Soon the entire White House grounds were engulfed in thick smoke. The string of M80s attached to the blimp then ignited, and sounding just like gunfire, a very loud crackling of fireworks commenced from within the thick curtain of smoke enveloping the White House.

Maddox was already back in the car. Rodriguez had quickly donned the drugged guard's uniform and was manning the guardhouse, M-16 rifle in hand. The handcuffed guard was placed in the trunk of the Crown Victoria, and Maddox punched the accelerator, sending the car crashing through the gate. Though spikes punctured the tires, Maddox kept his foot hard on the accelerator, and the car managed to make it to the portico of the White House.

Maddox couldn't see anything in the smoke, nor could anyone see him. He sprang from the car, felt his way to a window in the White House, and crashed through it shoulder first. Ricks followed close behind.

The sprinkler system in the White House had been activated and, adding to the chaos, there were people running every which way inside the building. Maddox shouted to Ricks to find the President, and then ran to the East Wing looking for Carpenter's bedroom. He tried several doors in succession, but found the rooms empty.

After kicking in another door, he found a group of scientists huddled around a computer. He leveled his gun at the men, but after scanning the room for Carpenter, the President, and Heather and finding none of them present, he quickly exited and continued his search. At last he came to the end of the hallway. Before him stood one last set of doors.

Maddox paused in front of the double doors, then, with a great heave, kicked them in. In the room, seated on the bed in urgent discussion, were Carpenter and Heather. The two looked up, startled.

Time froze. Maddox saw Carpenter reach for something that looked to Maddox like a mobile phone. Heather looked up, and seeing Maddox aim his weapon, instinctively threw herself in front of Carpenter. "No!" he shouted to her as he readied the first in a burst of shots. He paused for a moment, then reminded himself that she had betrayed him. She had become the enemy.

In an instant, however, before he could select a shot, his vision darkened and became clouded. A swarm was buzzing loudly all around him. *Hornets? Locusts?* He did his best to aim, but it was hard to see through the flying cloud. He found himself lifting his left arm instinctively to swat away the angry insects.

He felt stinging all over his face. Stinging in his arms. Felt the insects burrowing furiously into and under his clothes. He recoiled at the intense burning sensation they inflicted. He screamed. His vision became blurred and he felt faint. In desperation, he fired off two shots where he thought Carpenter was standing. He felt the gun kick in his hand twice.

He heard a scream before all went black.

EPILOGUE

Maddox awoke the next morning in a hospital bed. Thirsty, he reached for a glass of water only to discover restraints on his arms that limited his movement. He noticed his upper torso was covered with large red welts, and based on the reflection in his water glass, so too was his face. Otherwise, however, he felt fine.

His repeated pleas to his doctor and the nursing staff to learn what had happened to Heather, Carpenter, the President, Ricks, Lewis, Zach and Rodriguez, were all ignored. Requests to speak to Martin were also denied. Eventually he came to understand he was being held in a secret government interrogation facility.

He spent the next three months held incommunicado. It wasn't until a month into his detention that he was able to learn the result of the election: Drake had won a close victory. Shortly thereafter he introduced into Congress the Blueprint for America legislation.

The battle over the Blueprint had been close. Unbeknownst to all, Drake had wrestled mightily with a moral dilemma as he attempted to push the legislation through Congress. Several key congressional leaders from both parties had been infected with Carpenter's *microbots* and had been under orders from Carpenter to push the Blueprint through. For operational rea-

320

sons, Carpenter's demise was initially kept secret, and none of the infected congressmen were aware that they were free to vote on the bill as they wished. Needing every possible vote, Drake had been tempted to tell them of their newfound freedom only *after* the legislation had come to a vote. In the end, however, he bowed to his conscience and advised them beforehand that they were free to vote as they saw fit. In a rare display of bipartisanship, the Blueprint passed by a thin margin after garnering support from both parties.

Once Maddox's interrogators had sifted through the tumultuous succession of events that culminated in the assault on the White House, they eventually identified Maddox as the hero of the day. After three months as a 'guest' of the federal government, he was at last released from detention. To celebrate his heroism, he was even named the second recipient of the "Protector of the Nation" award. He also received a promotion and jumped two pay-grades higher, which was helpful but still insufficient to pay off his accumulated legal debt. As a condition of his release, Maddox was required to sign papers promising never to speak with anyone regarding any of the "recent events."

Towards the end of his period of detainment, he had been provided a phone-book-sized document containing the official version of events, to which he was expected to adhere henceforth: a previously unknown far-right domestic terrorist organization had launched a remote-controlled attack on the White House in a bid to disrupt the upcoming election. The group did not penetrate the White House proper and none inside were hurt. The subsequent "investigation" revealed the group had only a handful of members, and all were being detained under Patriot Act provisions.

Having been informed that he would be allowed to maintain contact with Heather, Maddox flew to Minnetonka to see her immediately after his release. The two had a subdued dinner at a local diner, and afterwards took a stroll by the frozen lakeside. The conversation was awkward.

The sky was a leaden gray, and scattered snowflakes fluttered in the chill air. Looking out over the motionless lake, Heather told him what she had seen transpire at the White House amidst the shouting, smoke and chaos of Maddox's rescue operation. Seeing Maddox level his gun at Carpenter, she had lunged instinctively to protect Carpenter. In doing so, she had received a bullet wound to the shoulder. The wound was significant, and she herself had only weeks before been released from the hospital. The doctor had informed her that she might never be able to play cello again or perform surgery. "I don't mind so much about the surgery: I'd be equally as happy as a pediatrician as long as I'm helping people, but the cello really gets me. It just hurts too much when I play," she said with resignation, a tear forming in the corner of her eye. Recalling that he had via video link watched her in rapturous duets with Carpenter, Maddox wondered whether the "hurt" to which she referred was primarily physical, or perhaps more so emotional.

Answering the question that had been foremost in his mind for months, she said she had no idea what had become of Carpenter either.

"I passed out after you shot me," she told Maddox matter-of-factly, "and when I came to, I was lying in a hospital bed, my entire right side in a cast.

"No one told me anything about what transpired that day, or what became of Carpenter, you, or any of the others. When I was released I was provided the official version of events and sworn to secrecy."

Maddox apologized profusely to her for having injured her. She said she understood and didn't blame him, but she also added, "Bill, do you have any idea *what* Carpenter was after?" He could only shake his head.

"All he wanted was world peace," she said in a pleading tone, a slight tremor breaking into her voice. She brushed away a tear. "Did you really need to shoot him?"

Maddox averted his eyes. "I'm so sorry," was all he could say.

"I know this isn't easy for you either," she added. "I'm sorry too. I know you were only doing what you thought was right."

He watched her lips mouth the words for forgiveness, but listening to the lingering hollowness in her voice, he sensed a distance between them that he knew would be impossible to bridge.

She asked him if there were any way he, as an FBI agent, could help find out what had happened to Carpenter. He told her, "Believe me, I wish I could tell you, but that, my dear, is way, way, *way*, over my pay-grade." The official report of the events involving Carpenter had been classified up to the very highest levels. "But," he added, "you can bet your bottom dollar I'll be keeping my eyes and ears wide open for a good long time."

At that, her eyes brightened somewhat and she looked out over the lake.

She told Maddox she had recently reconciled with her mother, and that Alice would be coming up to Minnetonka soon for a visit. She thanked Maddox for the role he played in bringing her together with her mother. It pained Maddox to hear Heather wonder whether she should explain to her mother about "her feelings towards Carpenter," or whether it would be best to avoid that topic altogether. "That's going to make for a really awkward mother-daughter conversation," she added wryly.

Following their rendezvous in Minnetonka and even knowing that his chances of success were slim, Maddox nonetheless tried his best to win Heather back. He was still taken with her, *badly*. He sent her flowers and a recording of him playing guitar, including *Guantanamera, Third World Blues*, and *Milkin' It,* as well as several new songs he had written. She thanked him and said she would treasure the recordings. The distance in her voice told him, however, that he was fighting a lost cause. No stranger to lost causes, however, Maddox vowed to himself that one day he would be back for her, regardless of the odds.

Returning to his FBI post in Los Angeles, Maddox never ceased trying to find out what had happened to Carpenter. He did so partially out of his commitment to Heather, and partly for his own peace of mind. None among his close circle had any idea about Carpenter's fate. Most intriguing of all, Maddox learned that the other members of Carpenter's team had also gone missing along with their families. There were no indications as to their whereabouts. The same was true of Lewis' wife Danielle. The official version of events had Lewis passing away peacefully in his sleep while traveling as part of his research.

Then, one day, Ricks took Maddox aside. In whispered conversation, Ricks said he'd heard from a friend in forensics that Maddox had shot Carpenter with the second of the two bullets he'd fired. But Ricks also said he'd heard whispers from other reliable contacts that Carpenter somehow had managed to escape in the smoke, commotion, and confusion of the day.

Later, Maddox learned more during a quiet stroll with Gottlieb, whose career was now in dramatic ascent after his Pulitzer nomination for coverage of recent White House events. The journalist told Maddox he'd heard rumors that Carpenter and his team were hard at work perfecting the latest generation of *microbots* in a top-secret government facility located on a mountain top somewhere high in the Grand Tetons of Wyoming.

"I think Carpenter's been Whiskey Delta'ed," Ricks whispered to Maddox over coffee one day.

"*Whiskey Delta'ed*?" Maddox asked.

"You know, the highest-level witness protection program? *Top Secret*. Makes the Federal Witness Protection Program look like a bunch of Vaudeville slapstick. Full cosmetic surgery, surgical voice and fingerprint alteration, the whole nine yards. If he's still alive, no way anyone's gonna find him now."